Advance praise for Miah Arnold's *Sweet Land of Bigamy*

"If I could have conjured a wild, wry, delicious story of bigamy, reversing the roles—the woman choosing one groom too many and a few other sweet sins, it would be Miah Arnold's *Sweet Land of Bigamy*. Gasping with laughter and and admiration, I wonder not if this book will be a hit, but . . . you'll pardon me . . . just how big!

Miah Arnold's Helen is not only a Utah cowgirl who just can't say no, but her poet groom number two is a Hindu, no less. Predictable mayhem ensues, but it's anything but predictable, and the secondary characters, including Helen's approving and unconventional mountain mama, spring off the page. Miah Arnold skewers every convention, from religious convention to social sedition, with a post-modern Austenian assurance."

—Jacquelyn Mitchard, author of
The Deep End of the Ocean and *Second Nature*

"*Sweet Land of Bigamy* is as weird as America, as absurd as our times, and as beautiful as our contradictions. Smart, funny, and utterly engaging. Miah Arnold makes a notable debut with a voice that seems to be just warming up."

—Mat Johnson, author of *Pym: A Novel*

"Reading *Sweet Land of Bigamy* is like listening to Tom Waits. Miah Arnold's book sings an American melody: the high and the low, the tough and the tender, the beautiful and the grotesque meet and marry. An arresting, inventive novel, so fresh, so full of images, of questions and answers."

—Adam Zagajewski, Nobel Prize nominee
and author of *Unseen Hands: Poems*

Sweet Land of Bigamy

A NOVEL

Miah Arnold

TYRUS
BOOKS

F+W Media

Published by
TYRUS BOOKS
an imprint of F+W Media, Inc.
10151 Carver Road
Suite 200
Blue Ash, Ohio 45242
www.tyrusbooks.com

ISBN 10: 1-4405-4189-2
ISBN 13: 978-1-4405-4189-6
eISBN 10: 1-4405-4161-2
eISBN 13: 978-1-4405-4161-2

Printed in the United States of America.

10 9 8 7 6 5 4 3 2 1

Library of Congress Cataloging-in-Publication Data
is available from the publisher.

This book is available at quantity discounts for bulk purchases.
For information, please call 1-800-289-0963.

For Jerri Ann

Acknowledgments

This is a book that my luck in family and my impeccable taste in friendships built.

I wrote this book over the course of several years, while my family slept. Between the hours of 9 P.M. and 4 A.M. two of Houston's finest literary nonprofits allowed me to write in their offices—I am profoundly grateful to Inprint and Writers in the Schools (WITS) for this twin generosity. I couldn't have finished my book without it.

I also want to thank Inprint, WITS, and The Houston Arts Alliance for sustaining me and countless emerging writers with grants, fellowships, and teaching opportunities over the course of decades.

My editor, Ben LeRoy, is a phenomenon the literary world needs. My agent Alia Hannah Habib is steady, and kind, and has a perfect head on her shoulders. James Kastely and Julie Kofford sorted out countless problems along my way.

My mentors at the University of Houston Creative Writing program pushed and bettered my writing, most especially Alex Parsons, Antonya Nelson, Hosam Aboul-Ela, Adam Zagajewski, Mark Doty, and Ruben Martinez. David MacLean lent me some humor, Irene Keliher and Nicole Zaza let me know when the book was dragging, and Keya Mitra helped me love it when I had given up. Julie Chisholm, Sarah Prior, and Dana Capell have believed in me long enough that it changed me, and they read versions of this book and helped me make it better, as did Mat Johnson, Kathleen Cambor, Gemini Wahaj, Maranatha Bivens, Hayan Charara,

Heather Bigley, John Pluecker, and Ira Sher. I am thankful to all of them.

I am indebted to Janira Umanzor who freed up my time with her tenacious help, and to Donna Kline, and to Isabelle Arnold. Indispensable friendships with Evan Cleveland, Christa Forrester, Jorge Galvan, Hank Hancock, Chuck Jackson, Jennifer Nelson, Kate Schmitt, and Steve and Diana Wolfe nourished me.

I thank Piper and Shelly and Scotty, and all the kids I grew up with, and their parents, and their dreams. I thank Myton, Utah.

I am grateful for my father's love of what others fear, and for editing advice begot of strange living. My mother Helen Forsberg taught me to write when it would have been easier not to have, and my mother Kathleen Cooper changed her life and it mattered to me and to a whole community. I am grateful for the powerful kindnesses of Vipul and Aparna Mankad. My grandmother Ludy taught me the strength of hope, and my grandfather Bud helped guide me through the world with his jokes. My extended Arnold, Cooper, Forsberg, Higley, and Mankad families have taught me to live in the world and to adore it. I am indebted to all of their love.

Most of all I am thankful to Lila and Vishwa who are horizons I will always write toward, and to my husband, Raj Mankad, for his love, for believing I could write a book before I did, and for reading so many drafts he might never get straight what finally happened.

Part One

Chapter One

June 26, 2004

With her husband Larry away at war, Helen Motes meant to make long-due amends with her alcoholic mother, but instead she fell in love with a young poet, and then agreed to marry him. Within the month, what began as the-accidental-acceptance-to-a-proposal-she-must-certainly-back-out-of transformed into this: Helen Motes, shivering inside her scarlet wedding dress on a cliff in Utah's Black Elk Mountains, scouring the rocky path below her for the first signs of her tiny wedding party. For her fiancé, Chakor Desai, and his two elderly neighbors.

Helen and the Hindu pundit who would perform the ceremony had climbed to Nuchu's Landing in the early morning so he could prepare and she could rest before the groom arrived. The landing was a ledge jutting out of the otherwise flat face of a cliff, and the cliff itself seemed to elbow its way from the earth after endless miles of burnt plains. Twenty miles to the north of the scorched brush was Smoot's Pass, Utah, where Helen had been raised; directly behind the wedding party's cliff, the Black Elk Mountains fanned out in piney-blue splendor.

It had taken the bride and the priest forty-five minutes to make the morning climb because it was a steep ascent and both were dressed in long ribbons of fabric—hers a shiny red sari embellished with silver trim, his a white cotton dhoti, like Gandhi wore. Though he sweated profusely on the way up and required a number of breaks, the priest had seemed unhindered by his attire. Helen was used to the hike, but worried that her sari would unravel and strand her inside an embarrassing puddle of silk. She knew there were seventeen safety pins holding it all together, but no expert had dressed her: the groom and the priest were men and had never learned to drape a sari. It had all been up to Chakor's New Age–hippie neighbor, Ida, and half a dozen different diagrams her grand-kids had found on the Internet.

When the priest and bride arrived at Nuchu's Landing without mishap it seemed to Helen a bout of undeserved good luck. What she deserved was for something to go wrong, she thought. She deserved something to prevent her from marrying a second hus-band, aside from her confessing her current marital state to Chakor, which she could not do. She had tried and it was impossible.

Behind Helen, in the cliff's shadow, the pundit was now engaged in a small war with the elements: the noon-hour wind was dead set against his lighting the sacramental fire inside his golden kettle. He hadn't spoken since their arrival, though on the way up he had confessed to being overwhelmed.

"Because I have never performed a puja in such an exquisite location," he had smiled, as he swept his hands toward the washed-out sky: blue and barren except for a few wisps of a jet's trail. "I haven't smelled air this clean since I was a boy visiting Mount Abu," he said. "You probably don't even notice."

"Oh, no, I smell it," Helen had countered. It was June after all, and the air was saturated with the competing odors of sage, cedar, and the sickly sweet Russian Olive trees that grew across eastern Utah like weeds.

"I am a priest as giddy as a bride today," he shrugged. "Strange."

"What's really strange," she wanted to tell him, "is that I'm already married."

* * *

Amos Monks had grown up among the scrub at the base of the Black Elks, a land he associated less with grandeur than the drudgery of home. As he was checking the traps he'd set to catch the bastard coyotes that had gnawed off maybe a dozen lambs from his family's herd since spring, he heard a disconcerting music. After taking a few steps closer toward its source he could tell it was drums. Drumming. Coming right at him, from the sky.

A few seconds later and he nearly fell over himself at what was playing out, plain as day, right in the middle of Chipeta County: an Arab prince or warrior or something was riding a great white stallion up toward Nuchu's Landing. His horse was covered head to foot in strands of orange marigolds. No shitting.

Amos blinked to give the possibility of heatstroke a chance, but it was no vision. Now Chipeta County was filled with both Utes and illegals, and either kind was as likely as the other to dress up his horse and head out on a spirit quest. But those types wouldn't be wearing glistening silvery white suits. They wouldn't know where to find a turban big enough to hold a bomb inside it.

"Shit," he whispered, and shrugged, and then he did a little dance of worry and excitement all at once. Here was this man, this, as incredible as it seemed, this *Arab* out in the middle of nowhere. Out where he clearly did not belong.

Da-ca-da-ca-da-ca-dhoon, the man's drums said. Were there drummers? Amos couldn't see. When he strained to hear the chanting beneath the percussion, though, his stomach turned at the realization it wasn't even English.

"Shit," he said again. He sighed. He missed his cool-headed older brother Frankie, away at war.

The man in the saddle looked happy swaying up there on his horse. He was holding his shoulders and arms out into the sky and dancing the best he could in stirrups. It looked ridiculous. Not like,

Amos tried to tell himself, a person trying to take down America from the inside. Maybe he was getting worked up over nothing.

"Bullshit," he said back to himself. Because maybe it would be a bitter kind of shit to swallow if Amos let the world whimper into oblivion without a fight.

He shook his head for clarity and held tight to the Marlin his dad had just bought him for his seventeenth birthday. The man and his drums would have to round a corner soon, and then Amos would sprint over to where he'd have a full view of Nuchu's Landing—there was no place else for them to be heading.

And the more he thought, the harder it was to deny that there was no place in America less prepared for the launching of a small nuke than Chipeta County.

* * *

Nobody would believe she'd danced the whole way up to Nuchu's Landing, Ida Meek knew, but she had. It was her one role in the wedding, and sixty-three years old or not, she'd made it. Since she had avoided keeling over in the process she felt invigorated—though just as soon as she and her partner Herman had been introduced to Davendra Dave, the priest, they'd both collapsed directly onto her emerald-green quilt. Now they were sipping cheap Merlot from foldout plastic wine glasses on this gorgeous Saturday morning, and she felt serenaded by the priest's lovely chanting. Even his name was luxurious and she kept repeating it to herself so she wouldn't forget it: *Dah-ven-drah Dah-vey, Dah-ven-drah Dah-vey.*

The priest believed Ida and Herman were the aunt and uncle who had raised Helen after her mother's death, a white lie Chakor had begged them to perpetuate. No parents, the priest had said, no wedding.

"I can't understand a word coming out of that dude's mouth," Herman complained when he'd caught his breath enough to begin paying attention.

"I told you, it's in Sanskrit," Ida said. "Nobody understands it but holy men."

"Not even Chakor?" he asked.

Ida sighed. Despite living with a woman who had studied up on all the world's religions her whole life, Herman remained willfully ignorant. She *had* told him earlier that very morning that Hindu ceremonies are still conducted in the ancient language because its very syllables are considered too holy and full of meaning to translate into any other language.

"Catholics gave up Latin and took over the world," he said, a long minute after she was through re-explaining. "I know *that.*"

Before she could scold him, though, he was already chuckling at her beneath his great, gray beard: just out to get her goat. She sighed again, and turned her attention to the young couple sitting on a pair of small stools, side by side. Dressed like royalty. Chakor was tall, dark, and handsome—and he was young. Just twenty-four. Though he was lanky, even feminine, he moved his limbs with athletic grace. His face was long and he had great black, expressive eyes with stretching lashes that reminded her of a mime's. His full, generous lips and large mouth took up most of his face, and he tipped his whole body backwards whenever he laughed. To top it all off, he had a slow, southern drawl, a relic of having been raised, the son of doctors, in Port Arthur, Texas. In the year he had lived in Chipeta County he had become Ida's darling. Helen was a lucky woman.

She was also the wrong woman for Chakor, but that was neither here nor there. Not because of the nationality thing, or the color of their skins, or because Helen was nowhere near as striking as Chakor in looks. The problem was one of misaligned intensities. Helen was a different sort of girl than Chakor. You could think she was haughty and she was a brooder. To Ida it made sense because

Helen's mother, Carmen, had been the town drunk in Smoot's Pass since before Helen was born. The girl hadn't had an easy life, and had found her own way to survival by taking up a serious, cautious nature. She'd done this the hard way, after a teenaged bout of carrying on like her mother, but of course Ida didn't fault her for that. Helen was a survivor. But still: Chakor was made for grand ideals and adventures, and Ida feared Helen might hold him back.

Of course, there was always divorce. Or better, Ida reprimanded herself, the chance that she was wrong. "How long is this ceremony going to last again?" Herman asked.

"I already told you it's not a ceremony. It's a puja," she whispered at her more grizzled half. "They call it a poo-jah. Poojah."

He sighed and poured them both another glass of wine. Ida took hers and decided not be annoyed by Herman's impatience. She did not want to taint the marital vibrations on this cliff.

Finally the pundit stopped his singing to speak in English, and Ida was as grateful as she knew Herman was. Davendra Dave instructed the couple to adorn each other with marigold necklaces as a sign of their mutual acceptance, and then to put their toes atop a nut. His voice was exceptionally beautiful, she thought, as he took up chanting again.

Although Chakor was East Indian, Ida couldn't help thinking that the last time this cliff had beheld such beautiful language, it must have been Ute.

"Or Anasazi, before they vanished," Herman nodded. It gave Ida the chills.

"Just think," she said, "the Anasazi's language must have been this exquisite. This exquisite and every day it was spoken in this land, and we'll never know how it sounded. It's just lost."

"Might have been the same language he's speaking now," her husband said, clasping his wife's giant, weathered hand in his own. "Who the hell knows?"

The old people sighed and toasted their fourth glasses of wine as Davendra instructed Chakor to tie a corner of his outfit to Helen's scarf so they could begin walking slowly around the matrimonial fire.

* * *

Davendra Dave said nothing to Helen's family about the wine. Chakor should have told them it was not auspicious to drink it, but already they had started. Both the aunt and the uncle wore long gray hair, frizzy and wild. They were old, but thin and crackling. A type he associated with India more than America. Best not to cross this sort is what he thought. And best always to be pragmatic: the damage was already done, why not let them continue drinking? This wedding was unusual enough in the first place.

Helen, for example, was white. She was visibly older than the groom. Her owl's face seemed too pensive for a bride's. Only her uncle and auntie were in attendance, and none of Chakor's family was. Nor were the hundreds of revelers usually adding gaiety to such an event. An intricately crafted, centuries-in-the-making ceremony requiring at least three, four days to perform properly was supposed to have been truncated, at the request of the groom, to an even sixty minutes. Davendra had secretly decided they would not notice if he made it a luckier seventy-one minutes long, but still: he had known Unitarians with longer weddings.

It was American, though, to the core to want everything done lickety-spickety. Like everybody else, he reminded himself, Chakor and Helen could not wait. Like everybody else, they had an impeccable reason not to wait. In this case the groom's widowed mother was on her deathbed in Ahmadabad and Helen could not accompany the young man there because this wine-drinking, mountain-climbing auntie was also gravely ill. Her vigor in the face of death impressed Davendra.

After the ceremony, of course, Chakor would return to India to take care of his own sick mother. A good boy. Maybe it would take a month, maybe a year: you never knew with this kind of trip. The elderly could linger, especially old mothers anxious to spend their last living breaths gazing at their doting sons. Chakor knew this, and he wanted to be certain the woman he loved believed he was coming back. That he loved her even in his absence. Chakor had promised Davendra they would have a longer, more proper wedding when life settled down.

It was good enough for the priest, whose own experiences with love had taught him the importance of securing a young woman's hand before making any long treks across the ocean—the girl he was supposed to have married twenty years before had eloped with a tiffin factory owner's son from Mumbai three months after the pundit had emigrated to the States. She believed her youth was too short to waste on waiting for him to make good and send for her. Good for her, the priest reflected. He'd always thought her nose looked like a child made it out of putty. Good for Chakor, he thought, for considering the flightiness of young women and securing a love that mattered to him.

Good for me, too. Who would ever have imagined him, fourth son of a lowly palm reader, presiding over this scene? Uniting this young couple in a landscape the Bollywood directors would gouge their own eyes out to film? Had he stayed in Mumbai he never would have found himself in such an unexpected place, marrying two children from opposite sides of the earth.

* * *

In the days before the wedding, Helen imagined herself as the fool who should have changed her name when she married the first time. The twenty-seven-year-old matron who ought to have worn her wedding ring on her left hand and not on a long silver chain around her neck. The desperate, childless woman making a fool of herself in a last-ditch grasp at happiness. But she had never imagined this.

Helen could not have predicted Chakor's rushed exit from the country, or his brazen insistence that they marry. She hadn't expected that since she and Larry had married in Hawaii, Utah wouldn't know she was already married. Or that she'd grown so distant from the people in Smoot's Pass that Ida and Herman, acquaintances of her mother's, hadn't an inkling about what had happened to her in the years since she'd run away from the region as a teenager.

What she *had* expected, what she was certain of still, was that the rules of the world would step into the picture and assert her unavailability. Somehow they would. And then they hadn't. And she ought to have spoken up, even now she could do it, but this morning was so spectacular.

Chakor had arrived on a horse! It was a detail about the Hindu wedding he'd kept from her until she saw him swaying on top of it, glistening and laughing down at her dropped jaw. Helen had been twelve when she'd chosen Nuchu's Landing as the perfect spot for a wedding. She'd told Chakor about the fantasy on a hike through the Black Elks. Marrying atop this ledge had been part of his proposal.

Not even her wildest childhood imaginings conjured a groom more exciting than Billy Cooper in a sequined cowboy shirt and jeans; than a bride wearing a sleeveless cotton dress that would billow up in the wind beneath a Stetson hat. Hers had been a simple fantasy, the kind a girl raised in Smoot's Pass might come up with and then give up on with hardly a pang in her heart.

What Chakor had produced was infinitely more romantic. That white stallion! The rosy incense from the priest's pot and the thin, ruby-red, silk sari teasing its way around her body: all details torn from the pages meant for a storybook princess. It was hard not to think of it all as fate, hard not to believe that at last her magical chariot had arrived.

Now, sitting next to Chakor on a tiny golden chair, she felt grateful, and then horrified, and then anxious, and then happy. She cursed Larry Janx and smiled into the eyes of her fiancé. Larry was the one who had given up on her, she reminded herself, but now here she was committing the abomination. It wasn't fair.

Because she wanted what she was not supposed to have, she wanted it more than anything she'd ever wanted. Larry was not her ex-husband, or common-law husband, or fiancé she left at the altar, but her honest-to-goodness husband of nine years. He'd left her alone to *hold the fort,* as he put it, while he used the Arabic skills he'd developed as a Mormon missionary in Egypt to translate for a contracting company in Iraq. And—this was the part that made Helen angriest—he had been a *good* husband. A wonderful one, a man she'd always believed would be a perfect father. However, they had spent six years trying for a baby and one miscarriage, early on, had been the only result. And now he was off at war: he had as good as given up.

Helen hadn't. When Chakor turned up in the middle of nowhere, out of nowhere, she had felt like dust. A layer of life Larry had left behind to settle into the furniture. Chakor offered her something better.

What a fool she'd be not to take it. Couldn't she cut things off with Larry after Chakor left to see his mother? She could.

"Helen," Chakor interrupted, pinching her playfully on the earlobe. She blinked to. The inquisitive pundit's face was waiting for her do something. Strands of oiled gray hair were flapping around his mostly bald head.

"Put the herbs in the pot," Chakor whispered, smiling indulgently at her because she was the center of his universe. She was and it was an enchanting place to be; Helen would not be ashamed of taking that universe. Even if every time Larry's name erupted into her thoughts it felt like she might be crushed into the earth she stood on, there was Chakor's ebullient face to steady her. The love in his eyes was muscular in its form. Any moment his whole body would explode into blossoms and drift off into the breeze before her. And if it did, she'd follow suit.

She *was* following suit, she had *chosen* to. So she banished Larry, again and again, in her best attempts to let this day be what Chakor deserved.

"Helen," Davendraji said, "Repeat after me: '*Sakyam the' Ghame'yam Sakyaath the' Maayosham Sakyan me.*'"

"*Suck-yum tuh gaaaaah may um,*" Helen tried, but couldn't remember the rest of the sentence. Davendraji repeated it for her, phrase by phrase, and she traced his words with her own the best she could. Then it was Chakor's turn, again, and after the two had spoken their parts, they took a step forward together: the first of the seven steps, of the seven vows, almost the last of the marriage rituals. Helen would not feel guilty, but she was grateful she didn't understand the meaning of the promises she was making, even if she did the portent: promise, step, promise, step, promise.

* * *

When at last Davendraji asked him to fasten the gold-and-black Mangal Sutra around his new bride's neck, it seemed to Chakor that only a few minutes had passed since the ceremony had begun. So many pujas just like this had seemed never-ending before. At his cousin Sunil's wedding he'd fallen asleep atop his mother's silk yellow sari before the bride had even arrived at the four-pillared altar. He hadn't woken until his mother rose to whisper secrets for a prosperous marriage into the bride's ear.

"That's what love's been for me, all along," Sunil had laughed, as Chakor's father chastised him in front of the groom. "Snoozing in my Ma's lap one day, waking up in the mandap with Mital's sari tied to me, and all you people making fun of my Sanskrit pronunciations the next. Don't you sweat it, little guy. Just look out for where you wake up!"

"Ba-ha-hah!" his father laughed, and Chakor had blushed, unable to imagine a day filled with such a surprise. But here it was. His mandap was the two spindles of giant aspen trees that punditji stood between. The hundreds of approving pairs of eyes usually adorning a marriage in human form were provided by the brown speckles on the milky bark of the aspens. If it wasn't traditional, this was at least a wedding over which the dreadlocked Lord Shiva, Chakor's favorite deity, would approve of from his home atop Mount Kailāsa in the Himalayas. Even the lie to the priest about Helen's parents being dead was just a shade off from the truth: Helen's mother was so sick and infirm that Helen hadn't even let Chakor meet her. Shiva would understand.

Now his bride focused on him as he faced her with the necklace, and she was trembling. He wished his father were with him, but he had died a few years before, and his Ma was sick. Too sick for him to even begin explaining his love for this girl who was neither Brahmin nor Gujarati, but a mongrel American white.

If he couldn't share its source, he vowed, he would at least spread the happiness of his life into the corners and receding shadows of his mother's last days. Maybe he'd even tell her about what he'd done, about his mountain woman buried so deep inside the United States that it was a wonder he'd found her. Helen's face was, now, unusually, ghostly pale, steadfastly refusing to flush in the day's gathering heat. Like Mital Auntie had before her, Helen had appeared. A blessing in an unsuspecting sleeper's life.

"Here I go," he said, embracing her with his eyes as he leaned in toward her. But then fastening the small clasp behind his new wife's neck turned out to be complicated. He fumbled, his wrists resting on Helen's cool shoulders.

"Take your time, dear," Ida called. "Marriage is all about patience," she laughed.

The more he tried, the further from fastening the Mangal Sutra he seemed, and even this difficulty filled him with so much joy that he laughed aloud at his own efforts.

"Patience my ass," Herman finally said, "Helen! Help him out before my back is crippled from sitting so long on the damned rocks!"

Helen smiled widely as she moved to help Chakor, but she didn't need to do anything. Chakor had finally clipped it, and had taken a step back to look at the woman he had just pledged his life to.

"Good! Then by the power vested in me by the State of Utah, I pronounce you husband and wife. I say you have earned a kiss from the bride." Davendraji smiled, and though she surely meant to gently rest her trembling hands on the sides of his face, she clasped his cheeks in what felt more like a death grip. He put his own hands over Helen's and leaned toward her for the kiss, but before he could rest his lips on hers, the morning's peace was shattered by an explosion. A mound of rocks came tumbling down from the cliff just twenty or so feet from where they stood, and Helen yanked Chakor to the ground by his face with a shriek.

"What the hell?" Herman's voice boomed as he bounded foolishly toward the side of the cliff. Two more shots smacked into the air, and the old hippie fell to the ground.

"Oh, God," Ida said, scrambling to his side on her hands and knees like a wildcat. "He's been shot."

"Bullshit," Herman said, swiping her away from him. He was already heading back toward the cliff's edge, this time in a commando crawl.

Helen had broken down into tears. "I'm so sorry," she said, "I'm so, so sorry." Chakor was too confused to figure out what she meant. He was entranced by the old hippie who'd spotted something.

"That little shit!" Herman called out, when he did. He stood back up on the cliff's edge in a rage. "You about killed us!" he screamed to whomever had shot. "What the hell are you thinking?"

Chakor heard some shouting from below, but not the words.

"What?" Herman screamed back.

"*God. Bless. America.*" The punctuated words traveled clearly up this time. Everybody on the cliff understood.

Herman's ease with whomever he was talking with, or at least the fact Herman hadn't been shot, gave Chakor the courage to stand. Helen, too. Ida was already at her husband's side.

"*GOD . . . BLESS . . .* " the voice started more forcefully, but then Chakor had made his way to the cliff, and "America" turned into a strange kind of squeak. It was a stubby guy in a baseball cap looking up at them.

"*GOD . . .* " the man screamed, and Herman dashed over to the empty wine bottle on the quilt and back again to the ledge where he shook it menacingly at the man, who started running, as if he'd forgotten he was the one with the real weapon.

Everybody stood looking a long time, nobody saying anything until Herman spoke, smiling somberly. "I'm sorry, kiddos, for all that."

Helen wasn't crying anymore. She had wiped the tears away, but her face was streaked and dirty because of them, and it made her look more beautiful. Authentic, somehow, it seemed to Chakor.

"He didn't say stare at the bride," Ida said, caressing the side of his face like a mother. "He said kiss her."

Chapter Two

August 31, 2003

In spite of the heat, Larry was finishing dinner with his wife out on the porch of their new home in Kingwood, Texas. He was waiting for the right moment to hand over his going-away gifts. It was his last evening in America.

Eating outside was Helen's gesture toward marking the night as momentous. Still, the meal was enshrouded by a silence disturbed only by the buzz of gargantuan mosquitoes, by the countless smacks they elicited. Painful welts quickly spread across Larry's allergic limbs. Needy as he was in terms of conversation starters, he was refusing to mention this to his wife. She'd blame him for moving them to Houston and not herself for insisting on the milquetoast, namby-pamby health-food-store repellents she'd always insisted they use. You could survive with them in Salt Lake City, but Larry could see that in Texas you had to buck up and use poison that nature had intended. He resolved to fortify Helen's Buzz Off with the backwoods deet repellent he kept hidden in their camping supplies the first chance he got.

Focus, he told himself: he had worked too hard to do something nice for Helen for the whole thing to flop. The right gift was a hard thing to find. The right gift would lessen her fears about his departure. It could help her see that his being in Iraq at sextuple his

25

stateside pay was really to be here with her, working on the family she had begun obsessing over in increasing degrees since he'd signed on with ThunderVox. Because his wife could not understand their family was in a *bind:* she would not see it. No man wants to go to war, but Larry Janx had no other options.

Larry's friend Bill thought the solution was simple: *"Semensicles."* He swore a buddy of his had produced progeny using some old *Hustlers* and a couple run-of-the-mill ice cube trays. Though the idea of it had thrown Larry off icy drinks for a week, one miserable Tuesday later he found himself on the phone with an actual fertility clinic, inquiring about a more considered way to do what his friend had suggested. He was halfway through the most humiliating conversation of his life when he'd come to and hung up. But that was how desperate he was in the search to calm his wife.

Of course Larry had known Helen would fight against his leaving for Iraq—a man would feel mighty small if his wife didn't. But then the woman was supposed to fall in line. All the other wives had.

"This meal sure is delicious," Larry blurted out into the silent night. He rotated his clenched jaw muscles to relax them. He smiled at her, took her hand into his own. "You did a real good job with the sauce this time."

Helen pulled her hand back and used it to slap her bicep so hard he flinched. She held her hand up to him like the mashed and bloodied mosquito's corpse was a Rorschachian condemnation of Larry himself.

He breathed in and counted to ten. "I was hoping we could relax tonight," he said. "I was hoping we could be lighthearted."

His wife raised her eyebrows.

"You're forty-one and childless and leaving for a war zone tomorrow," she said in a controlled, breathy voice. "It's time to start a family and you're letting a midlife crisis destroy us."

"I may be an old man," he joked, "but you're not even thirty. You've got a decade left—more—before we have to begin worrying."

"That's bullshit."

Larry cringed: he hated obscenities, and Helen knew it.

"We've gone over this," he sighed.

"I *need* a family, Larry."

"Okay. So do I. But how do you plan on taking care of it?"

"We'll manage. I have the job at the Blue Hope. You can start another business here."

"Come on, Helen."

"I don't even believe in the war."

"Come *on.*"

"We never even discussed this. You made the choice and now you're about to disappear and I had no say. No say at all. And it isn't okay."

The gift was a series of objects, all waiting in a file crate in the garage, ten feet away, for Helen to say anything that wasn't confrontational.

Larry whacked a mosquito. It was warm outside, the air heavy and unpleasant. He forced himself to explain his reasons for going, yet again: with the money he'd make in two years' work in Iraq he could regain half the savings he'd lost in the downturn. They'd have enough money to seed the new business in Houston, or any city she wanted to move to when he got back. He'd be able to provide for the children he never doubted they would produce, *in God's time.*

"We don't even know what's the matter," she said, her face glistening beneath a sudden barrage of tears. "We don't know why . . ." she said, and then stopped. She swallowed her words, stood, and gathered their finished dishes.

"I'm sorry," she said into her filled arms. "I know I should be able to pull it together for your last night, but I can't. It's not like you joined the Army—until the moment you're on that plane I feel like your leaving is something I can stop. Something I have to stop."

"I know you do," he sighed because he heard the verge of tears in her voice.

Moments later, Larry was left alone to consider the hum of insects and the paling of the suburban sky. She knew he wasn't bloodthirsty. That he wouldn't take stupid risks. That he would try to do more good than harm. She knew their lost fortune was his fault, and he was of a strong enough character to admit it. His own cocky decisions were as much to blame as the downturn: she knew it, and had forgiven him.

What Helen didn't see was that he wasn't ready for defeat. Moving into a smaller house, in a less becoming neighborhood, was out of the question. He'd worked like a machine for too many years, nonstop, for that to be all right. His business was gone now—sold to keep them from losing everything. But a downtrodden, defeated father was not the one destined for his children. Why couldn't his wife understand this?

"The right path always comes along for the man with his eyes open," he said to his wife, who was still inside and could not hear him. "Mine are open."

He stood to help finish clearing dinner. He was right about what he had to do, and he even suspected deep down that Helen knew it. Goodness knew he hated the thought of leaving his wife so disheartened. If he had it to do over, and he told Helen this most every day, he would have made smarter choices. But he was leaving. He was forty-one. There wasn't time to amass his fortune the way he had when he was younger.

"My eyes are open," he repeated to himself, as he gathered the salt and pepper shakers, the salsa. He knew people at ThunderVox and Halliburton because of security work he'd done for them in Idaho and Utah. Before that, he had been called to serve on a mission in Egypt for the LDS Church. He had fretted the whole time because although the Mormons were allowed in as a physical presence, the missionaries still hadn't been allowed to proselytize. A few years after he served, despite the ties he'd tried to make with local institutions, the Church was kicked out for good. He'd learned Arabic, but gotten no converts, and no leg in for the Church, and so he had felt like his service was wasted. Now he realized it had all happened for a reason, albeit the celestial kind you aren't meant to understand until just the right moment: and that moment was now. He had learned the language well, and he had come to love the Arab culture. It was as if he had been molded by Heavenly Father himself so that he could undertake this kind of special mission—this service to God, to the freed people of Iraq, to his wife, and his progeny.

Sextuple pay. It would be insane not to go. Two years, during which time he could return home twice a year to see Helen.

The distance, he reflected, might even do the woman some good. Since her miscarriage a few years before, she had begun moving through the world like it had teeth. He had begun to worry that this anxiousness was affecting her womb. Allowing her room to rediscover who she was and what she deserved would strengthen her, he hoped. It would allow for the kind of psychological distance a body needs to regenerate itself. A couple years down the road, then, she'd be ready. They could begin growing the family they both yearned for.

Helen would understand in her own time, he thought, heading for the back porch. He opened the screen door with his elbow, annoyed at the sting at his ankles, the mosquito he couldn't slap because his hands were full.

Chapter Three

June 28, 2004

Two days after their wedding, Helen and Chakor faced the sky in buck-naked splendor, their backs warmed by a boulder that kissed the waters of an unnamed pond near Chakor's cabin. They had skinny-dipped in the freezing early morning water for as long as they could stand and then made love on the rock. The rising sun bore into their bones to offset the chill of mountain air against their wet skin. Flocks of birds hid in the giant pines. Their lazy chirping filled the air with squawks and shrieks so randomly placed that they sounded like wind chimes.

The pond was a glorified puddle of melted snow in comparison to the dozen or so lakes adorning the Black Elks. The key to the place was the rock beneath them: it was granite, not sandstone, and that was a geographic impossibility. There were no other instances of granite in the surrounding mountains. Something, at some point, somehow had to have moved the monstrosity to that unlikely location. This mystery had drawn people to the pond on and off for years, and it was what drew Chakor, though Helen let him believe he'd discovered it himself on a walk they took a week after they'd met.

Her new husband didn't need to know the substantial personal history she already associated with the boulder: that she and Billy

Cooper had shed their virginity on top of it, for example. Still, Chakor knew more about what happened with her teenaged lover than Larry ever did. He knew about the boy she and Billy had given up for adoption when she was fifteen. Larry's religious background had scared Helen away from telling him when she met him, and by the time her courage caught up to her it didn't matter. Her husband's views on dredging up the past were plain: "You got to let it go," she'd overheard him counseling any number of friends. "I never met a happy man sinking in his own feces."

The next day Helen would return to Texas to tell Larry their marriage was over, though her new husband thought she was only going to pack her belongings in a U-Haul and head back to Smoot's Pass. Chakor's flight would touch down in Houston just a few hours after Helen's, on his way to Paris and then Mumbai. The cost of taking the flight together was honeymoon-sized and so they settled on the romance of nearly crossing paths.

Figuring it all out had been acrobatic. Helen would only be in Houston a day before she was supposed to pick up Larry from a flight he had planned months before. To even get there on time, she'd had to convince Chakor to leave for India a week earlier than he'd planned. If his mother was so sick, she'd said, it was wrong to spare that time for themselves when they'd have the rest of their lives to spend together.

Her concern for his Ma had touched Chakor.

"You'll never get to meet her," he said.

"I know," she said, and cupped her hand over his.

Chakor turned toward Helen, and brushed the hair from her eyes. His uncircumcised penis pointed down at the rock, shriveling in the brisk air.

"Every day we'll write," he said, "and the pads on my fingers will press into the plastic keys on my uncle Amit's ancient computer, and yours will caress the keyboard in my cabin."

Helen remained splayed out, like a scarecrow, and Chakor touched her lips with his fingers.

"And we're not going to feel all these rivers and deserts and countries separating us. At every impress of the buttons we'll be electrified by our physical connection through our fingertips."

Helen smiled. She'd married Larry when she was sixteen, and had skipped young adulthood entirely. She'd matched her older husband's steady gait and been grateful—her marriage to him was like a long, luxurious sleep after a childhood of bad magic. And Chakor, because he was so unconsciously outrageous, Chakor felt like waking up. Like a spell breaking, though not broken because sometimes she still heard her new husband through the ears of her responsibly grown, adult one. That couldn't last forever, though.

Now he had moved onto his stomach and was resting his giant hands onto the hot surface of her chest and abdomen. His fingertips felt intricate.

"My palms will be as good as pressed up against you like this," he was saying. "I'll smell the cold water in your hair. You'll wonder why you can smell so much rain and cow dung in the cabin. I'll laugh, and my cousin Amit will pop his head in the room and ask what's so funny and I'll jump from my seat, terrified that he can see the flesh of your presence as clearly as I can. As I *will*."

"Jesus!" Helen finally said, and burst out laughing, but she could feel her face blooming into blush. "Who talks the way you do?" she teased. "How did you survive high school talking like this?"

"Barely," he shrugged, a half-smile glimmering. "I talked like this *and* I was the only brown kid in a private school for rich, white southerners. It was probably an actual miracle."

"A miracle," Helen gave him, nodding. "I'm glad you survived."

"I'm glad *you* did," he said.

Her young poet thrilled her. He believed that he needed her, he felt the pangs of their upcoming separation so cruelly. Helen loved him, and she loved these things about him. The pain she was about to cause Larry somehow amplified the pleasure she felt.

* * *

Within twenty-five seconds of walking into the Grill, Carmen Motes figured out just where Helen had disappeared to these last few weeks. Call her what you like, but she was not raised in a bucket. In no time, she and Terrible had joined the lovebirds at their table.

"Three scones, one Earl Grey, and a coffee that better not be from the bottom of the pot," Carmen hollered at the waitress across the room. To the young fool sitting with her daughter she said: "Well she got my manners, that's for sure. I'm the dear mother, this is Terrible, and you have to be the skinniest damned Ute I've ever met."

"Jesus Christ," Terrible said. He leaned back into the too-small chair, and smiled over at the boy. "Helen," he nodded.

"Hi," Helen said, standing like she believed escaping her mother was a possibility. "Nice bumping into you, but we have to get moving."

The boy was not moving, however. His eyes were fixed on Terrible's doll: a two-foot-tall plastic girl sitting quietly in his lap. "That's Vera," Carmen sighed. "Helen's little sister. You don't want to ask."

The boy blinked. He said, "I've been looking forward to meeting you a long time, ma'am."

Carmen laughed so hard she almost fell out of her chair, only partly for the effect.

"You smell like a distillery," her daughter observed, collapsing back into her chair. "You both look like you slept in an ashtray."

Her young friend's expression gaped at Helen in open horror.

"Oh, I raised her to have a mouth," Carmen explained to him. "It was supposed to be her dowry but then . . . ."

"This is Chakor," Helen said. "He's the Poet in the Heartland."

"From India!" Carmen said. "I read that article in the *Standard*. I was dying to know whether or not you've figured out a way to save today's youth. God knows I'm sick and fucking tired of a bunch of momo Mormons trying to do it with their heads stuck so far up their asses that everything they have to say smells like shit."

"Jesus," Terrible said.

The group of self-righteous hens over at the next table fluffed their eavesdropping feathers at her pronouncement and so, being good-natured, Carmen cackled over at them as offensively as she could. The fine Mormon ladies of Chipeta County were a bunch of tight-assed hypocrites, as far as she was concerned. They were all decked out in matching red sweatshirts with so many American flags on them Carmen felt like singing the goddamned anthem. Like letting loose some fireworks.

"Bah!" she screamed at them, over her shoulder, and watched them start.

"Christ," Terrible said, again. If you didn't know him you'd think he was criticizing her, but what he was doing was egging her on, putting out his own version of a call-and-response. It's why she loved him.

Helen crossed her legs and rested her head between her hands like she was all priss and *not* stepping out on her self-righteous husband. Not that it wasn't a relief to see her doing it.

"You look like shit," Carmen nodded over to her. "Poor thing."

When Helen didn't bite, Carmen lit a Pall Mall since it was the next best thing to a sparkler. The lunch went on from there, with the uptight waitress and fat ol' May Bell demanding the cigarette be snuffed, Helen looking like she was about to bolt, and Terrible uttering "Christ" every fifteen seconds to keep her going. Which she did: she was the sole person at their table keeping up conversation during the half hour it took for her food to be slammed down in front of her and eaten. On the upside, the boy seemed as taken with her as he was speechless. It was a quality she found endearing.

"Is it true your people sniff seawater through a little teapot?" she asked. "I always wanted to try that for my allergies but I never could figure out how it works."

Helen groaned, but the kid laughed. He'd said that if he ever came across a neti pot with instructions he'd send it to her. Now wasn't it just like her daughter to find a man with a sense of humor about one hundred years later than it mattered?

"You're a good kid," Carmen said. "A nice little boyfriend for Helen."

"He's *not* my boyfriend," Helen spat.

The boy's face fell hard enough to shatter the ground beneath them.

"Don't be rude," Carmen said. "You've spent the last seven days with him, not once stopping by your bed to sleep."

"Mother!"

"Oh, right," Carmen said, turning and smiling into his pretty eyes. "Don't you worry about that tightass who's sapped the spark from my girl. *You've* got everything over Larry, already. Plain. As. Day."

"*Shut up!*" Now Helen's voice was turning heads, and it made Carmen happy to see it: like mother like daughter.

"Well, I'd love to hear all about your platonic wanderings. And I've got some good news to share myself, but it needs a glass of champagne. Why don't the two of you come to dinner, Friday?"

"Busy," Helen said.

"She's going to Houston tomorrow," the boy added.

"I'd forgotten about that," Carmen nodded, because she had known her daughter would be flying back to meet up with her waste of a husband. It had just come up sooner than she'd thought.

"And I'm going to India, tomorrow," the boy went on. "But I'm coming back."

"Of course. But what if you don't? And I've got something that won't wait to tell Helen in person. Terrible. *Terrible.*"

"Mmmm?"

"We can have them tonight?"

He was smart enough to know it was her house, not his, and she wasn't asking. He saluted her.

"You'd like that, wouldn't you, Chuckker?" Carmen said. "To see Miss Helen's childhood home?"

* * *

The newlyweds were now riding inside Helen's car, an out-of-commission Ute Cab, on their way to Carmen's. Helen relented about having dinner at her mother's house at the last minute, but had spent the entire day railing about her mother's untrustworthy character. Chakor kept to himself the irony he found in Helen's words: had not she, herself, told him her mother was dying in a bed in Smoot's Pass? It seemed such an insensitive lie to tell a man whose mother really was dying. A visit to Carmen's, he hoped, would help him understand.

The cab was an old Cadillac and still smelled of stale cigarettes and the sweat of strangers and adventure. It smelled like Helen—it had been among the first details of his now-wife's life that he loved.

Chakor was a poet, after all, and he was drawn to these sorts of details. He had never expected to be paid in dollars, but he believed the universe would watch out for his well-being so long as he held true to his love of the particulars. So far he had been right about this. None of the handful of Indian children he had grown up with in Port Arthur were now driving 1985 Ford pickups on their last miles, as Chakor did. They drove Lexuses and Toyotas and even Mercedes sedans. He had chosen poetry; they had chosen medicine or engineering or law. However, if Chakor's truck broke down he could walk through a landscape adorned with clear skies, horses, country creeks, and flowers, and find a neighbor who would help. In the same kind of predicament his old friends, wherever they ended up, would be run down by the first highway motorist they tried to hail down for help.

They would be run down by *each other*. They lived in luxurious apartments packed into great towers where nobody knew each other. He lived in a log cabin next to a cold stream he could jump into on hot days, on a mountain he could cross-country-ski across when it snowed. Neighbors brought him basketfuls of corn and tomatoes all summer long. Nights, Chakor grew delightedly dizzy looking up at the infinite numbers of stars he felt himself drawn into while his old schoolmates saw a faint smattering of the brightest planets and galaxies through the polluted haze of the cities they lived in, and called *that* the sky.

A garage full of BMWs, or the universe. That was the choice life had offered, and Chakor was no fool: he'd taken the latter. He'd moved to the country and spent his nights learning constellations, fantasizing about how he'd tell his mother about his Native American wife—one hundred percent Indian, like he'd always promised. That's the kind of woman he thought he'd marry when he was called out to Indian country.

He had never imagined Helen, who was Native American like most people in the States—one of her great-great-grandmothers, on her mother's side, might have been half-Cherokee. She didn't know her father, not even his name: so still, he thought optimistically, you never know.

You didn't. Helen wasn't what he expected when he began to fall in love, but she was what he was meant for. When he got the call about his mother's illness, it only confirmed his love's intensity. As the world took the first woman he had loved from him, it was introducing him to the one he would live the rest of his life with. She wasn't Ute, but she drove a Cadillac with a picture of a Ute brave still showing through the shoddy maroon paint slapped over the doors. That was some kind of sense, at least.

"She was drunk at one o'clock on a Monday," Helen said, interrupting his thoughts but picking up on the conversation they'd been having all day where it had left off. "Smashed."

"But she was still kind of amazing," he said, and his wife set her jaw and stared down the road.

"It's our last night together," she said. "And you're letting her ruin it."

Of course Chakor knew about Helen's terrible upbringing, but the way he saw it, no parent deserves to be locked out of their children's lives. The lines on Carmen's face told him there were many parties she'd stayed overnight for instead of raising her little girl, but he could also read in her shifting body that her life had slowed down. It would be worth helping Helen allow Carmen back into her life: there was still time for them. But the time for letting his own mother into his life had come and gone. All Chakor had was time for goodbyes.

They pulled off the half-mile of dirt road they'd been on, onto something paved. They began passing the large, scruffy ranch houses on the sides of the small road. It was still light out and would be for another couple of hours.

"You just don't know any other drunks," Helen finally said into the silence. "That's it. You just don't know anything."

"I don't," Chakor said, annoyed. "I don't know anything and if I told anybody from my life what's going on they'd say: what do you expect? You married a girl you knew less than a month!"

Helen flinched, and he was shocked when a tear ran down her cheek, which she tried to wipe without him seeing. He touched her face with his hand: "I keep thinking this whole thing, our wedding and everything, is just a dream," he said. "That I'll leave and it'll puff up into a cloud of smoke and you, and the cabin, and even all Chipeta County will all be gone when I get back." "This is so hard," Helen said, shaking her head. "It is."

Helen was speeding down the mountain roads, in the opposite direction they usually headed. The Grill, the grocery stores, everywhere they usually went was in Franklin, not Smoot's Pass. Chakor himself had never even driven into the little town. He'd passed it on the way to Salt Lake City from Franklin, of course, but it was just marked by a green sign naming it, and one gas station. Sneeze, and you'd miss it.

"Thank you for taking us," he said to her. "She is my *Sasu*. Paying my respects—maybe even getting her blessing . . . ."

"A what?" Helen said. "If she finds out we're married, do you know what she's going to say?"

"Congratulations!" he laughed. "Come on! What else?"

"She'll tell *everybody*. Your whole family will know how you lied to your sick mother, how you *excluded* her from your marriage. My mother isn't sick in bed, but she's sick, Chakor. She is. She can't help it."

"But you can at least tell her you've broken it off with the guy from Houston," he said, and the sentence surprised him: he hadn't realized how heavily Carmen's jabs about Helen's two-timing had hit. He had known Helen had come from Houston after a bad breakup. They'd been together for years: an older man and a younger woman who never wed. The man was a warmonger. Helen had left him for Chakor, no contest. Still, it was now occurring to Chakor that he had pushed so hard for a marriage before he left partly because of that specter of her former lover.

"Let's not even bring Larry up," Helen said. "Just not yet."

"But she already did. And you're not cheating," Chakor said. "You can tell her *that* at least."

"This is impossible," Helen said, and Chakor sighed and held her hand in agreement as they drove into Smoot's Pass. After all, he was getting this meeting. He was getting what he wanted.

Franklin was small and rundown, but this city was worse. On the main road he counted one green lawn—the rest were weeds, or just plain dirt. Nothing seemed to have been painted in thirty or forty years. He saw a small group of kids smoking cigarettes on a picnic table on top of a merry-go-round in a tiny park. They were at least five or six years younger than the high school students he taught.

And still, he was glad to be there. It felt a little like driving into a Western, except for all the cars. And there was no way to take the marvel from the simple thought that he'd *married* into this town.

* * *

Inside the sweet trailer that the city let him live in free for being assistant handyman, Jimmy Hendrickson was frying up small chunks of venison steak for the world-famous spaghetti sauce he'd invented. His teeth were still in a cup on the windowsill. He was only thirty-five, but an affair with crystal meth had rotted the pearlies he was born with into rotten, painful jags. After working for Smoot's Pass City a few months, the mayor had found a dentist to pull them out for him. A year later, she got him new teeth, but they sliced into his gums and tongue. Mostly they jiggled around his front shirt pocket these days, only making it into his mouth when he spoke to the mayor herself. No way would he let her think he wasn't grateful.

Tonight he'd put them in before Sue Crofts came by—not because she hadn't seen him plenty without them in (she *liked* the feel of his soft mouth when they kissed)—but so that he didn't have to swallow the meat in hunks that would get stuck in his chest for hours, no matter how much water he drank.

Joni Mitchell was like an angel whispering from the tape player. The cassette turned out to be the only good thing about the Datsun he'd bought for three hundred dollars from a woman in Franklin. He'd almost thrown it out. First, though, he'd pushed it into the truck's player. Her voice made him feel taken care of, the way the mayor did, the way nobody else in the world had done before he moved to Utah.

He dumped canned tomatoes over his venison, and added some cinnamon and sugar. When he heard a car pulling up he rushed over to the tape deck to eject Joni Mitchell and plunked in *Houses of the Holy*, about the only music Sue liked that he did too. She was mostly a Slayer/Anthrax/thrasher-metal kind of girl, which was not such a bad thing inside the sheets.

After checking to ensure the sauce was okay on simmer, he covered it, and cracked open the front door, holding it hard so the wind wouldn't smash it back into the side of the trailer. It wasn't even her: it was a lady and a man climbing out of a red junker. Their car had a muffler problem as bad as Sue's, that was all. He kept his door open, looking out, waiting to see what they wanted, but then they didn't come to *his* place. They walked straight up to the Murray home and started banging on the door. Maybe Willy Murray had gone and sold out, sick of waiting for Jimmy to save enough to pay for what would be the first house without wheels he'd ever lived in.

But if that were it, they wouldn't be knocking. They'd know old Mrs. Murray had died earlier in the summer.

Jimmy closed the door, put on a pot of water for the noodles, then looked out the tiny window where his teeth were. The skinny brown guy was straight-backed and smart; he looked like the junior high Spanish teacher that Jimmy had had the year they'd lived in Boise. The woman was just a regular woman a-knocking away like she believed in ghosts.

He opened the door and let the wind do its thing: it banged hard against the blue paneling of his trailer. The couple jumped.

"Como estas amigos, yo Juanny." It was the best he could remember. They stared blankly at him, and he wished he'd been a smarter student. He walked down his stairs grinning so that his gums felt cool in the wind. He pointed at the door. "Nobody vivas en that casa no more, you know?"

"Excuse me?" the man said. "I don't speak Spanish."

"Me neither," Jimmy laughed. "You saw how I don't speak it, man, I never could."

"*Go away,*" the lady said. She whispered something to the man, pointed over at him with her head. He studied her long nose and ponytail and tried to remember doing something nasty to her sometime in the past. In the distance, he heard the muffler he'd been expecting and looked for Sue's Mustang.

"We're having dinner with Carmen and Terrible," the man said. "They must be out at the store, or something. We'll just wait on the porch."

"He's on drugs and they're drunk," the woman said. "At the bar. We'll be out here all night. Let's go."

"I think," Jimmy said.

"We're *fine,*" the lady snapped. "Leave us alone."

He watched them argue on Mrs. M's steps, and then head back for their car. Sue was pulling up, so he yelled over the noise of her muffler, "Well, I guess you got the wrong house, then."

The man turned.

"What?"

"That's not Carmen's house."

"You think I don't know where my own parents live?" She grabbed the man's hand and pulled him toward the car.

"Clear on the other side of town is where they live," Jimmy said, "right next door to the Ute Petroleum. That's where they've *always* lived. And they don't got kids, that lady is whacked."

Sue climbed from her car wearing a hot miniskirt and bright orange tube top.

"Carmen and Terrible live down next to the gas station, don't they, Babe?" he asked her.

"Duh," she smiled, hitting her forehead.

"Where you from, anyway?" Jimmy asked the man, who was just staring at them.

"Texas," he said, and climbed back into the car.

* * *

If Helen had had another forty-five seconds at Mrs. Murray's, Chakor would have believed they'd gone to Carmen's and missed her. He would have believed Helen had *tried*—which she had. It had taken her the day to come up with the idea of the detour-house, and it should have worked: since when did people in Smoot's Pass look out after each other's interests?

"I know you feel cheated," she said, reaching out toward him. He moved away from her hand. "A week after I knew I had to come to Smoot's Pass," she sighed, "I arrived in Salt Lake, rented my car, and drove here."

Across the street, inside the tennis court that had no net, a group of kids were kicking a red rubber ball. Chakor's eyes were following its movements instead of her face. She explained how she'd driven through the Wasatch Mountains toward the scrappy sagebrush of Chipeta County. From civilization to a town with two churches, a cemetery, an elementary school, a post office that didn't even deliver mail, and no ATM. Carmen's place bordered on the right by a trailer that Bud Cooper rented out to a revolving series of drunken oil workers, and to the left by the town's only gas station.

The house had transformed since Helen had last seen it, two years before. Carmen had proclaimed that Terrible owed her almost a decade's worth of back rent. An ordinary man might have thought her mother was ending their relationship, but Terrible wasn't normal. He wasn't crude or violent like all the other men Carmen had dated. He was more upsetting.

"He seemed nice enough," Chakor said, the back of his head facing her.

"You saw the doll," she said, "He rescued it from a river and began *talking to her* ten years ago. And once Carmen pissed off a group of men in suits at the Salt Lake City Hilton's bar so much they wanted to fight. Rich, buff, meaty guys wanting to fight skinny old Terrible. And so Terrible slammed his beer bottle onto the bar and shattered it. He didn't use it as a weapon," Helen said. "He ate it. To scare the pricks away, he ate his own damn beer bottle. And it worked. And when Carmen demanded back rent, he read nothing into it. He used to be a carpenter, and just set to work on the house."

"That's impossible. I don't believe it," Chakor said. He was now only half-facing the window, but still not looking into her face.

What all this meant, Helen said, was that the weeds in the front yard that Carmen and her friends once threw beer cans into, like they might grow Miller High Life trees, had been pulled. New beer cans were hidden inside a tin garbage bin with a pig painted on it, and Terrible drove them to the recycling plant in Warren twice a month. The two junk cars that had served as Helen's playground equipment had been disposed of, except for the hood of the old Chrysler onto which Terrible had painted a yellow smiley face and stuck behind a small cactus garden he planted in the yard. He had even scraped the last bit of pink paint left on the house—though that couldn't have been difficult since most of it had already peeled back into tight curls. Now the house's exterior shone a milky caramel, the color of a crème brûlée. Lilac bushes lined the perimeter of the house.

Even the sculptured, antique maple screen door Carmen had inherited from her father, and which had fallen off before Helen was born had been resurrected from its longstanding position behind the bushes in front of the living room's window. Sanded, re-hung, and painted a pale cornflower blue, along with the rest of the house's trim, it crowned the home. It served as the renovation that marked the property as being cared for by its owners so much that when Helen first saw it, she didn't believe it was the same home.

"I thought our house had been torn down, for just a second. That Carmen was God knows where, and I might never find her again."

"But she was there."

"She was," Helen nodded. "And the inside is still being made over."

"That's wonderful."

"Maybe. But I thought I should at least get to tell you that, as far as I'm concerned, it's as much the wrong house as Mrs. M's was."

Chakor's attention had moved away from the kickball game as Helen told her story, but he squinted back over at it when it was clear she was done talking. Helen watched as the group of little Ute boys, all with the same buzz cut, were shouting. A reddish pink ball soared through the air. Helen turned back to Chakor before waiting to see if somebody caught it.

"You think it's me, but this is how it always is with her. You think it's all accident and happenstance. The tiny percent of our lives that my mother has been part of has been our worst. It started our first fight, it ruined our last day together. These aren't results of anything we did."

"It is too!" Chakor almost hissed. "It's a result of your lies, not hers."

"You think that because you haven't always seen her. These are the results of spending half an hour with my mom, and it is always the same results, and I know you're mad, and don't want to trust me, but you've got to believe me when I tell you: we can't go."

Helen started the car's engine again, and drove in silence. It was finally dusk.

Chapter Four

June 8, 2004

Instead of vacationing in the Bahamas, Helen was sprawled out and unsettled on her mother's sagging couch. Terrible had been halfway through installing built-in bookshelves on one of the walls for a week, and everything was overrun with power tools, extension cords, and planks. She had missed Larry's first call from Iraq, but he'd promised to get hold of her again at two, and it was a quarter till. It was their tenth anniversary.

On the television in front of her a whale documentary was playing out. She hated hearing the pained concerns of scientists predicting the sea giants would disappear entirely if humanity didn't change its ways, so she watched the show on mute. She missed Larry. As ever, she was desperate to know he was all right. This morning she had been at the meeting for the arts center when his call came in. The answering machine had captured the tinny echoes of his distance, the soft, static outlines of his voice. During real calls, her anger welled up and strangled conversation within minutes; having his voice on tape felt luxurious, and she listened to his message half a dozen times to soak him in.

Chakor Desai, still new to her, had tagged along for the morning's meeting. They'd met the week before, and seen each other twice since then: once over lunch, another for a hike to the Picnic Cliff petroglyphs. Helen had needed a friend—she hated seeing people she knew from her past and took great efforts to avoid bumping into them—and Chakor was funny. He told her the most unbelievable things—for instance, that when he got the assignment to teach in Chipeta County, he'd made plans to marry an Indian lady, a Ute, by the end of the year.

The idea, he had told her, came to him like fate. He'd never felt fully American nor fully Indian growing up in east Texas. After his father died of heart failure and Chakor had graduated college, his mother moved back to India to spend time with her cherished younger sister, and he had felt completely alone. Connected to nothing. Then the Poetry in the Heartland program sent him to rural Utah, in Indian country, and he knew it was in order to meet his wife. Her Native American-ness, he had told Helen with a straight face, was supposed to have fused with and completed his own Indian American-ness.

"I can't imagine that worked very well," she'd said, and wondered who admits to such weirdness? It seemed sordid, except that he didn't think it was.

"I knew it was crazy," he had said. "I shouldn't have told them my plan, really. I just liked it. There was one woman I really, really liked who thought teaching two traditions would overwhelm her, and then a couple other people I dated told me to buzz off, but not so nicely. And then nobody else would say yes to a date."

By the time Chakor claimed interest in the arts center project for the Blue Hope, Helen understood he was as interested in her. When she'd picked him up this morning from Union High, where he'd parked his truck so they could carpool the thirty minutes to Chipeta, she'd felt butterflies. She felt she'd earned the flirtation after the torture Larry had been putting her through.

During the ride Helen told Chakor stories about her boss, Emmaline Harris. The Blue Hope had been her brainchild, funded through her husband's oil wealth and her own inheritance. "Her grandfather had some patent on a certain kind of vibrating water-bed that was popular in the late seventies," she told him. "There are supposedly a half dozen of them in the Playboy mansion."

Chakor flushed and Helen laughed at him. At the meeting she introduced Chakor as the Poet in the Heartland and a possible collaborator. The county educational coordinator, Tad Lemon, was short, dressed in yellow, and altogether reminded Helen of a half-used pencil. When they sat at a brown, plastic table, she launched into an explanation of the Blue Hope's mission to expand into Chipeta County.

"Seems odd she'd choose here," Tad said, looking at Chakor instead of Helen.

"Well, for a decade it's been a purely Texas-based institution," she said. "Ms. Harris wants to celebrate its tenth anniversary by expanding, by bringing experts in the fine arts to our underserved community." With that bit of information, the condescension that had been hovering in Mr. Lemon's green eyes from the start became pronounced. Still she continued on, offering her vision of the arts center that Emmaline and she had plotted out.

"Maybe it could be mechanical arts. Or even the technological, computer arts," he grinned after a moment's hesitation, nodding at his own suggestion. "Now that would be of use to the kids out here. But not even the Indians make money off their jewelry or whatnots, right? If they did, I can tell you now, we'd have a very different kind of community and your idea would make more sense."

Helen listened politely, overcome by a perversity she'd felt as a teenager when she would ask friends to her house for dinner. Instead of defending the project, she let Tad Lemon spew. If Chakor hadn't been there she would have cited the statistics linking art to healthy communities, to college graduates. It was her job and she was good at it. But Chakor was there. He was sort of hers, and so she wanted him to understand the limited vision she associated with everyone in Chipeta County. She milked Tad for his blandness by nodding, encouraging him to go on. The corollary, in her teen-age years, had been to make her mother's drinks twice as strong when friends came so they could *witness* what she lived with.

"I won't stand in the way of money," Tad said to them with a confidence that suggested he didn't doubt he'd get his way. "But I'd rather it not be wasted."

"How do you work against that kind of thinking?" she'd asked Chakor once they were back in the car, heading for his truck. "You're a poet. You must get the same kind of response from half the people you work with."

"I don't know," he sighed, after a long silence. "I always figure I can convince anybody of anything. If I try. And then I do." She detected disappointment, even reprimand in his tone.

She dropped him off with a limp, annoyed wave, and headed home with the realization that Chakor thought *she* had been the moron.

At home Helen had turned the television on to erase the whole morning from her mind, and when the PBS documentary finally came to an end after a long segment devoted to whale dissection, she began flipping through the channels: a fat man cooking, a spaghetti western, court television. She let all the faces dilute her own thoughts and mellow her mood.

When the phone rang, she was ready for Larry. She was ashamed about how flustered she had been by Chakor's presence at the meeting, and grabbed for it eagerly.

"Larry!" she said.

"Yes, I'm calling for Helen Motes," the voice returned. She feared that in the few hours between her husband's call and the one she was now receiving, something awful had happened.

"This is she."

"Did you know Chipeta went to Washington?"

"What?" Her sinking stomach was replaced by confusion.

"Chipeta did, to testify, and beg for the rights of her people in front of Congress." It was Chakor's voice, she realized, talking like a lawyer. "Chipeta was the only Ute woman who'd ever gone. This young, visionary woman half Chief Ouray's age."

"Excuse me?" Helen sighed, still peeved. Chipeta and Ouray were names from Utah history to her, that was all. She knew the local Utes labeled the pair sellouts or unlucky prophets because they'd tried preparing the tribe for the oncoming hordes of white settlers.

"A few years after that Washington trip a group of Whitewater Utes attacked and slaughtered almost an entire town of settlers in Colorado—all except the women and children, because Chipeta sheltered them. She took them into her compound and waited out the raids, and none of the raiders could fight it because she was Ouray's wife."

"So she became a hero," Helen said. "Okay."

"They tried to *hang* her," Chakor countered, "and they would have except the women she saved made enough noise on her behalf to return the favor."

"I didn't know that," she said. "That's amazing."

"This *land* is amazing. It's full of these people looking out for each other, you know? But those aren't the stories people tell. Those are the ones that get lost, and people don't even know. They don't know what they have to be proud of," he said.

Helen was speechless.

"What I'm saying is that if I were you I'd use the grant money to set up a *cultural* arts center out here. Utes and white kids, even the migrant Mexicans could come to it and learn about each other. I mean, throw in a website, a couple computers for that guy in Chipeta, but then *fight for it*, you know? You could make something really wonderful."

"I have no idea what to say," she admitted, and Chakor laughed, long and easily, the laughter of the ridiculous and the naïve and the beautiful. Chakor, who she would discover could name and sing the benefits of the scrappiest weeds. The contrast between the immaturity of his plan to marry Pocahontas to fulfill his own destiny, and his real knowledge and love for the land in which she'd grown up, delighted her. A few weeks later he would convince her to marry him and her yes would be contingent on all these things.

But on the day of the conversation about Chipeta, when the call she knew was Larry's interrupted the one with Chakor, she'd excused herself. She still wanted to hear Larry, she wanted to tell her husband about Chakor Desai. And so she'd hung up to take the incoming call.

"Larry," she said when she clicked over.

"Happy anniversary," he said. "You are still the woman of my dreams."

Chapter Five

June 29, 2004

"House on fire?" Terrible asked through the door's crack. He was trying to adjust his eyes to the absence of darkness the sun had a bad habit of creating. Runner kept ramming wicked claws into his bare legs, and he had been woken from a stone dead sleep.

"You're here," the Indian guy said with a giant grin.

"You're twelve hours late," Terrible squinted back, raising a hand to shield his eyes in an upside down salute. "Food's cold and in the refrigerator, and I'd stay out of Carmen's eyesight a few days if I was you."

"He wants a house tour," Helen said. "Then we're off to the airport."

No part of Terrible's unshaven face and sleep-swollen eyes could have possibly suggested guests were welcome. It was his god-given right to sleep past six-thirty, especially after having tired himself out cooking for the two no-shows all night. But having survived a near-decade alongside Carmen meant that Terrible could read the vibrations of a Motes woman with his eyes closed and his ears sealed shut. Right now, Helen's demeanor announced that she didn't give a shit about his rights.

"Your mother's gone to cook at the senior center already. Gone with her feelings still hurt."

"We tried to call and cancel," Helen said, bald-faced.

"We *didn't,*" the boy stammered. "I'm sorry."

"Christ," Terrible sighed.

Except for the sadness it caused Carmen, Terrible had been glad the kids ditched—he had no desire to watch them squirming around about the tryst Helen was bound to deny having. It was undeniable that the girl's asshole husband deserved what he got—Larry had long spouted the virtues of "family values" at the same time that he did anything he could to sever the relationship between Carmen and her daughter. Still, a person ought to end one thing before beginning another.

"Well I'm buck naked behind this door," he said. "What do you want to do?"

"We'll go. I'm sorry we woke you, it was stupid," the Indian said, looking dejected as all get out.

"Oh, Jesus *Christ,*" Terrible groaned. He was prone to taking pity, and that's what he was going to do. "Just wait out here a goddamned minute."

His clothes were stacked for washing in the hallway, so he creaked into a pair of dirty Levis and an old Gill's Hardware T-shirt.

Just before opening the door he saw the stack of bridal magazines on the coffee table. Carmen had spent the night torturing them with scissors once she realized Helen wasn't showing up for her big announcement. Now, Terrible did his best to pick up the magazines and the largest of the shreds. If her daughter found out they were going to tie the knot from anybody but Carmen herself Terrible would be in a world of trouble. He smashed all the evidence into the junk drawer beneath the television.

"As you can see, I still got the dishes to do from last night," he said to the couple when he finally bade them enter. "Do me the favor of pretending you can't see them, and I won't have to ask you to mind the mess."

"What'd you cook?" the boy asked.

"Roast beef," he grinned, and Helen elbowed Chakor in the ribs, her smart-aleck eyebrows raised. They wandered back to her old bedroom, where she'd been staying during the summer. Truth was that Carmen had demanded Terrible fix a dinner with no meat. She wouldn't even let him use chicken bouillon to flavor the rice. She'd read in the article on the boy that his religion didn't allow it. They'd bought fake hamburgers at Safeway and Terrible had intended to crumble them into a nice pasta sauce until he realized they tasted worse than the C-rations they'd fed him in Vietnam. So dinner had turned out to be all veggies, pasta, and rice: a dinner about as close to starving as eating could get. He refused to give Helen the pleasure of knowing how much they'd tried.

Terrible sunk into the muddy green armchair that Carmen had pilfered from the old-folks home, Runner jumped into his lap, and he scratched the old dog's ears. The lovebirds wandered through the house like they were thinking of buying it. He looked to Vera, who was sitting in the hard-backed chair against the wall. *Not my problem*, the doll's little blank face was saying.

"Thirty seconds more for the tour and I'm back to bed, kids." Of course, they ignored him. The boy was studying the house like an artifact.

"It's creepy," he complained to Vera, and Runner wagged his tail. By the time the intruders had their fill he was still scratching Runner's sore ears.

"Well, your mom had something she wanted to tell you, but I'm fairly certain she won't talk to you for another week or two," he said.

Terrible stood to open the door for them, then, and a cutout picture of a bride in a silk wedding dress floated from somewhere that was stuck to him. It fluttered and landed atop Helen's shoe. She picked it up and then dropped it like it was diseased.

Guilty, guilty, guilty, Terrible thought, and let them out.

* * *

If a collision was imminent, Chakor thought half an hour later, let it not be due to an ordinary deer—at least it could be a lone moose, even an antelope. Give his family the detail of a uniquely American creature to dwell over, to pass down to the small cousins who'd tell their own children of the giant moose that had run their mad poet uncle from the road.

"Slow down," he said.

Still, he braced for an animal to leap in the Ute Cab's path, turning man, woman, and beast into a jumble of blood and antlers. Nobody in India would know he had died married. They'd just wonder what in the world he was doing letting this crazy woman drive him down a winding road at ninety miles per hour.

Helen had tried to make up for not only refusing to take him to her parents' house, but for taking him to the *wrong* house by promising he could see the house she'd grown up in this morning, while her mother was at work. Chakor had taken her up on it—what else was there to do, at this point? And then the trip to Carmen's was all disaster. Helen had demanded he get down to smell the beer and old cigarette ash she said was still caked inside her bedroom carpet.

As if that was supposed to prove something. As if following her directions made Chakor feel anything besides foolish. He had found himself there, on his elbows and knees, sniffing the long strands of early-seventies brown shag for nothing. He couldn't help but feel set up. Like he was in a mob movie, or maybe something *noir,* and he was about to be shot in the back by the woman he never should have trusted.

"It smells like carpet," he'd said shrugging up at his wife, who was not brandishing weapons. Helen was just staring out her window, chewing on her bottom lip. "Let's go."

"Whatever," she'd said, and it must have been the tone of her voice but the patience he had mustered for her so far had just vanished with that word. Whatever? Is that really all the explanation she was going to send him out of the country with? *Whatever?*

Outside the cab, now, the tumbleweeds and rust-colored earth that marked Smoot's Pass were transforming into alfalfa fields. Within twenty minutes the fields would be overcome by the desert, by sun-bleached blue sky, sage, and cedar trees. The Utah summer presented the landscape as a planet not quite earth. The dry air sharply delineated the smallest details of every growing thing they passed. Chakor was in love with this vividness of Utah.

"Jesus, it's like somebody set the brightness too high on the TV," Helen said, rummaging for her sunglasses in her purse. Not reading his mind, but on a parallel track with it, as usual. And her observation was true, as well: the blinding light outside was the landscape's only imperfection.

He wanted not to be, but he was mad. Lines of black tar crisscrossed the roads in front of them. Earlier in the summer he and Helen had walked barefoot along the squishy strips on one of the side roads leading to the cabin. Their feet had sunk into the burning, sultry black, a feeling so sensual he'd had to step out and crouch by the side of the road. Helen hadn't caught on, and she had kneeled beside him, watching to see how long it would take for the last of their tracks to puff back up, for the traces of themselves to fully disappear.

Were things as they had usually been between them, Chakor would regale Helen with the memory and then top it off with something over-the-top and poetic. He'd say: *the imprints you've made in the hot tar of my heart will remain unchanged through the entirety of our separation.* Helen would laugh and kiss him and they'd hold hands and talk nonstop until the moment where if he waited a second longer, he'd miss his plane.

Things weren't as they had been, though, so he said nothing. He let his mind wander along a different track and thought about how the tar lines were just the signals of all the places the asphalt hadn't been strong enough to hold together.

* * *

They had crossed a dozen small creeks, the Cedar Pinnacles, the tiny desert community of Orchard, and were now ascending into the pine forests leading up to Crustacean Reservoir. They were an hour from Salt Lake, and twenty minutes from the turnoff to Mumps Lake, which was more a tiny, glorified swimming hole than anything. Taking him there had been her plan the last couple of days, a romantic surprise on his last morning in the United States.

A year or so after she'd married Larry she went to a computer class in Salt Lake City. After introductions the first day, a worn-looking woman had sought her out at the break: "Oh my God, you're alive," she'd said. "I can't believe you're alive."

According to the lady, Carmen had once dropped the toddler Helen off at her house one Sunday, and not come back for a week. The lady didn't even know Carmen, was the worst of it: she was the cousin of Carmen's boyfriend's mother.

"I cried when your mother came back for you," the lady said. "I wanted to keep you. And then I always worried—I have always *wondered* about what ever happened to little Helen Motes."

About now it was driving little Helen Motes mad to think of Chakor going home to India thinking of Carmen as a harmless, sorry old soul. Mad he would be angry at her when she was about to destroy a man she owed everything to, to be with Chakor.

She looked over at her new husband and wished he'd say something about Chipeta. About the beliefs the Utes and the settlers shared without knowing it. About any of the things he was wont to bring up. His face soaked in the passing scenery, the random houses, the cows, the salty earth.

A few days before he'd told her the town in India he hailed from was more like Smoot's Pass than anybody would imagine.

"Same stars," he'd said. "You can see all of them there, too, and the same crumbling houses, the laughing, running dirty children. Same coloring to the dust."

What was there for her to tell him, now? She wondered if anything would even sink in. There was something willfully ignorant about Chakor that she was starting to fear. His poetic nature seemed like a kind of autism, sometimes: he knew the story of her growing up, he knew the broad details of her teenage pregnancy, and it should have been enough. She had walked him through Carmen's, where she'd thanked God the dishes hadn't been done, the kitchen was a pigsty, and her mother had thrown three or four outfits into the hall deciding what to wear for work. He'd soaked it in. He couldn't repel from it the way she thought a husband ought to. In her bedroom, she'd said: "Last night the house would've looked perfect, it would've been a mask. But three weeks from now the house will be all this, plus three more weeks of dishes and clothes."

"They were probably too hurt to think of doing dishes," he'd said.

Helen's boy had almost been born outside in a blizzard because of Carmen, on a January night. The sticky sweet smell of alcohol, the atonal chortling of drunken men and women, and especially her mother's own slurred and blaring voice had compelled Helen to take things into her own hands after her water broke. All the *I'm gonna be a grandmas* that slithered toward her from beneath her closed bedroom door revolted her. *We're gonna gather boulders at Moon Lake and make a front-yard playground,* she'd heard her mother say, *We'll use those abandoned irrigation pipes for tunnels.*

The spot where she'd thrown a comforter below her bedroom window, in the crack between the house and the mounding snow on the lawn, was now covered by Terrible's lilac bushes. But before all that beauty it was there that she thunked down onto the wet ground, wrapped in a wool blanket—wild, living belly and all. Her moans were caught up in the droning of the wind, and she began praying that the drinking and partying she had done to make this baby disappear hadn't fucked it up beyond repair.

And with that Jack Grimshaw had come stumbling out into the moonlight, unhitched his belt and pulled out his penis. He shrieked when he heard Helen in the throes of what had become her screams. And then Carmen and what seemed like dozens, hundreds of other people came running out to find her crouched and panting like an animal in the snow. A hundred men's drunken arms lifted her, a hundred men's voices argued as they maneuvered her into the back seat of her mother's car. And then she and Carmen zigzagged down the icy roads.

The black of that car in the blizzard, the strong smell of bourbon on her mother's breath, and all these words her mother was screaming back at her—but that she'd decided not to hear was enough for her, then. It had been one thing to be raised in the afterthoughts between hangovers. It was an entirely new and unacceptable thing when Carmen's response to the soused and pregnant incarnation of her daughter had been to insist she make good use of the vodka by using it to down three horse-sized prenatal vitamins a day.

Tough love is what Carmen had called it, and tough love was the explanation Helen had given herself for not going home once in the first five years after she'd given the baby up for adoption and run away—she wouldn't return until she'd already married Larry. Until she was pregnant with the baby she didn't know she was going to lose, and some kink inside her needed her mother to be part of it. And then again now: Larry went to Iraq, and her nightmares became unbearable, that same kink pulled her back home again.

"That's not a mother," Larry had said seven years before, just a few hours after meeting her.

"That's not the kind of man you marry," Carmen had said about Larry, loud enough she was sure he'd overhear on his way to the bathroom earlier that same evening.

He saw her as oblivious, dangerous, and egotistical; he was judgmental, priggish, and unimaginative to her. A drunkard, a momo, an emotional asp, a personality leech. In their three or four meetings in Helen's decade of marriage, the only thing her mother and husband agreed on was that their hate for each other was mutual.

The brilliance about Larry, a brilliance that Chakor did not share, was that she'd never needed to tell him anything and he knew. He knew, upon first sight, that his mother-in-law was sick; he knew from Helen's posture how sick her mother, in turn, made her. It was a fidelity she knew only now that Chakor didn't have it in him to muster.

In the Ute Cab, they were just a few miles from Mumps Lake, and Helen glanced over at her husband to gauge whether or not she should call visiting there a bust. Against the window his profile wasn't angry, just dismally sad.

"I'm sorry," she ventured.

Chakor cocked his head, but remained looking out the window. She took it as a positive sign.

"I never wanted to start the marriage out with lies," she said.

Chakor sighed, forced a smile. "I'm just confused. I wish we had another week."

"Do you wish you hadn't married me?" she asked, a little bit to lighten the mood and a little bit because she thought he did.

"I wish," he said, and then shut his mouth, and closed his eyes long enough to unnerve Helen. "I wish we'd had more time before I had to go, but I wouldn't have spent the time we did have differently."

"I get it," she said.

She couldn't pull out the words to introduce where she wanted to take him so she didn't. She just waited for the moment, slowed down, and took the turn into a tiny, pine-enveloped road.

"What?" he said, and curiosity and fear both crossed his face and it mortified her.

"It's Mumps Lake," she said, pointing up at a sign. "I planned on stopping here before we were even married. A surprise. A tiny honeymoon."

"There's no time," he said, sounding slightly panicked. She heard, but she kept going because the swimming hole wasn't five minutes from the road—though once there it felt a million miles from nowhere: too small for the fishermen and motorboat people to care about, and hidden just enough for most tourists to miss. She'd made pilgrimages to the lake throughout her years alone, before she'd ever come back to Smoot's Pass for a visit.

It was cold, crystal-clear water you could see through all the way to your toes. Since the car was sputtering along the bumpy road at just a few miles an hour, Chakor rolled down his window, and smiled into the mountain breeze, looking out for the lake. But he never found it. They rounded the last corner, toward where the swimming hole was supposed to be, and Helen gasped.

"What?" Chakor said.

"There," she said, pointing at a depression of earth, feeling a depression in her own heart for the entirely ruined day. "The water's gone."

She felt punched, but her announcement seemed to excite Chakor, who had hopped out of the car almost before she'd stopped it, and run over to the side of what used to be perfect, purifying water.

"You can see the outline of where it used to be," he shouted over to her from its edge, grabbing a large branch from the ground.

Helen crawled from her seat, and then leaned against her closed door watching him try to insert a stick into the former lake's bottom. She heard a tapping of the wood.

"No mud," he shouted happily. "Just hard clay. I wonder if we can follow the riverbed leading up to this and figure out why the water stopped flowing. Look at that, the way the bottom is cracked into a million pieces of dirt."

Helen, who wandered slowly over next to him, thought it looked like a rash, a disease, but didn't say so. If he were going to take this dried-up lake as a blessing, she'd let him. She said, "I'd love to. You'd miss your plane," and he smiled at her like he was still in love, and her heart started up again.

"But we can still have our picnic, right?" he asked, and she nodded. No water, but the tree she always lounged in front of was still there, reaching its arms out toward the vanished lake the way she felt it ought to. She could make lemonade if Chakor wanted, and so she helped him heave the cooler out of the cab's trunk, and filled her own arms with the blankets they'd brought to lay down for the picnic she'd told them they'd have in Sugar House Park, in Salt Lake. She dropped her load and began spreading blankets out beneath the tree, as Chakor scrambled down to the lake's bottom with the cooler and said, "I say we join ranks with merfolk and picnic on the bottom of a lake."

He stomped at the designs the dried earth had made, and she tossed the blankets over the lake's edge. He chose a spot still under her usual tree's branches, beneath the rope swing that looked creepy without the water's innocence to dress it up.

"That's great," he said, when she'd laid out the blankets, and dropped down onto them. "It's beautiful. I love your little swimming hole. You are the only person on earth I know who could have brought me here."

"You can write a poem about it."

"I will. *An Ode to My Bottom on the Lake's Bottom.*"

Helen groaned.

"Very romantic," she said, but then by the time they unpacked the grapes and the sandwiches and their fancy bottled ginger beers, she was feeling like it *was*. Birds flew overhead, the smell of pine filled up the space the water left. They ate their meals, and they undressed each other in full sight of the sun, daring any passing fishermen or campers to discover them.

* * *

June 30, 2004

"What can I get for you?" Lizzie Urisk asked the skinny Indian, or maybe Pakistani, at the Terrace Grill in Salt Lake City's airport. She had been serving flapjacks and coffee five hours straight. Against policy, her cell was set to vibrate inside her apron. Lizzie didn't usually break rules, but she was waiting for a doctor's opinion.

"I'll have half the Salisbury Steak special," the man said, "minus the steak. Just the mashed potatoes and greens."

"That's diff'rent," Lizzy said because it was. "I'll have to charge you the full price, though."

"I can't be charged for just the special's sides?"

"Maybe," Lizzie said, because the guy was cute. He was a browner-looking version of her son Jaydon's deadbeat dad. "If you order it as sides."

"Sure. And I want something special to drink."

"Beer, wine?"

"A chocolate shake," he said. "My flight was cancelled."

She smiled. There was an earnestness about him, and now he was reminding her more of her son than his father.

"Air France?" she asked, and the guy nodded. The mechanics in Paris were threatening to strike again.

"They're always threatening something in France," she told him. "It's mostly all show. You could fly out tomorrow."

"They said it'll be a couple of days. They're getting us all vouchers at the Hilton."

"Hope it doesn't ruin your European vacation."

"I could use the time alone," he said. "I think the world's looking out for me."

Lizzie laughed, but in her pocket, the cell started vibrating. She jammed her thumb on the silencer.

"And I'm going to India," he said but Lizzie heard it with her back turned to him. She was halfway to the kitchen to drop off her order. Then she was flashing two thumbs down at Lin, the wisp of a woman who was her manager, before heading into the airport corridor. It was the agreed-upon sign for declaring a womanly emergency.

Which it was. "This is Lizzy Urisk," she said into the phone once she'd shut herself inside the tiny bathroom that was supposed to be reserved for families traveling with small children. Which she was. "Somebody from the office just called about my son Jaydon's tests, but they didn't leave a message."

She waited four minutes on hold, then, expecting Lin to snap over and chew her out. It was bad news that the nurse hadn't left a message, the same way it had been bad when chilly Dr. Harmston had suddenly become gentle with her after noticing something about her son's blood work. They'd sent the tubes out to the University of Utah. That night, after Jaydon was asleep, Lizzie spent half an hour vomiting in the back yard.

Lizzie hung up her cell and called the office back. She was sent straight to voicemail. After hanging up and calling back again twice in a row, to the same effect, she left a message asking that the doctor leave a specific message about the results on her machine. There was no way she could get away again until after the rush.

Chapter Six

May 10, 2004

In the months before she left Houston, Helen would pull into her driveway nights, after having worked late helping her boss sift through grant applications at the Blue Hope Emergency Center in downtown Houston, and an orange set of eyes would gleam out at her from beneath Larry's unused Lexus. The beast they belonged to looked like a football with a rat's tail: an opossum. It looked unfriendly. She felt that any moment it might grow gigantic and shred her into a pile of clothes, scraps, and flesh for the water meter reader to find sometime later in the month.

Online, she found that the creature had more teeth than any other mammal in North America. Everything else was complimentary: it was a harmless eater of roaches, rats, and snails who didn't burrow or cause other types of garden upsets. Opossums were intelligent survivors that adapted to city life rather than being locked out by it. They didn't attack people. The country's only marsupials, they hung upside down by their tails and carried their babies in pouches. Nothing to fear, only to respect. It was all good to know, *but,* on the nights she encountered one in her driveway nothing could convince her not to throw her zipped purse into the driveway as a decoy and then leap from her car and run full-tilt for her kitchen's back door.

When the opossum wasn't around to upset her, she found something else to do the trick. There was the pair of mostly empty garbage cans judging her from their perch at the side of her house, for example. A real woman would have stinky plastic diapers and wasteful toy packaging enough to top both cans, weekly, they whispered. A woman who could keep her husband with her and make babies would need a *third* can.

Finally Helen's self-respect demanded she rid her yard of one of the plastic bullies. As she rolled it out behind the garage, though, she nearly backed her head into a wasps's nest. The size of a fist when the real estate agent had pointed it out earlier in the year in recommending she and Larry have it removed before it posed a real problem, it was now larger: the size and shape of a mummified infant.

That's the sort of place Helen's mind took her these days, and she panicked. She stumbled forward and her elbow almost impaled what she imagined would be the mummy baby's crackling and somehow-still-breathing lungs. The millions of years of death inside it would sink into her skin and pollute her. Would snuff out any chance of childbearing she had left. She ran inside so fast and terrified she had to sob all alone to herself, on the couch no guest had ever even sat on yet, until she slept.

In these days before Helen left Houston, the minutiae of her quiet life could so terrify her because she had locked the rest of the world out. Since Larry left, she had refused to watch the news or read the newspapers for fear. For fear that her very reading about the war would curse Larry. It was irrational, she knew it, but she was all alone in the world and the man who had given her the only sense of safety she'd ever had was now gambling it away, and she could not stop him.

So that she would not worry nonstop about his life or her womb or the future they may or may not have together, she worried about insects and trash cans and the grant projects on which she spent her days working. But then one day, as she was on her way into her boss

Emmaline Harris's office at the Blue Hope Emergency Center to deliver the mid-May grant checks which needed signing, she heard her boss whisper: "Oh no. Oh my *heavens.*"

Helen, thinking there must have been some family trauma or emergency, hurried to her boss's desk, and put her hands on Emmaline's shoulders to comfort her. She raised her eyes to the computer screen Emmaline was glued to and saw some shadowy figures onscreen struggling with a screaming young man in orange fatigues. She squinted, and then she looked deeper, confused. It looked like the men were trying to slit his throat with a kitchen knife.

She wondered if it was a scene from an Internet movie, something that was supposed to look real, like the *Blair Witch Project.* Just as she was about to ask Emmaline about it, black words in yellow highlighting began blinking at the bottom of the screen: *Kidnapped American Contractor Beheaded in Iraq.*

Later, Emmaline would explain to Helen later she had shamefully, willfully disregarded all her instincts and pushed the triangular play button on the video her brother-in-law sent her to watch. If she didn't look further than the headlines, she thought, everyone in the world would know something about life she was too cowardly to know. And so Emmaline lost in her struggle with the horrific magnetism of the gruesome and clicked over, like that.

None of these questions occurred to Helen: the men sawing away at the neck ligaments of a living man were just there in front of her, and she had no way to back out of what she'd seen, though she literally tried to. She anchored her back against the wall between the two windows in the room and slumped down it. Her fingers gripped the dusty green fringe lining of the carpet protecting the hardwood from being gouged by the wheels of Emmaline's chair. She sank her head atop the heaps of her knees and trembled.

She was furious at Emmaline for subjecting her to such bile: a kinky, gruesome, twenty-first-century pornography. War pornography. Her head was filled with the sound of a thousand hornets.

"I'm so sorry," Emmaline said, fumbling her high-heeled and short-skirted form down next to Helen. "I can't imagine what you're thinking. I mean, I feel *ruined*, somehow—but I'm not connected to this. Not like you are."

Helen blinked. She opened her mouth, and a stumped, cawing sound came out.

"The world is so hard," Emmaline said. "Things have been so hard for you."

The words felt like they might suffocate her on their way out, but Helen finally made some: "I want to go home," she said.

Chapter Seven

June 30, 2004

Larry's newfound fear of too many people—despite the sparse nine P.M. crowds at Houston Intercontinental airport—made his arrival feel like a blur. Even Helen, smiling in her pretty blue dress and yellow heels, had seemed like a vision from a postcard. There she was, right in front of him: unreal, untouchable. Even though she'd cried. Even though she'd hugged him, told him how glad she was to see him.

He had not seen his wife in nine months and Larry Janx had to try not to wince when she touched him. He wasn't going to ask her why her communications had lapsed in the last few weeks because he knew: with the date of his first trip home looming, Helen had withdrawn. Worried about what she would say to him, unsettled by the news reports about what men like him spent their days doing, she had withdrawn. If he confronted her, that's what she'd say. Only cruelty on his part would make her put words to these fears and Larry had been proud, and maybe not thoughtful enough, but he wasn't cruel. Never intentionally.

That he was changed he couldn't deny, and she had called it before he left: in the days she demanded he not leave she had warned him he'd fall into a shell of who he was, that he'd spend the rest of his life trying to untangle himself. Look at Terrible, she'd said. He'd only been in Vietnam a few months before the war ended and he was shipped home: look at him.

"*Terrible,*" he'd scoffed. "My heck, give me more credit than that. Let's look at John McCain if you want to do some looking. *He* was a *POW* and then a senator and then he put in a bid against Bush to be the president of the United States of America!"

How arrogant. Everything Helen had said, he'd shot down. Now he wanted to say: *you were right.* A forty-one-year-old man had no business leaving his wife and future family behind. Going *wasn't* comparable to leaving on a business trip in Italy (had he really said that? He had). The money was sextuple what he would have made in Houston, but he knew now that eight times as much wasn't worth it. Not for Larry Janx. He might never get over what he'd seen. On all accounts she was right.

If he said so, though, she'd try to convince him to stay, and he couldn't do that either. He was in the middle of something in Iraq, some small little thing that might help him to regain himself. If he didn't follow through there might be no restoration of his balance.

"How does it feel to be back?" she tried to ask him in the old Lexus, a question for which there was no answer he found acceptable enough for her.

"I missed you," he said.

The words weren't there to tell the story she needed to hear, and he hadn't thought of that possibility. The jumpiness he felt whenever cars passed on the highway enraged him, he wanted to swipe out at something. He didn't dare look Helen in the eyes, he didn't dare open his mouth: anything might spill out, and he wasn't ready. She was Helen, though: thank Heavens she was Helen. She held back. It must have tormented her to do so, but his wife knew enough not to make him talk when he couldn't, and she gave up trying.

He choked back a complicated sob in the middle of I-45 and forced himself to ignore all the blinking lights, and to focus on just the yellow line ahead of him to make it home. In the driveway of their house in Kingwood he thought it looked like a cardboard person's home. He wished it were the home in Salt Lake City they had lived in most of their marriage. That eighty-year-old house with worn wooden floors and creaky stairs was a Korean War vet's before they'd bought it. That house might know how to take him in. This one was so flimsy. He'd convinced Helen to move into it when he began interviewing with the contracting companies. It had seemed like the least complicated thing to do.

Inside, they sat on the couch he bought her at some furniture warehouse that had provided free hotdogs and soft serve ice-cream to the customers. They'd bought a whole house full of new things to go with their new life, he'd insisted their old stuff would look shabby in the new home.

"We have to start dreaming *big*," he said, like a man who had just lost their one million dollars of retirement in a blink. Now their house had a feel less lived in than a hotel room. And yet: he'd *loved* it, he had loved it before he left. Before he left, it had only felt not quite lived in yet. Like something to grow into.

"Larry?" Helen whispered, finally. A single floor lamp was lit and the house was otherwise dark. She was staring at him from the other side of the same couch he sat on, and he'd hardly realized she was there.

His head was buzzing so much, and he realized he had spoken all of a dozen words to her since returning.

"I'm so sorry I've been so. . . . "

"I'm not mad," he said, and to his great shame tears erupted from his own face.

"Oh my God, Larry," Helen said, almost jumping into his lap to comfort him. He was trying to take back the tears as soon as they were released, and pushed her away. He hadn't cried in front of her before.

"I'm, I'm very exhausted from the flight," he said, angrily. "I'm sorry."

She kissed him like a dart. Her hands rubbed his wet face, clutched onto the hair he'd let grow out a little before coming home. It was a kiss like the ones when they first dated, when she was wilder, and still teenaged, and less predictable. His body remembered. His blood remembered he was a man returning home from war sitting in front of his beautiful, devoted wife for the first time in nine months. His arms scooped her up, and running up the stairs with her in his arms he almost tripped when her feet bumped into the banister, almost sent them both backwards and down into oblivion. On the bed he tore clothes from both their bodies. Her eyes were wide and maybe scared but when he hesitated, she pulled him toward her.

He kissed her body like it was oxygen he'd been deprived of, and he entered her without thinking, without remembering what he'd decided until the last moment: he pulled out only a little late. Most of his sperm sailed into the sheets between her legs.

"What happened? What happened?" she said, concerned, and he didn't answer yet. He crawled next to her and hugged her the way he did when she awoke from nightmares, but this time he was the one shaking. He fell asleep demanding that his limbs become still.

* * *

July 1, 2004

"You have to come to *our* house," Helen had said to Emmaline Harris early the next morning, in tears.

"I haven't even done the shopping for tomorrow, yet," Emmaline said. "No problem."

"You have to come *tonight*." The tension in Helen's voice was enough that Emmaline didn't even mention the plans with the Wilkins's that she'd have to cancel at the last minute. She'd just read an online article about the challenges, even the dangers that the wives of returned Iraq veterans face, and Emmaline had no intention of ignoring this cry for help.

Now she was sitting inside the godawful living room in Kingwood, and Helen was upstairs trying to convince her husband to come down for dinner. The house was built for a family of eight or nine, and was brand new. No lovers, no children had ever slept in it before: she could feel it. It was a terrible sort of suburban gothic. There were no foreboding shadows, secret chambers or dark corridors, of course. (And Emmaline didn't like to judge, but she couldn't help thinking those kind of throwbacks would have at least been interesting.) No, in Helen's house, almost every wall contained windows twice as tall as a man. Even at six o'clock the rooms were awash in sunlight. But that was it: she had this feeling that the light . . . that it was the wrong kind of sun getting in. It felt eerily like a corollary to cheerful music in horror films.

She checked the list off in her head: bad sun, immense home, suffocating suburb, no friends. No wonder the girl had hated Texas so much. If only Emmaline had visited before, she might have saved Helen grief. Insisted that she take an apartment in the city and sell this monstrosity—she could even have stayed in her own empty maid's quarters, in River Oaks.

The smell of the volatile organic compounds in the new paint, of the fire retardants soaked into the carpet and the tacky new furniture was overwhelming. Emmaline worried she might get a nosebleed— her body was *very* sensitive to environmental toxins.

"He won't come down," Helen said, startling Emmaline enough she jumped. "He's not himself."

Helen's eyes were puffy, and she might have looked wan except for the deep tan she'd picked up in Utah. On Helen the tan didn't look slutty, Emmaline thought. It became a woman like her.

"Why don't we go outside?" Emmaline suggested. "We'll make our plates up in the kitchen, and then we can talk where we won't disturb him."

Outside, Emmaline was relieved the developers had been at least sensible enough not to tear down the old live oaks that shaded most of the chemically fertilized—she could smell it—lawn. Its mossy branches sprawled out over the yard like a slow yawn, and Emmaline felt more at home. Helen began hosing the wrought-iron table caked in a season's worth of dirt. Although she was only forty-five herself, Emmaline was more worldly and educated than her protégé. She always felt like she was talking to an intelligent teenager in Helen, who was nothing like Emmaline or the women she knew: she was more like the people the Blue Hope helped. It's why Emmaline had hired her and her GED over the liberal arts–educated girls who had applied for the job as her assistant. Helen's steely eyes, her unabashed skepticism about a number of the small projects the Blue Hope ran, convinced Emmaline that the risk might pay off in street smarts.

"How's the arts center project looking?" she asked, so that they might move more slowly into the subject of Helen's aching husband. When Emmaline assigned it to Helen it had been to give her something to do instead of fret over him, to allow her a small income while feeling somehow useful. After all, Helen was hardly trained. But the girl had taken to the project, arranging meetings with the Utes and the county government, with the various educators in that area.

Most intriguing to Emmaline was having a strong, arts-based institution in a community that would ordinarily never have access to such an endeavor. It seemed the perfect way to spearhead Blue Hope's reach into regions outside Texas. Helen told Emmaline the details of her meetings as she toweled down the dripping table, set it, and served dinner. Talking about it seemed to relax her, and Emmaline was grateful for her own foresight. They had e-mailed about all this, but hearing it all come from Helen's mouth made Emmaline think, for the first time, the project might actually become something. It might take.

"Logistically," Emmaline said, "I would fund it for two years, and we could re-evaluate then. If we find a strong, visionary director of the project who could write grants—and I *do* have a local personality with expertise both in the nonprofit world and the area in mind, if she could get her husband to move back to Utah—we could start something transformational."

"It's not totally my idea," Helen said, after a long pause. "I've had a helper."

And that's how innocently the conversation rocketed out of control.

Emmaline was all for lovers in theory. In books. Even in the case of her friend, Bianca, who was always fooling around with Ashtanga yoga teachers or old high school boyfriends. But not in the case of a woman like Helen, who claimed to have fallen *in love with* her helper. This Emmaline could not accept. After all, Helen was a soldier's wife: stoic, unappreciated, sinned *against*.

"You don't mean you're having an *affair*," Emmaline whispered to be sure.

Then, right in front of their plates of lukewarm pasta with sauce that came out of a bottle, Helen nodded yes. "I have to leave Larry." Her big brown eyes seemed to be drowning in confusion.

"That's rash." Emmaline couldn't stop the words. "You're emotionally vulnerable."

"Maybe," Helen said. They sat staring at each other a long moment while Emmaline's thoughts arranged themselves into an acceptable order: this girl, who had been married to the same man since she was seventeen, had been left suddenly on her own. A cunning Don Juan had homed in on her naiveté, on her loneliness, on her anger even. And he had exploited it.

"I know you and I agree that Larry made a terrible decision getting caught up in this war," she counseled slowly. "But: I know you love him. Any man worth his salt would never have seduced a woman under the duress you're under. Do you see that?"

Helen pressed her lips against each other, sighed, and looked up into the live oak branches that tangled above the table like an old wizard's fingers.

"If he were a good man," Emmaline continued, "he'd see how much you *love* Larry. How much you two have *cared* for each other. He's taking advantage of you, Helen—men like him exist the world over. Move back to Houston if you have to but *Larry* is the man you love. I've seen it, I've seen you two together: I know what I'm saying."

"I can't move back," Helen said very quietly. "And Chakor's gone, anyways."

"You mean you've already ended it?" Emmaline felt immense relief at the prospect. Helen's eyes teared up, and she took this as a yes. "And so then you feel *guilty*, is all? And you want to *end* things with Larry because of it. It's not necessary. I think, I think that given the *circumstances* right now, I wouldn't even tell Larry if I were you. You don't need to—just, just promise yourself you'll look out better for yourself now that you see how you're vulnerable."

Helen remained silent, but she was crying now, eyes still focused on the tree above them.

"Oh, God," Emmaline said, grabbing the girl's hand. "You haven't already *told* him?"

"No," Helen shook her head, finally letting her gaze rest on Emmaline's face. She looked sorry. Like she thought Emmaline might never understand.

"Helen, what you did, it isn't extraordinary," Emmaline promised. "It isn't unusual even. And you regret it—I see that. Don't *leave Larry* for God's sake, though. Anybody, *anybody* else in your shoes might make a mistake like yours."

"Larry doesn't even want to touch me."

"Convince him not to go back. Get him into psychiatric care. He's your *husband*. It's your *job* to look after him."

Helen's face clouded over, and Emmaline could see it was a conversation maybe best picked up when what she'd said already had sunk through.

"You and Larry love each other," she said. "If you didn't love each other, I wouldn't tell you to stay together."

* * *

July 2, 2004

Moist, smelly air clung to Chakor's skin inside the red convertible he'd rented at George Bush International Airport, in Houston. He had driven toward Kingwood with the top down, in the roar of traffic. His plan was simple: surprise his wife and take her blueberry-picking at a farm twenty minutes from her house.

When the Air France mechanics went on strike he had called his mother but not Helen. He wanted the time to consider the unexpected turn their relationship had taken and had used it well: he turned Helen's actions over and over in his head, and compared them with his own. What he had discovered was that while he had claimed the high road, his actions were no better than hers.

He neglected to tell his dying mother about his wedding—or even to invite her to it. He intended never to tell her. Intended for her to die thinking he was unmarried because he was ashamed of what his mother would say about the white girl from a family of drunkards in Utah. Nothing Helen had done compared: she had overstated her mother's illness, and then begged him to wait until later to meet her. Chakor had pushed, and she had shoved, and now angry French workers had made way for the two of them to have one more, sparkling afternoon together in which he would tell her now that he had forgiven her. That they were in this together. That he understood it was, as she said in the car, *hard.*

The time alone revived his spirits enough that he impulsively finagled a fourteen-hour layover in Houston, in lieu of the hour-long one his original itinerary proscribed. Because he relished surprises, Chakor had spent thirty-nine dollars on the Internet to procure his wife's former address from just her name and her geographical history—the fact that she'd been a resident of Salt Lake City and then Houston.

What it all added up to was this: that Helen made him capable of incredible things. Of creating a wedding atop a remote cliff in the middle of nowhere. Of showing up on her doorstep when she thought he was on the other side of the world. She made the magician in him emerge, breathed life into the person Chakor had always imagined becoming when he was a child.

Now he pulled up into her driveway, palms sweaty from nerves and heat both. It was at least one hundred degrees outside. He wished he wasn't sweating. He wished there was some way to surprise her more sweetly than just ringing the doorbell. He felt he owed them both a grand entrance. He walked up to the front door and then didn't knock. At least he could appear: a vision in the backyard.

He tiptoed over to the wrought-iron fence—fully aware there was no reason to try and be quiet—and that's when he saw Larry. He knew instantly it was him, that he hadn't just stumbled into the wrong back yard. Chakor stood beneath the hanging vines on the fence, and waited, in a panic. Larry was singing something low and howling, he thought, but then Chakor realized it was sobs.

"Oh my God," Chakor whispered, and tears came up into his own eyes, too. This trip home he'd known about—Helen had *said* when they first met, Larry was due for his return at the beginning of July. She'd told Chakor that Larry had canceled the trip when she told him she was leaving him. Chakor knew now, on sight, that Helen had been unable to be so cruel.

Of course she had. At a certain point before they wed, the thought that Helen could end an important relationship so simply, over the phone, had panged briefly at Chakor's own heart. It didn't upset him much, or for long, but he had registered the injustice of it.

No wonder she'd been such a mess before he left: she was dreading the pain she was about to cause her former lover. No wonder she was so confused and she'd behaved so stupidly: she had this big, horrible date looming over her and she hadn't wanted to worry Chakor with the details.

Larry was sobbing, his head in his hands at a table Chakor could barely see. From his position behind the purple vines blooming around the fence, Chakor ached for the man and tears welled up in his own eyes. Chakor felt sorry for the guy, there, felt his sense of doom. What worse fate could there be than having the woman you love tell you she'd already married another person, that there wasn't a last chance for anything? Chakor's chest constricted as if it were happening to him.

He thought of knocking quietly on the door. Of letting Helen know he knew why she'd been acting so strangely. To tell her how touched he was that she'd been unable to let down a man she'd loved a long time over the phone, while he was in a war zone. But the loneliness of Larry's sobs in the backyard stopped him from doing it. He had already interceded in this man's life enough; it was only decent, in a universal sense, to allow Larry this letdown without interference.

Having made the decision, the red car in the driveway behind him suddenly stood out. Any moment Helen might come out to see whose it was—so he hunched over like the spy he'd been all weekend, and ran back to it. He threw his jacket over his head inside the car and pushed the button to bring the top back up. He drove away from the neighborhood fast, heading for the airport.

Before he met Helen, Chakor would have laughed if he were told what his life today would look like. It had been a long hard day, but he was glad he'd come. More so than if he'd actually found Helen alone and eager for his company—his faith in her was restored. His wife's depth was murkier and more complicated—and maybe more terrifying—than any woman's he'd ever met.

On their wedding day, they had circled the holy fire together four times: for Dharma, Artha, Kama, and Moksha—duty, prosperity, passion, and self-realization. He and she would work through these all-important aspects of life together, and help each other to become whole. The woman he married wasn't the expected one: she was infinitely more complex and nuanced. She was the right woman, the one he had unearthed in the middle of the sage and hot rocks of Chipeta County. Especially after having seen the misery her rejection had caused Larry, he was elated that her steady gaze was set on him.

* * *

July 4, 2004

At only nine-thirty, Caroline Lee's patience for the month's Fast and Testimony meeting at the Church of Jesus Christ of Latter-day Saints in Kingwood, Texas, was waning. Instead of listening to Harvey Oswald deliver *another* lecture on the three degrees of glory in the mind-numbing drone he always did, she was thinking about the Mia Maids class she would be teaching after this meeting was over.

Last week after she dismissed the girls, she had overheard Mindy Horn declaring her mother happy in the passenger seat of her marriage. "Mom navigates and Dad *listens. She* wouldn't even *want* the responsibility of wrecking. He doesn't have a choice, though: it's the responsibility Dad *has* to take."

Caroline had been trying to leak some feminism into her classes awhile, and Mindy's bright idea was disheartening. Caroline was nervous about the lesson she planned in response to Mindy later in the morning. The lesson she'd give *if* she survived the torture of Harvey's testament: he'd been at it fifteen minutes, a slightly altered version of what he said every month, and *still* Bishop Floyd was too intimidated by the old man to tap his shoulder and ask him to wind it up. It killed Caroline. The only thing going for the ward this month was the absence of Jim Woods—who more often than not would jump up and offer countering interpretations of whatever Harvey said. Luckily, he'd broken a hip.

What a thought to have at church! Caroline commanded herself to pay attention until Harvey sat, and Katie Harrisburg took her turn. Katie was a Utah Mormon—she still dressed in a high-collared, short-sleeved, mid-calf length dress and flats.

"Each and every one of you has made a difference in my life," she started. "And so I would be truly remiss if I didn't get up here and share with you the prayer I had answered just two days after I prayed for it."

Today Caroline would be teaching Chapter 16 in the first *Young Women Manual*, "Women and Priesthood Bearers." Her girls had started spouting analogies about submission six months before, *en masse*. There was the driving one, but it was the biological one that got Caroline the most: since women got to bear children, the marriages would be unequal if they *also* got to lead men in the church.

It was the Fourth of July today, and she felt her duty as an American was to bite these trends in the nub. But she'd decided to revamp the official lesson so much she was worried she might not get called to serve the teenagers again.

Nobody was as good as Caroline for delivering a last-minute meal to a sick Brother or Sister or showing up for work in the canning factory, she reminded herself. Bishop Floyd always backed her. Some of the parents grumbled when she strayed from the lesson guidelines, but she always got the calling to lead the teenagers. He appreciated, she knew, her attempts to change the church from within instead of rejecting it entirely: his own wife had been a Sunstone feminist and had nearly been excommunicated in the early eighties. He'd back Caroline as far as he could.

For the first twenty years of the church, women could perform blessings, heal, and prophesize—they held priesthood keys. Women had *lost* power and authority in the last hundred years, *despite* Joseph Smith's own views. It wouldn't be *becoming* liberal when women regained their authority in the church. To desire it wouldn't be coveting something not prophesized or modeled already by their foremothers. It would be *returning* to the vision of the church's founder and first prophet. Caroline wasn't power-hungry; she just felt the priesthood inside her. She'd seen it in her Sisters, and yet twelve-year-old boys held more clout within the hierarchy than women who had returned from their missions and had raised families.

Becky Perkins, a spitfire also in the Young Women's group, stood up when Katie sat down. "Just to say how much I love my mom, and my dad, and my brothers and sisters, and my best friend Jill who you don't know, and who is happy, but I guess would be even happier if she had the gospel in her life. I say this all in the name of Jesus Christ, Amen." Her mother or father had obviously made her do it.

Sometimes a Fast and Testimony meeting was good, and Caroline would be moved. Or she would hear something that made her see the real good bearing witness could do for a person. In general, though, she was a bigger fan of the usual sacrament meetings, when just a couple of people prepared talks, which were thoughtful and generous as a whole. Her favorite doctrine of building the city of Zion came up a few times a year. Today, though, Caroline looked at her watch and sighed when she saw another twenty minutes left to go.

"I haven't borne testimony in at least five years," a voice she didn't know said then, making her look up from the notes in her lap. It was a prickly looking tall man with a red rash all around his neck. She'd met him briefly a few months back, when he and his wife had come to introduce themselves to the ward. As far as she knew, they hadn't returned. The man looked like he'd been sick, and Caroline worried their family had been in need and that nobody in the ward had known to help them. She couldn't remember his name, but the woman was Helen, like her own mother.

"I have a long story," he said, in a shaking, small voice. A desperation about him kept her from returning to her notes. She could feel something was about to happen. The last time she'd felt this was when a man nobody had ever seen before had come into the Sugar House ward she'd belonged to in Salt Lake and said, "I know a lot of you don't think much of the way I dress or the way I conduct my life, and to you guys, I say"—and then he'd flipped the ward off old-style, with his third finger held straight up and the rest in fist. "And I *do* say this in the name of Jesus Christ, our Lord, Amen," the man finished, before marching out of the church.

The man at the microphone today didn't seem out for revenge. But there was still something. He was staring quietly out at everybody long enough to make people squirm.

"I have had this story to tell to my wife, and it won't come," he said, finally. "I woke up this morning and it's the Fourth of July and it's God's day all at once. I thought maybe if I came I would find the spirit, that Jesus would help me find the words. If he hadn't already walked me through this morning, I wouldn't be here, that's no joke."

"I'm back from Iraq for just this week," he said, running one of his hands compulsively through his hair as he spoke. His voice was still unsteady, almost a whisper. "I prayed all winter, though, without any response. I figured the requests sent out to Heavenly Father from that part of the planet were just too overwhelming for even Him. I know it's wrong, but I can't believe a loving Father would find it easier to bear what I have seen than the rest of us."

Maybe it would be an anti-war rant, Caroline mused: now that would be *something*. A young boy whimpered in the front row and his mother carried him out. The soldier was again staring, waiting for the words from Heavenly Father, which was normal enough at a Fast and Testimony meeting: the Latter-day Saints could be a patient lot.

"I've been afraid to look at her," he finally said, still sounding unsure. "I see worry in the lines around her eyes and this great wall around her. But I have thought about it, and I want her to know that even the filth suffocating our world can offer clarity. The way a blanket of snow shows you something new about the world because of what it's hidden. And I will take whatever strength I can from what I've seen. I will take the positive and not the negative strength, like I have always done, and with the Father's help I can still do that."

He paused again, "Please, Heavenly Father," he said, "help me get this story on track." And he waited again while the people around Caroline shuffled in their seats, looked to each other.

When he started speaking again his voice *was* stronger. "I came into the house of God today to share one story. A little bit of good I am doing because even when I am at my worst, I want to be the person Helen thinks I am. I keep seeing myself like this rotted walnut inside an unopened shell that looked fine from the outside. It's crazy. But it isn't in me to feel this way forever: I will not be that man, and I want you, I want Helen to know it. And so here is the story that is my only proof:

"I got off work a couple weeks back and felt like heck. I was worried already about this trip, and went to the mess hall to eat but I was too sick to do it. I just sat there, staring at my food. Listening to voices all day long is all I do, and that's enough of that. But when I don't work, I don't talk to anybody. I don't listen to those stories the guys tell—most of them are service workers that cook or clean or drive things from place to place, and they just tell these stories that drive me insane, and I won't listen.

"But this night, you know, it was doctors who came in and sat at the other end of my table. Kids who looked younger than my wife, and one older lady who was a few years older than me. The mess hall they usually go to had lost power. That's how I know, now, it was by sheer grace that they sat next to me.

"It was just jokes, talking about back home awhile, and then one of them started talking about this little girl they were all worried about. Her daddy had managed to bring her across the entire country, from Karbala, through Baghdad, and to Balad. He'd heard some medic at our camp could help his little girl. . . . "

"This daddy, this man for some reason trusted his child—and you hear of girls mistreated, that's what they say—but this father trusted our American doctors to save his child's life. She'd been growing sicker and sicker for a year, and he had gathered her up and traveled across this very dangerous world they lived in to save her. Maybe he thought the American bases were the safest places in Iraq to bring her, but who knows why he didn't bring her to a camp closer to Karbala. That's what those doctors were saying.

"And they were worried because he'd done all that, he'd gotten to base, but his English was very limited. He spoke it, just not enough. And none of the doctors spoke Arabic. The doctors at the table were worried they didn't have a good enough understanding of her case history, they had very little access to interpreters, none who could spare time for this family. And that girl was getting sicker and one of them said she would probably die, after all.

"And here is the part meant to prove to Helen, to you all, that the core of me is not all rot: because I spoke up. I offered my services. 'I work fifteen-hour days here,' I said, 'but I'll give you all every one of the nine I'm free.' And when I said that . . . and when I said that . . . "

The man started crying, but he didn't stop: "When I said it to those healers I swear to every soul in this room that I felt Jesus Christ, who I told you had been gone, I felt him press his lips to my lips and kiss them.

"I wouldn't make that kind of thing up! If I were lying I would have said he came to me and I heard him, but I'm telling truths now. Heavenly Father has provided me with the words, and what I say is that Jesus Christ kissed me on the mouth and it almost stopped my heart and it was so obvious something had happened to me that the doctors stared like I might spontaneously combust.

"'Please,' I said, 'I don't know if you boys believe in any kind of God, but I do.' And it was the lady, the older doctor, who started talking to me first. Asking me questions, asking how good my Arabic was. My words for the anatomy have been terribly increased since my time in Iraq, and I told her that, and I told her why. Told her that my job is to translate stories torn from the youth of Iraq for ThunderVox. I didn't lie and tell her I knew how to say gastroenterological in any language but English," he said, and a couple people in the pews tittered, relieved at the straw of humor. The laughter was good for him; he began smiling through his tears.

"I told her to give me one chance, and that it would potentially be a blessing for us all. And that is what I have done twice, now. I talked to that girl's dad, Mossily, and I talked to that little girl, who keeps two stuffed animals the nurses gave her when she arrived tucked into the crooks of her arms on either side. A Mickey Mouse and a giant, pink bunny. The details of what ails her aren't so important to this story as the fact that I helped her get diagnosed with a liver problem that could have killed her, and the doctors are now working on convincing the father to take her to one of the hospitals in Baghdad, where after all, they have the best equipment to care for her, and where one of the doctors has some sort of connection that might get this girl seen. They have begun giving her the right medicines, she has been spared the torture of random, hopeful tests that may never have come up with the answer the doctors needed.

"I am trying to avoid imagining her life after she is cured— whether or not she will just be shredded by the war in a year or two more, or how hard life will be even for the survivors here. All that I have to offer I have offered up to our Heavenly Father and to this child, and the rest I leave to Him, who I trust will protect this innocent since she has already suffered so much. I admit that when I came to her bed before leaving for home and saw her sleeping, I wanted to slip her inside an envelope and take her with me. We have wanted a baby so long, and she needs a safe place to grow up. But she's not an orphan, not some unloved and mistreated Arab girl. She is the daughter of this skinny man who looks to be in his seventies but who says he is only forty-six, who says she is the beloved middle child in a family that has already lost two children on either side of her age which is seven.

"I cannot deliver her from the war zone and her family. I have come to deliver this girl's story to you as my testament to the greatness of Heavenly Father, and to ask that you pray for her, too. And that you pray for me and my wife, and the worlds between us. And I am relieved to let you know that though I am no person's hero, I have found some little hope in this relationship with Dr. Frank and her team, who are my first real friends in this place after almost a year. When I work with them I do it for Helen and Jesus and I feel a little bit like a living man.

"Helen, I love you. I will not rot inside and ruin you through association. I want you to love me, to know always I am trying the best I can to be worth your love."

"I say this in the name of Jesus Christ, Amen."

It was ten past ten, the meeting had run over, and people were sobbing. It wasn't abnormal for a Testimony meeting, but even Caroline was swallowing tears. He put the microphone back, and walked quickly to his wife, who stood and went to him. Her sobs were moans. People crowded around him, to thank him for his testament, but the couple shot out of the church as fast as the man who'd flipped it off had done.

Caroline, too, left the room without speaking to anyone. Today's lesson would be particularly on the poems of Eliza Snow. The poetess had revered not only Heavenly Father, but Heavenly Mother—who Caroline regularly had to remind her students, was as real a presence in the Church as the Father. She was as divine and as holy as the Father. Eliza had first prophesied her, but Eliza was no heretic—she was, in fact, one of Joseph Smith's wives, and then Brigham Young's. She laid hands on people and healed them like the woman in this man's story had healed him. The woman doctor *let* the man into her specialized world, and he benefited, and she did, and the children did. She shared control of her car—there was no giving it up, or taking it over. That's what she'd say to the class, she decided, as she began arranging their chairs. As she took the minute alone to imagine the lips of Jesus Christ pressed up against her own.

* * *

Even as he escaped the prison of so much unsaid, a plain and rapturous light embraced Larry Janx. It coated his soul with the strength of angels: the power of a sincere testimony. Its reward. And good heavens, was he ever grateful. He had spent the entire night before trembling in his bed, his ears stuffed with toilet paper, because of the sound of fireworks. Talk about a patriotic irony. But now, *goodness*, was he relieved. Changed. Satisfied that he had watched the heat of his words thaw the anger that had built up so heavily around his wife, toward him. When they left he was filled with the sense that God's forgiveness still resided inside himself.

Helen, however, was quiet and seized up. She listened to him, but said almost nothing the whole car ride home. It had felt like they'd reversed roles. She'd silently slipped directly into the kitchen to make lunch when they'd gotten to the house. After half an hour or so, Larry poked his head in after her because it was so quiet in there. The ingredients for his mother's corn soufflé were laid out on the counter. He knew she must have planned it to help snap him back to himself, and now here he was: but there she was, dead still, staring at the eggs and the ceramic cooking pot like they were unwelcome intruders.

"I'll make the lunch," he said, startling her. He walked slowly to her and cradled her head in his hands. She smiled, made an effort at raising her eyebrows to look skeptical. "I taught *you* to make it," he reminded her.

"Flopsy and Mopsy?" she asked, the real smile lines finally cropping up in the edge of her eyes. It was true: both his soufflés had collapsed. He'd been a terrible instructor, but then she'd figured out how to make the soufflé just like his mother, anyway.

Larry leaned against the kitchen counter and watched her, still smiling, as she started searching out mixing bowls. Helen was as beautiful as he'd ever known her, a woman who improved with age not so much because of her looks, but because of her growing comfort inside her own skin. That's what it seemed to him now.

"Thanks for coming to church," he said. Helen's jaw tightened, and she looked up at him with a grimace meant to be a smile.

He was leaving for Iraq again Wednesday. He finally felt himself. He could not let her withdraw. And with this thought he remembered what it was he'd hidden away so many months before, kissed his wife on the nape of the neck as she stirred, and walked out to the back yard.

An item of mine that she loves. When Larry had come to a dead end on gift ideas before he left for Iraq in the fall, he had stumbled upon a mother's blog post. Love Baskets, it was called. He swallowed the title like a cup of vinegar, but the idea behind it all settled in him. The writer had to travel to Sudan for a week, once a month, for some project. Her seven-year-old daughter suffered nightmares, refused to eat, and hardly spoke to her for days after she came home. The baskets, she said, went a long way to helping the girl cope.

An item of mine that she loves? Larry had chosen his black terry bathrobe, which Helen enshrouded herself in from time to time because, she said, it made her feel safe. It smelled like him. He'd doused it in his Old Spice to be sure. Wrapped it with Christmas paper turned inside out.

A tape recording of me singing her favorite lullabies, the blogger had written. That didn't make sense for Helen, but he fished the only mix tape he'd made in his life from her jewelry box. He'd given it to Helen a few months after they started dating. (Three different female coworkers assured him it would make him seem hip, that it would impress a younger woman like Helen, and it had.) He listened to it and chose the songs he remembered her liking, that seemed right for the occasion, and that he thought he had a fair shot at singing: "I Want to Hold Your Hand" by the Beatles, "You Were Always on My Mind" by Willie Nelson, and, as a joke, "Hungry Like the Wolf" by Duran Duran. Following the Internet lady's advice, he didn't practice and didn't record the songs more than once. It wasn't supposed to sound like he was a rock star, just like an ordinary man. He placed the recorder and the original mix tape in an old shoebox and wrapped that, too.

Her favorite sweets. Finding them had required a trip to IKEA: she loved a kind of strong black licorice shaped like cats. They were Dutch. Helen used to buy them at the novelty Swedish Deli in Salt Lake City. The candy colored her teeth a deathly blue and he'd never told her.

A photo of us doing something she loves. When he was rifling though the box of loose photos they kept he had found something even more valuable at the bottom of the box: a receipt he'd gotten from the MacFrugals where Helen was working when he met her. The date on it was November 15, 1993—and though he didn't know Helen then, her name was on the receipt. She had been the cashier for his order of Doritos and five plastic garbage cans. He'd scanned the receipt, printed it, and then had both the copy and the original laminated. The copy he took to Iraq as a talisman; the original was housed in a regal red envelope.

He had never claimed to be the creative sort, but he knew how to search an idea out and take it on when he came across the right one. But these goodbye trinkets, the planning he'd done, had come to nothing. By the time they were ready for Helen, he was no longer ready to give them. He was angry at her, she was angry at him.

Not today, though.

After he left the kitchen, Larry walked directly to the garage. The garbage bag he'd angrily stuffed with gifts in the fall rested, dusty and anonymously, on the low shelf on which he'd left it. Of course it was untouched, although he had imagined Helen would somehow accidentally discover it. Maybe she'd be looking for the croquet set next to it, or maybe for some reason she couldn't describe she'd be drawn to the mysterious bag. Or perhaps, he'd considered, he himself would give in. Maybe his wife would need special consolation and he'd direct her to the bag—a hidden treasure that would lift her spirits when she most needed it.

But then their phone calls were silent and awkward and full of not enough information. And then she fled. He'd never dreamed she would do such a thing, that she'd end up in the hometown she'd proclaimed she wouldn't return to if there were a nuclear holocaust and it were the only habitable place on earth.

"Because you know it would be, right?" she'd nodded to herself. Heck, she wasn't twenty-one yet when she said it.

His gifts for Helen were stolen ideas, but the right ones. He'd once promised himself to soften Helen's pessimistic nature, and for years he had. But then he let it get to *him.* Now he repented for having done so. As he snuck back into the house in Kingwood— through the front door since she would see him coming through the back—he held the black plastic bag over his shoulder like Santa. Helen clanked around the kitchen on his second-to-last morning in America, while Larry Janx scooted a large red vase with dried wheat in it from its place next to the door into the center of the living room. He dumped the presents out in front of it, and arranged them around it. On impulse he raided the Monopoly game in the coat closet for a little green house, and left it at the bottom of the pile.

The living room would smell like sweet soufflé any moment, and she would call him into the dining room for lunch, and Larry looked forward to that. He was starving.

* * *

July 10, 2004

Helen woke to screams the following Saturday, for the second time that week. She awoke to the sensation that somebody had wrenched his fat fingers between the muscles connecting the sides of her ribcage, and ripped. Consciousness saw Helen sitting upright in her bed, eyes open tight, at three A.M. On her bedroom wall, a black web formed by the light falling against the tree limbs of the black gum shifted reluctantly in the slow breeze. Even the *shadows* in the Gulf Coast were wet. In Utah they were sharply edged and clean-cut, separate from and indifferent to the worlds they danced upon. In contrast, the diffuse edges of the Kingwood shadows looked like they were trying to grip the walls, trying to take hold of the worlds they traversed.

Wednesday night she'd woken the same way, to the same scene, and Larry had been there to hold her. The way he had been there when they'd first met and her nightmares were so frequent she thought she'd scare him away. He sat behind her, curling his legs around her hips and his arms around her shoulders: a human life vest. An hour inside church and Larry Janx had been returned to her, like that, the man she married. His naked stomach pressed into the bones of her back, and the heat of his body seeped into her terror-stiffened muscles. He waited for her body to relax and give into his own. In the past they would have made love on such a night, but in Kingwood he just hummed to her—a slow, slow rendition of a song that sounded vaguely country and western—and he rocked her soundlessly, swayed her to sleep.

Nobody on the planet made Helen feel as safe. It was her terrible secret because nobody besides Larry understood how much that mattered to her, or how hard Helen herself had worked to be safe. Chakor had resurrected the recklessness inside her she thought was long dead. He thought it was the essence of who she was: it's why he loved her, and it was why he was foolish. He was fireworks when she closed her eyes, and Larry was all the black in the sky behind them, the surety of stars and everything in between.

He had reminded her about all this too late. There he was with gifts, six months tardy of their making a difference. The story of his hope for redemption, the admission of his own mistakes, the defense of his humanity: everything came too late, everything came just in time to make asking for the divorce impossible.

The thought of succumbing to another bout of fitful sleep mashed too terribly into Helen's mind on this Saturday. She slid onto the carpeted floor, instead, found Larry's cologne-drenched robe, and wrapped herself in it before wandering into the dark hallway. The small tape recorder was in one of the oversized pockets, the other smaller gifts in the other. They bumped against her thighs as she clomped down the stairs. She walked straight to the back door and opened it, turning her back to the cave of her empty home. The warm air outside felt like a stranger's too-intimate breath. *But I'll take it*, she thought.

In her pocket, she fiddled with the little Monopoly home. He'd urged her to sell the house that neither of them would ever come to love, and rent something in Salt Lake until he returned and they could choose something new to buy together.

"You need a home base that's all yours," he'd said. "I can see that."

The brawny, tangled live oak sprawled out across the back lawn and tonight it was haunting. There were things she would remember forever about Houston, nightmarish things she would miss. The thought of forever abandoning her old nemesis, that opossum, already upset her. Her time away had transformed the small beast into something less monstrous in Helen's mind—less werewolf, more stray cat. Right now she wished she had it near her to cuddle, rat-like tail and all. She'd hold it in her arms and its warmth and its short breaths would be so forgiving.

The beast was absent, though; probably busy with her own life, raising a magnificent litter of joeys in the utility alleys between people's property lines. Helen was left to herself in the darkness of her backyard and, as ever, its loneliness overwhelmed her. She soon found herself walking toward the garage and her wasp's nest: she needed to see something *living*. It was even less cuddle-appropriate than the opossum, of course, but at least the starlight might transform it into something more hopeful than she remembered: a paper lantern, maybe, or a small and unassuming satellite of the moon. Barefoot, and naked beneath her robe, she felt vulnerable, but she went.

Even in the dark it was immediately obvious from the corner of the garage that the nest was gone. It was so obvious that she sped down the dirt path toward it, hit a cobweb, scrambled around in a short panic, and was by then one hundred percent certain there were no wasps: not a single angry buzzing sound emerged from a sleeping silence. There wasn't even a piece of wasp's nest shell she could see. It had all vanished. The colony had probably been murdered as it slept.

Helen stumbled back out the way she came, fumbled through the grass, and onto the concrete driveway where she sunk to her knees, and hugged her elbows. The neighbor on the other side of the fence might have heard it, might have been bothered by the wasps, and figured they were doing her a favor. More likely it was somebody she knew and it was her fault for having failed, for never really attempting to explain her attachment to an object that she'd found so terrifying.

At Helen's core existed a careless person who paid attention to the wrong details, who fell in love with the wrong things, and who was embarrassed for the wrong reasons. Lying on the pavement, she looked up at the small remnants of the night sky. The lights of Houston blotted out most of the stars, and though Kingwood polluted the sky a little less, she imagined the astonishment of native Houstonians the first time they encountered any sort of real wilderness, the first time they realized just how many stars hid behind city lights.

She didn't mean to be in this situation. Men did this, men married twice: not women. Horny truckers took wives, started families with both of them. Polygamists did it for God, at least in Utah they said they did. Maybe some other kinds of desperate people did, too. But Helen wasn't desperate or religious or sex-crazed. She was a woman who had been totally determined to live the dullest, most ordinary life in the world. A safe life. For years she had managed, until all in one swoop she undermined it. She wanted Chakor.

Chakor, who she'd known since June. When she thought about him, though, he set off the same synapses in her mind that thinking of her childhood did. He seemed a relic of growing up—a best friend she'd always loved but had to leave behind—and this thought sent a pang to her heart. She wished she could delete him.

To put him out of her mind, she pulled the tape recorder from her pocket. Though she expected to hear a new mix tape when she hit play, she was astonished when Larry's voice itself warbled out into the night. She balanced the recorder on her chest, and let his deep, pitchy, tone-deaf recordings vibrate into her. And it felt to her like he was coming through for her, it felt to her like the thing she needed.

The only warmth besides the recorder available to her at this moment was the concrete's stored heat—no substitute for a husband's arms, but better than nothing. She spread her body out in ginger-man fashion, as she had on the impossible rock by Chakor's cabin earlier in the week.

As a child she had had a wonderful, profound thought once, while looking at all the stars above Smoot's Pass. When she ran in to tell her mother, the idea had completely vanished from her head, but the memory of it, the glory she felt when she knew that thing, she never forgot. So Helen did what she did whenever she found herself alone, facing stars: she tried to remember that idea, that beautiful observation she had lost so long ago. When she woke up it was dawn and she started packing, again, for home.

Chapter Eight

January 25, 1994

It was the coldest night after the coldest day on record in the Salt Lake Valley, a night Larry Janx got caught outside and almost froze to death. He had always loved extreme weather. Every summer he spent a few weeks leading Eagle Scouts through the canyon lands in Southern Utah on survival trials. They'd scoot down thirty- or forty-foot-tall crevices with their backs to one wall, their feet to the other in the July heat. They packed in two weeks of water and learned to dig at the base of cactus plants to find more, if they needed it. Insane, Helen would later call it. Spiritual exercise is what it was. But snow—heavy, blizzarding snow—was his favorite. He loved how fast the snow fell, the way it pelted his face hard, like the world was trying to transform him into some wondrous creature whose hot insides were at war with its icy surface.

On the coldest days, when most people bundled up in their houses, he'd pile on two or three sweaters, top off with a generic black cap that made it look like he was about to go out robbing drugstores, and disappear for hours. These were the days, he always said, when history confirmed he would discover the most essential and incredible parts of himself.

The night of the blizzard in question he had, as usual, left his down parka on the coat hook, didn't check the weather forecast, and set out into the snow. Since he'd never been a man to permit himself to do something for the joy of it, he invented an errand. Computer peripherals. MacFrugal's was having a sale on computer peripherals and the data management business he was building up from scratch could always use another USB cord or two. Driving was impossible since the roads hadn't even been plowed.

He set out from his house at the bottom of the Avenues in Salt Lake City, and headed for the MacFrugal's downtown, a mile or two away. It was five-thirty, already dark, and his footprints were the first everywhere he went, a feeling he relished. He relished the way the walks of some people were already covered in two feet of snow, while other folks would never allow more than a quarter of an inch. This latter sidewalk he assumed belonged to old men or the neighboring invalids they shoveled for—and he admired that World War II generation that believed it their civic duty to keep the walks clear. But he didn't hold grudges against the nonshoveling sorts, the loafers, the renters: the world needed a little of everyone. Larry could acknowledge this clean fact when he was out in the briskness of winter, not so much anywhere else.

Truth be told, Larry liked walking in the deepest snows best. For one thing, it was less slippery, but mostly it trailed his thoughts into other time periods. He thought about the pioneers, for example. How the prophet Joseph Smith was murdered, how twenty or thirty years of the man's thoughts had been stolen by his early death. How the prejudice and hate from people who themselves had fled the Old World because of the same hate, forced whole families, an entire community across the Great Plains, over the Rockies. Not many old people, though, he suspected, and thought about how it must have hurt the elderly to be left behind. It was for the greater good, but still it must have hurt. Maybe those old men with the eternally shoveled walks had this in mind. They wanted to make sure even they could follow on the next exodus.

Larry wandered through the streets toward the MacFrugal's, a thirty-two-year-old businessman deep in the childish kind of snow thinking he rarely allowed himself. There were no cars out, no people, and when he made it down the hill to North Temple Street, he was awed by the way the streetlights kept turning from green to yellow to red. Every change of color glowed on the snow below him like the harbingers of varied desolations: foreboding red, like the world had been wiped out by war; a sickly yellow that felt like the past and the plague; and of course, green felt extraterrestrial. All his streetlight scenarios left him the last man on earth, a thought he relished. He wasn't the type to hit the malls and play with all the toys inside. If he were left all alone, he thought, maybe he'd finally sit back in front of the television and watch some movies. He'd feel safe, like anything he'd been born into the world to do was already finished.

The light evening snow he'd stumbled out into had slowly picked up to a full-on storm. And it had gotten colder, the degrees dropping. He turned around to look back at his tracks when he was just a couple of blocks away from the MacFrugal's and they were already nearly erased. He liked that, but he knew by then that he'd picked a stupid night to buy peripherals. He realized the MacFrugal's was likely to have closed early, if it had even opened at all, and began making an alternate plan: he'd hole up inside the McDonald's on the same lot and drink the grayish hot chocolate. He wasn't a fast-food kind of man, especially downtown, where the restaurants were liable to be filled with the homeless, whom he didn't like. He hated their apologetic smiles.

The lights on the MacFrugal's were on when he turned onto 400 South, and there were three cars in the parking lot in front: lucky. But of course, when he made it across the parking lot, which seemed to be the only plowed space in Salt Lake City, he found the MacFrugal's locked. He knocked even though he couldn't see anybody inside, and all but the store's window lights turned black at the same time. There was no avoiding the idiocy of his having wandered out into a windy blizzard with a few sweaters on and nothing else. He didn't even have gloves on and his hands were already chapped from his shoving them into the pockets of his too-tight Levis.

Just about the moment he decided to cut his losses and high-tail it back home he saw a pudgy, small figure creeping up one of the store's aisles. He was a regular enough at the store to recognize her gait: it was the teenybopper sales girl with the Raggedy Ann-colored hair and thick black eye paint. She'd always amused and disgusted him all at once, and he'd never figured out why the store management let her get away with such confrontational hygiene. He watched the girl, maybe a high school senior, put a big blanket right on top of the sales counter in front of the store and lay down on top of it, gazing out the front window to the other side of where he was hunched.

His feet were wet, the snow had soaked down his pants and into his boots. His walk to the store had taken half an hour, and he knew the walk home would be longer, a lot more miserable. He'd even misjudged the McDonald's: the giant M loomed darkly over the parking lot, deserted. Of course, no buses were running. He was a dope, not really in danger of freezing, he thought, but in danger of being stupidly uncomfortable.

Crouching down into the corner between the door and the building to rub his hands and warm up, he was most afraid a police-man would come by and mistake him for a homeless person. But of course, no cops were even out. It'd be a good night for a robbery, he thought, and tried to get his mind off the cold by imagining the kind of criminal who waited for just this sort of storm. This train of thought was rich enough to ride all the way home and he stood, finally, only to be startled by the fat face of the punk rock clerk staring at him through the door. The condensed air on the store's window made her whole face look streaked by black lines, and she stared at him a long time after he regained his composure enough to stare back at her. He'd been the son of a single mother, and was acutely aware of scaring a lone girl, which is why he hadn't knocked again when he saw she was the only person in the store. He'd realized she was snowed in, alone, vulnerable. And he probably terrified her, and so he smiled, saluted her, and turned back into the parking lot, now a whole inch deeper in snow.

"Are you stranded?" she asked.

Larry turned to see the girl's head outside the door—he realized her face was actually smeared in her black cosmetics. It hadn't been a trick of the water on the store's door.

"I guess so," he said, shaking his head. It was cold.

"I guess you ran your car off the road," she said. "You must be a real dumbass to think you could drive anything but a tank on a night like this. Don't you watch the news?" Her red hair was clinging to her sweater from static. She'd taken it out of the usual ponytail she held it in and she looked to him more and more like a little girl's abandoned doll.

"Well, you better come in," she said. "It's fucking freezing out there. I would've shit my pants tomorrow if somebody found you outside, frozen to death, and I'd just let you do it."

Although her vocabulary left something to be desired, she was right: it would be immoral of her to let him go. He felt like a jerk for putting her in this position, but he accepted what he'd done. She touched his face with fingers whose stubbed and bitten nails were covered in chipping black paint, just as soon as he stepped in the door,

"A fucking Popsicle! Jesus Christ. You better go run your hands under the cold water in the bathroom. You know where that is?" He was amazed she didn't seem to realize how obvious it was she'd just been crying, that the black lines drying to her face looked like prison bars. She was wearing a giant brown sweater and a black wool skirt and black pantyhose and army boots. He said he knew where the bathroom was, and found it without her.

Somewhere between the bathroom and the aisles of hair leg disintegrators and hair dyes he fell in love. That suddenly, that dumbly. Not because he was saved but because he'd found somebody who needed saving, somebody in an obviously bad place, but who hadn't lost the ability to reach out and help a total stranger. She was righteous in the old sense. In this moment what he'd seen as pudge and fat became girlish curves, the eyeliner was a barrier he would help her past, and the hair the last remnant of what looked to be a tough upbringing. Though usually a person thinks the words that will one day sink their heart will be in a more poetic vein, somehow Larry realized that she'd said exactly what he'd been waiting for somebody to tell him his entire life. *I'd shit my pants if you died.* It was a beautiful thing to say.

Chapter Nine

July 11, 2004

Dear John, Helen began late Sunday evening. She was already back in Utah. She was already at the edge of Salt Lake City, steering around the grand, wide curves of Parley's Canyon. *Dear John, I didn't have a right to marry you because of the love I've always held for my first husband, a difficult and wonderful man whom I neglected to mention. I can't imagine living without him. I think there's still time to annul.*

Dear John, she thought half an hour later, as she turned off the interstate, toward the highway she would follow until she turned off for Chakor's empty cabin, *I know this is a bad time for you, wherever you are, but things have been wrong a long time, between us. Our needs have changed, and for one of us to have our needs met, the other can't. I wish we had spoken about this more when you came home, but there seemed no space to do so. I love you, I will always love you, but I don't want to be married to you anymore. I've found a new love with somebody who shares more of my desires. I can't imagine life without him.*

Dear John, Helen tried as she slid out the ashtray at a stop light in Heber City, tore her second wedding ring free from the duct tape that had secured it there the past week, and slid it over her first wedding ring. Even when she turned Larry's three round diamonds inward so they wouldn't dwarf Chakor's slim 22-karat band, the differing golds clashed preposterously against each other. *Dear Johns,* she exhaled as her thumb played with the new arrangement on her finger, *If you knew me better, you'd be writing this letter.*

You shouldn't have left, Johns, she was dictating to herself in the Ashley Forest, and by the time she climbed into Daniel's Canyon, passed the turnoff she and Chakor had taken just a week before.

The first waves of real panic had set in when she'd woken on the driveway and her life was exactly as she'd left it the night before. Right before the flight from Houston she'd swallowed two of the Xanax that Carmen had given her when she'd first arrived in Smoot's Pass complaining of nightmares. She'd been furious that her mom wanted to solve her problems with drugs: today she knew for certain she couldn't stand to be conscious on an airplane, cooped up with her increasingly violent conscience. She'd slept the whole ride home, and the drugs made her too nauseous to buy something when she landed.

Dear John, I married a second husband, I hope you'll like him as much as I do, she tried as the Orchard General Store slid into view. *You admire Joseph Smith so much, I thought you wouldn't mind.* The previous twenty miles her gas tank had been crying empty as persistently as her bladder had been demanding release. And she was starving.

She was worked up into such a weird and heightened emotional state that when she got close enough to see the Orchard store's lights on this late on a Sunday, she almost laughed. Craving stillness, her physical body actually lurched forward in the seat in its efforts to help slow the car down.

She opened the car door to the smell of cold mountain air. When she stood, her knees were unsteady as her psyche, and she leaned against the car as she filled the tank in perhaps the last place in the universe that didn't require paying before pumping. She almost tripped on her way to the bathroom, which somebody had left open, but felt much freshened by the time she approached the store with an emptied bladder and a face glowing from cold, cold water being splashed across it.

A sign on the door announced: *Out of beer, quarters, and worms.* Gas had been crossed off the list earlier in the day: she was lucky. She jingled the wooden door open.

* * *

Hettie Gallagher's boss was way too cheap to pay for the pumps where people could just fill up and leave. Too worried that his employees might luxuriate in the tiny bit of time on their hands if they weren't always having to ring up whatever idiots hadn't filled up in Heber or Chipeta, where anybody with half a brain could see the gas cost five or six cents less a gallon. But Hettie got that if you *were* stupid enough to have forgotten, and that if you ran out of gas *between* the two cities, you'd have no choice but walk into the gas station at Orchard and pay. Even if you *were* in the middle of a long, snotty crying fest, you'd have to do it. You'd have to suck it in and let whoever was behind the counter see your puffed-up face and red nose even though they'd wonder what kind of shitty existence you thought you had that was worse than anybody else's—but then you'd run right back to your car totally humiliated.

What Hettie did not understand on this Sunday evening was why a woman in said predicament would prolong her contact with the public, who had a right not to have their space invaded by crazies. What she did not understand was the type of person who ordered tuna melts at quarter past seven, when the tuna has obviously been sitting around all day. Well, Hettie wasn't making a new batch: this was not the Ritz-Carlton. She just slapped the funky seven o'clock tuna onto two pieces of toast—she wasn't about to turn the grill on at this hour—stuck a piece of Kraft on top, put it in the microwave for thirty seconds, and walked it out to the table.

Of course, of all the seats in the store, Weepy Smurf had chosen one of the few directly facing the cash register. Some people were just born rude.

"Thanks," the lady sighed pathetically with a smile that didn't melt Hettie's heart.

She'd have felt more sorry if the woman were an escaped polygamist from the ranch at Cedar Break. That's who Hettie was waiting to save. She'd give the running woman the keys to her own car, and then tell the search party the runaway hitched a ride with a trucker heading for Cheyenne.

With the runny eyes and empty gas tank and all, a less trained eye than Hettie's might have thought Tuna Melt was one of them. But at the Break the women called themselves *liberated*. Liberation was jeans and plaid shirts passed down from one person, male or female, to the next, over and over again until they were rags. Not what Hettie considered freedom, and certainly a situation Hettie herself would cry over.

But Hettie would shed no tears for this woman staring at her sandwich like maybe it would bite her if she put it in her mouth. She was one of those people that wore the exact sort of modern-day, earth-hippie clothes that pissed Hettie off. No makeup, frizzed-out curly hair, and a puddle-brown shirt: all paired with too-big, sage-colored pants she had no doubt the woman paid a hundred dollars for. Hettie was all too familiar with the type.

One hundred dollars, in Hettie's hands, would pull together two outfits cute enough to make a dead man sit up and whistle. High heels and accessories included.

"We close at eight Sundays," Hettie called over. The woman had drunk half her OJ but hadn't touched the sandwich.

"Yeah, okay. What time is it?"

Hettie dignified the idiocy of such a question by lifting her hand above her head and pointing her thumb at the clock right behind it, bulls-eye ahead of where the woman sat.

It was bad enough she was working the weekend, let alone the night shift. Not her fault old Swanson couldn't hire an employee besides her who didn't start pilfering from the registers before their first work week was up. Even the one lady they'd hired from the Break stole so many six-packs of Sprite you'd have thought those polygamists required carbonation to multiply.

Hettie was about the only person she knew who could think an entire sentence that made any sense. She'd thought Lewis could too, when she met him at a kegger in Chipeta. Of course, love served a whole hell of a lot of good when she was cooped up inside this hellhole on the mountain, slinging gas and burgers sixty hours a week, and he was always working at his daddy's ranch.

But he *knew* about the polygamists out here: his uncle was one of them. They'd talked about infiltrating the compound as a couple. All it would take to break it all up, Lewis said, was a few dozen battery-operated televisions to show the kids the world they were missing. They were going to hide the televisions in bushes and such, where the adults wouldn't find them. Hettie had even researched how to weatherproof them with duct tape and garbage bags. She still liked the idea of kids finding televisions like Easter eggs in the desert.

"Is everything all right with your sandwich, ma'am?" she asked. That woman still had not even picked up her sandwich and it was seven forty-five.

"Oh," the woman said, smiling. "It's fine. Thank you." She lifted the sandwich in her hands, stared at the plastic insulation over the window, and didn't even nibble it. At least she wasn't a jabber mouth.

Ding, ding, ding, is what that kind of thought earned her. It was the bell over the door, and, speak of the devil, one of the polygamists had come wandering in: the cute teenaged one who always came for spare groceries Wednesday nights. He wasn't alone, though; a whole host of them were outside in a white suburban.

"Hi, Enoch," she said, which was what she called every single one of the men.

"Hey, Cheerful," he smiled back at her, touching his hat.

"I thought Sundays you weren't allowed to buy anything."

"I'm not," he grinned, "I thought you might loan me the key to your restroom, though. We're just coming down from the mountain and the little girl can't wait until we get home."

"Your girl?" she asked. She knew they had them young, but this Enoch wasn't a day older than Hettie herself. She thought the guys had to wait until they were older to be chosen to marry.

"My niece," he said, and she was for some reason relieved.

"Oh, whatever," she said, pissed off her face was for some reason flushing. She threw the key to the men's room at him. "Do *not* leave it poopy." He burst out laughing. This was her life.

* * *

Helen might have enjoyed the view from the small wooden table she'd collapsed in, except that it had been weatherproofed for winter with a thick layer of translucent plastic. Nobody had bothered removing it for the summer. Now it filtered the last remnants of the sun's light into an opaque glow, and Helen couldn't see anything but foggy forms through it.

A young man came in and flirted with the counter girl, and Helen followed him out the store with her eyes—there was a small hole in the plastic she could see through if she cocked her head. She watched a woman drape a small child between her arms and head off toward the restroom while the guy seemed to be joking with the rest of the kids in the car. He leaned into the opened door of the van spreading his arms wide, then hunching himself quickly up, telling some kind of story that made the kids squeal loud enough Helen faintly heard them. Then the woman was back, and buckling the child into a seat, and the family left as quickly as it had materialized.

"Don't tell me they just drove off with my key!" the salesgirl shrieked, running out the door to wave them down. But they had, and the girl came back inside, slamming the door.

"Jesus Christ!" she said, glaring at Helen. "Jesus Fucking Christ." Her lips glowed like Snow White's—she must have just reapplied her lipstick.

The family's van, Helen noticed through the hole in the plastic, had been hiding her cab. She didn't want to climb into it. The teenager had stormed into the kitchen and was now on the phone whispering angrily to somebody, Helen could see her through the large service window.

It was time to go but she wanted to crawl beneath the table and blend in with the chair's legs so the girl would lock her inside the store. Nobody would see her, nobody would know where she was, and she'd be walled safely away from the world she had made such a mess of. Just for one night.

She might have tried for it except a shadow emerged from the dark field across the highway, pausing as it seemed to take in the café. It crossed the street and stood in front of the cab. Helen stuck her finger in the plastic's peephole to widen it, to see more of what she thought was happening but couldn't believe since it was the stuff of urban legend: wasn't it enough her life was already the stuff of tabloid filth?

"Something the matter?" the girl asked, and this is where Helen made the mistake. She didn't cry out, or faint or point. She didn't do anything sensible.

"No," is what she said.

"Then get your damned finger out of my window." The girl sounded weary, finally, and sad. "That's good plastic. And it's closing time."

Helen didn't need prompting to leave. She abandoned the sandwich and juice as she left to meet the figure she felt certain, the moment she saw him opening the door to the Cadillac, she shouldn't go see. A man she saw climbing into the back of her car in the last remnants of twilight: she *saw* him. And for no good reason on earth, she let him do it.

Maybe it was precisely the legends, those tales about the men crawling into the back of cars at truck stops, that drew her forward. In all the hours of deceiving men she loved and fretting herself sick and driving down the canyons which always led to home, Helen had not once asked God to help her out. She understood she was undeserving.

But now, now she was thinking, maybe, *maybe* He was making the first move. He'd tried smiting her on the mountain the morning of her second wedding and it hadn't taken. So here He'd sent a messenger. Or maybe *She* had. Heavenly Mother, finally. Or maybe the man was sent by Chakor's family's mother god—she rode a tiger, he'd told her. Ambaji had ten arms and held weapons in most of her hands: a fierce protector, a force to be reckoned with.

Or maybe Helen hadn't seen anything. Maybe she was only tired and overwrought. Either way, she swallowed hard before opening the driver's door, and she was too afraid to look down at what might lay hidden in the back seat.

Maybe there was a man who thought she was really driving a cab. Maybe he was sitting there behind her now—she had swooped into her Cadillac's open door and sat in a single movement, the way she'd remove a Band-Aid. The way she'd jump directly into the depths of a freezing lake instead of inching in. Maybe he was waiting to give her directions.

A tortured look into the rearview mirror revealed no stowaway in sight.

He's hiding, she thought. *He doesn't want to be kicked out. He's just looking for a ride.*

The adrenaline surge slamming the car's door shut called up was complicated—she was afraid, but she'd been afraid. Now there was something pressing, an immense and immediate reason for her current fears to eclipse the ones she was already so exhausted from. As she inserted the key into the ignition and revved the engine, she had proof that somewhere along the way this summer she had truly lost her mind. She ran from opossums, married a second husband, and followed this shadow into her car: undeniable symptoms of a disintegrating sanity. Of an injured brain.

That had to be it. She might have a tumor like the one she'd heard about earlier in the year, where a shrewd and greedy rich man's brain tumor had transformed him into a romantic philanthropist who loved his wife. His children had sued their parents to have the tumor removed and won.

These things happened, Helen thought, idling a long time in the parking lot. Idling minutes. Losing heart now was too late: if her passenger was a murderer he wouldn't let her leave, or he'd follow her back to the locked store and kill her and the clerk both. The tale of the trucker driving behind a lady's car and flashing his lights and honking his horns every time the killer in the back seat raised his knife didn't make any sense: who stabs the driver of a moving car?

Dear John. Dear, oh dear. She pulled onto the highway. She did. What else was there to do besides drive? She could hardly contain her fear and nausea, her growing realization that she might finally have gone too far. She adjusted her rearview mirror to show her as much of the backseat as possible: all clear. Stupid, stupid. Driving around with a bomb in her backseat, why couldn't she hear it ticking?

If he were a murderer, why wait? A robber would have stolen the car, a murderer would wait for a stretch of dark highway to make his move, to demand she pull to the side of the road (she wouldn't). But all they had passed through the last ten or fifteen minutes was empty and desolate, and the night was truly descended now, as if on a film script's cue.

She should have said something to the girl in the store. Obviously. But would she have believed her? They could have called 911 and what if the police arrived and the backseat was empty, and they took down the information on Helen and figured out, somehow, about her double life.

She should have said something.

"Sit up." The sound of her own voice, she found, reassured her. Maybe the man in the backseat just needed a ride. Maybe he was a runaway, like she used to be, and her kindness was the break he needed to save himself. Maybe he was as scared as she was. Maybe he was waiting for her to stop at another business and go inside so that he could melt back into the landscape when she left.

If he would make the tiniest of sounds she would know, but he wouldn't and so she drove, drove miles and miles, ears straining to hear a second set of lungs or a muffled sneeze, but she couldn't. The car's engine, its wheels on the highway, made it difficult. She was driving and driving through the night, and taking comfort in the idea that she could still veer off the road and into the starlight if he tried jumping her. He wouldn't expect her to know she could do it. But she could.

"I never learned the constellations," she said, looking up into the gaping mouth of jagged stars above her.

A few minutes later: "If we hit a deer you'll go cannonballing through the window. You should put on a seat belt."

Helen was following the glowing yellow dividing lines of the highway to avoid missing the curves. If this were her last night on earth, and if the person in the back seat were an actual person and not an angry god, and if they caught the man who killed her, he'd say: "She made small talk."

She was not a banality, though. She had tried to be. Tried for simplicity. For the opposite of the life she grew up in, but not even her mother had pulled stunts as stupid as Helen's. Crazy-drunk, or crazy-drugged, or crazy-sped-up was so much better, in the end, than just crazy. Would her mother accept that her daughter had finally out-Carmened Carmen?

"I'm a . . . a . . . *bigamist*," she said. "I married this poet on top of a mountain—because he was the one I was supposed to have married all along even though he's young and he's got no, no *gravitas,*" she said: it was the word Emmaline always used to describe Larry.

"But he's got that spirit, that eagerness to live that you're supposed to have when you're twenty-something. When I'm with him I have it too. And I'm not forty, like Larry: I'm twenty-eight. Chakor is young, but I am too. He makes me *hopeful.* I mean, who asks a girl he's known three weeks to marry him? I said no and no and no, and the possibility of my saying yes was so impossible my guards weren't up, that's all I can think. There was no reason for me to think I'd do that sort of thing."

Once she'd started, it was hard to stop. Good.

"It was all just supposed to be a problem with a timeframe that I'd fix.

"I mean—

"But when I did, I *was* going to tell Larry. I thought I could tell him it was over and nobody would know the difference, but he was fatter, and all the skin around his head and neck was chapped and red, like nothing I've seen. He'd had some reaction to the sand, he told me, and then didn't say a word for three days, not until he woke up one morning and demanded we go to church, and then he looked out onto all these strangers and told them this, this *story* about how much he wants me to love him, and how he's saving kids in Iraq because of me."

"After the church visit he said he didn't think he was fit to be a father, anymore. He told me he didn't want children like he was reminding me, like it was something we'd already discussed, and then he started using a condom when we made love. I had been barren almost our entire marriage and he used a condom and I thought I might suffocate somehow inside it, but I *still* couldn't tell him I wanted a divorce. I didn't tell him that."

Helen finally took a breath. Her heart was racing. Here was her murder's chance to pipe in, to say: by God yes, I've chosen the right woman to kill. She was almost to Freedom Reservoir when she heard him sneeze.

"I got married two times to save myself and I don't know what to do. I am open for suggestions."

It felt good, talking. Letting one fear cancel out the other, feeling like if she was going to die, she'd do so confessed.

"I keep worrying you're going to kill me," she said. She was careening through the small canyons before Freedom, hoping now that she wasn't alone, despite what she said.

"He said he didn't want to have children, anymore. He said it, but I knew it already. I knew it just as soon as he left for the war. I knew Chakor would have a houseload of children."

Helen didn't decide to pull off the road when the black waters of Freedom Reservoir sparkled into the purview of her headlights, so much as she just did it. She didn't announce the reason behind the car's slowing. The vista in front of them was stunning in the daylight, but was just black now. The gaping, toothless mouth of a body of water at night. She surveyed its shine intently during the long moments she didn't dare turn around.

She wanted to cry. Confusion and terror seized her movement, right up to the point she heard a body unfolding. She repressed a scream as she squeezed the steering wheel and stared up into the rearview mirror, all this happening at the same time. The eyes that her eyes met through the mirror was one eye, was *her* eye, it was a *her* she saw, not a him. A her leaning toward Helen, watching her face through the dark mirror Helen watched hers through. What Helen saw was a short, dark, frizzed perm: weird hair framing a square head, doughy white skin, a devastatingly blank expression.

It was a face intensified by tears that dragged, honey-like, down its cheeks, tears haunting the green and yellow bruises on her cheeks, but especially the deep black one obscuring most of her right eye, by making it gleam terribly in the moonlight. Helen took the woman in, watched her good eye moving, looking for her own battle scars.

"What happened?" Helen whispered, and the woman didn't answer, or even respond with a new expression: she just stared through the mirror, shaking her head, no, softly, and so gently that Helen kept quiet. She was mesmerized by the physical nature of the woman's bruising, by its strange tenderness, by the sense that she looked the way Helen felt. Her inside was on the outside of another human being, and this woman clearly hadn't done this to herself. She was maybe in her thirties.

"I'm sorry," Helen said, turning her shoulders, her whole body so that it faced her stowaway's and she could see her with her own eyes instead of through the mirror. But the woman scooted back into her seat as she turned. Helen froze. The woman held a white canvas bag in her lap, was wearing a dirty sweatshirt with fake pink flowers. The flowers were glued to it, but peeling off from the front. The shirt clashed with her bruises, Helen thought, and felt nauseated.

"I'm not sure what to do," Helen finally said to her, "I don't know how these things happen." The woman was still shaking her head that gentle no, her lips were moving slightly, but Helen couldn't hear what she was saying. She tried, though, and she reached back, her hand reached back toward the woman's face, her bruises Helen wanted to touch, but the lady thrust her body back into the corner behind the passenger's seat with a soft yelp, still expressionless.

"I wasn't going to," Helen started to say, but then the pistol came out of the bag, and was in the woman's hands, pointing at her. It confused Helen. It was the wrong thing. She stared at the woman's dried, red and wrinkled fingers curled around the polished oak handle. It was to the gun's barrels that Helen said, "Oh, God."

Helen was the one backing up, now, slowly, while the woman held the gun at her head. She sat like that for a few minutes, facing the stranger's hands until she had to move her eyes, until she had to bring them up slowly, to the woman's face. Tears drying, but the same nothing expression behind them.

"Are you going to . . . " Helen asked, and the gunwoman whimpered. But Helen was the one shaking her head, now.

"Take my rings," she whispered, pulling off her finger in a single motion and holding them out in front of her. "Take my rings and the car and I'll just get out here and you can go." She didn't want to die, the thought a too-late revelation. "They're worth thousands of dollars, I promise you. I won't call anybody and report them gone. They're yours."

Helen set the rings on the dash, and moved, slowly, to open the car door, but the lady spoke up. "Don't move!" she whispered. Then, in a voice that sounded like a rabbit's: "It ain't real."

Helen took her hand from the car's handle, looking at the gun. It was real.

"It ain't, I swear it ain't," the woman said. "Just close your eyes."

And then Helen knew, easily knew, she had been too forward. She had gone too far, and she started crying. It was painless. She was crying tears like the woman's, slow ones, and it felt good, somehow, it helped her to breathe, and so she was breathing when the woman said again, "Please, just close your eyes, ma'am."

She just watched the woman with the gun, who watched her. The gun seemed to be controlled by nobody, it seemed a force of its own, hovering between these two women. How long did they wait? How long until the woman whispered, "She won't, she won't do it, she won't," until the hands holding the pistol moved, took a U-turn and delivered the gun's barrel straight into the woman's mouth.

"Oh, God, don't do that," Helen said, and the woman herself closed her eyes, tight, the way children do when they pretend to sleep, and Helen couldn't take it, she jumped under the steering wheel, of all places, she hunched down beneath the pounding sound of gunpowder she imagined would come. She waited, and waited, though, in silence. Alive, glad of it. She wanted to stay alive. The backseat of the car opened, and she heard the woman climb out. Helen was still crying, sobbing into her den by the car's pedals, she was waiting for the driver's door to open, for the woman to kill her. Waiting, and waiting, and waiting. How long? Until she heard a series of gunshots. They sounded a long ways away, and she bolted up into her seat.

Helen drove fast as she could out of the alcove, alive. What could anyone do for the beaten woman, she wondered as she decided whether or not she should stop at a pay phone and call the police. If the woman was dead she wouldn't be harming anyone. If she was alive—and the number of gunshots Helen heard suggested this since a person can hardly shoot themselves more than once or twice—she had already shown that she wasn't trying to harm anyone.

Helen sped around a hairpin curve too fast, and her wedding rings jerked off the dashboard and somewhere into the dark cracks of the seats: the wedding rings even a desperate and terrified woman who needed them believed were already too cursed to touch.

Perhaps the lady would be fine without them. Maybe there was a plan Helen couldn't know, and right now her armed passenger would climb through the rock formations surrounding Freedom Reservoir and find shelter: a makeshift cave to keep her until the next morning. Perhaps she'd awaken. Pull her broken body through the icy waters to cleanse herself, and re-emerge into the world without the fear she'd been trying so hard to flee.

Part
Two

Chapter Ten

Date: Thur, 08 July 2004 02:50:22 -0600
From: "Cha Cha Kor" <desipoetics@hotmail.com>
Subject: RE:
To: cmotes@yahoo.com

I ask: who is the fool who defined distance as a force that might separate two lovers? Chakor is, part of me answers. He is the one whose joints ache with the lack of your caresses. Me number one wonders if I kiss the screen and you kiss the screen at the same time will we explode, the way they told me as a child that falling from a cliff in a dream at the same time you fall from your bed will kill you. But me number two is too suffocated by the cruel and immense emptiness I have suffered in your absence to wonder anything at all. And Good Lord! It hasn't yet been two weeks since we parted!

Oh my love, my moon, my Lady of the Missing Lake! Disembarking the plane in Mumbai was breathtaking. It's a city of car fumes and bodies of the poor and the rich and the young and the old, the land of rotting fruits and fragrant flowers, four-legged creatures and their fresh milk, horns, shouts, ocean waves, and wind. It is New York City multiplied by thousands of years and peoples and ideas and gods and dreams. You hear all cities in the "third world" are alike but there is no other like Mumbai. It buckles my knees, Helen, as it always has, as it did when I was a child and a cow in the street pushed me up against the wall to take my samosa. I shrieked. My mother rescued me but said: "Imagine if he hadn't tried, and you had never smelled a bull's breath."

I am in Gandhinagar now. It's more pastoral, but still the capital of the state of Gujarat, where my mother now lives with her brother, my Amit Mama. Just writing this to you I feel like you're seeing it with me. And that is lucky because a lone body feels like no match for mighty India.

You are by now thinking: how can he go on and on when all I want to hear about is the health of his mother and whether or not he made it home in time. I know that, Helen. I have been selfish so far in this letter, and I don't have an excuse. The truth is that I seem to be able to explain anything except what I have come home to see.

To my own eyes, which are yours since you can't be here to offer another vision, there seems to be nothing wrong with my Ma. She is the same as always except that she is wearing salwars instead of the jeans and sweatshirts of these last twenty years in America. She's returned to the clothes I remember from childhood, from when she was still new. I like the change. She looks more like the mother in my memories than she has in a long while.

Is she thin? No. Pale? No. Weak? Does she appear to be in pain? Not more than headache pain, and she's had migraines her whole life. But is she dying? Is the glint in her smile a sign she's moving closer to the place she was before birth than to any mortal place? Amit Mama says yes. He says a tumor is growing in her brain.

Is it scandalous to admit I don't believe him? I don't, but I haven't told anybody. I think they lured me here to find me a wife. I know that sounds crazy. But they're both old and they worry I won't marry. And two different unmarried girls have been brought to tea in the week since I arrived (I wasn't going to tell you, but I can't help it). When they leave my uncle's wife asks, "Did you know Priti sings classical music and garbas? She's so artistic, she would make such a good wife for a boy like you. Did you not think her beautiful?" I love Shruti Mami, she has always treated me like a younger brother and so I just shrug. I say, "You will love the woman I marry." (She will.) And then she pinches my cheeks and says, "Priti cooks the best rotis. Don't you want to marry an Indian girl who will hide your bones with fat?"

Don't worry, I am not tempted! I won't be one of those Saturday Afternoon Special stories men who tries to keep two families on two continents! You have demonstrated, quite adequately, that one wife is more than enough to handle :). I only tell you any of this so you know why I feel like everybody is lying to me about my Ma. Don't you think they would have told me it was a tumor over the phone in America—not that it was just old age—if it were really a tumor? It's a slip up, you know?

I find it harder believing she's even sick here than I did in America. I'd imagined her wrapped in cotton blankets, slowly moving from this world to the next, the way people are meant to. It was a death I could grasp. A happy death in a way.

The thought of her being taken against her will is too horrendous.

Family is everywhere, a tiny cousin always hiding in the bushes or the trees, an antique auntie always surprising me when I think I'm alone. I wish you weren't a secret. I wish I could call you from the living room of my uncle's home and my mother could hear the voice of the woman who will bear the children who would call her Dadi.

I feel like a liar. I feel bad for having judged you for keeping me from your mother. I miss you, and now I feel I might have depressed you. I guess it is your duty as my wife (what a beautiful word) to let me depress you sometimes, but I want to leave you with a better feeling, a feeling like you are here with me already.

And so here is the secret most worth sharing: do you know how birds are born knowing where to fly and when? When I walk the streets of the cities here, I have always felt the magnetic pushes and pulls of four dozen generations guiding me through the streets, shepherding me around hidden corners, leading me to the mysterious and mundane and sometimes terrible wonders that have shaped so many of my ancestors. Of course, the people here can see at a glance I'm American, and I can only drink the bottled water in my family's houses, but my connection, my deeper connection, is omnipresent and exciting.

You and I will one day walk these streets together, and I'll tell you the second big secret now, but you will feel it for yourself when you're here: feel the way a world undeniably, and one hundred percent different than the one you're reading this e-mail in, in my cabin, is also and at least equally one hundred percent the same as the world of Chipeta County. It is textured differently, but amazingly the same.

People are starting to wonder and poke their heads in. I could write you for days. I know the letter is long: you have married a writer. Maybe some of this I am just writing down so that I can see it stare back at me in print. Would you forgive me if that is so?

Helen, I will e-mail you the very next chance I get, and by then, I hope, I'll be able to tell you more about my mother's condition. I love you, I love you, I love you. I think I will actually kiss the screen,

Here I go,

Chakor

Chapter Eleven

Mid-July, 2004

Helen slept and woke, tucked into the fake leather beanbag she'd lugged from its place by the chimney to a spot directly between two corner windows facing up toward the south side of the mountain. Had she chosen to sit in front of the bay window on the north side of the cabin she could have watched Starvation Creek eke its way down into the valley below, felt the grandeur of life up on a mountaintop, but she wouldn't have felt hidden. In her corner, concealed from passersby on the road below by the steep incline of the mountain, she could look out into the world and feel sheltered from it all at once.

She watched a visible population explosion in the jackrabbit community from the window she was stationed in front of. They congregated half a mile up the mountain, right where private property gave way to state park. It appeared some evolutionary fluke had enabled them all to sense the line that was supposed to shield their kind from little boys with pellet guns and rifles.

Occasionally Helen rose to drink water. To pick through handfuls of walnuts and raisins. To relieve her bladder or her bowels. Otherwise she remained wedged in the tiny lifeboat that was her beanbag. Worry troubled her too much to miss more regular meals, but at the same time, her mind avoided the troubles she needed to be facing, and instead dug up the deepest memories.

* * *

When Helen was in second grade, she remembered, a little girl and her grandmother moved their trailer into the lot next to Carmen's house. They dropped into existence from nowhere while she was in school. The trailer had a fold-out aluminum porch the likes of which Helen had never seen and a dozen different kinds of bee-themed wind chimes hanging from it.

"Characters have moved into the backyard," Carmen had said. "I can tell you that."

The girl was plump and harassed. Kids teased her like they did Helen in those days, like they would until she'd grown her razored, teenaged teeth. Her own deformity wasn't pudge but dishevelment: she looked like a girl whose mother didn't take care of her in a mostly Mormon community where mother care held the greatest cachet. Even the girl in the trailer always came to school with perfectly braided hair and clean, pressed dresses though her family didn't even own a car.

With their inevitable friendship Helen began spending afternoons in their home that smelled of sugar baking. The grandmother was a rail-thin, mostly silent woman who called their house "the hive."

"We just think it sounds *nicer*," the girl said. Helen had challenged the name on the way to school—it wasn't golden but blue and white-striped, shaped like a rectangle and not a pyramid, only two people lived inside it, and the girl was so allergic to bees that Helen could make her skedaddle by just mentioning a buzz.

The girl rolled her eyes but seemed otherwise unbothered by Helen's observations, and Helen liked that. She liked learning to crochet in the hive—its inhabitants created magnificent doll dresses to sell at county fairs while Helen slowly graduated from a long smooth line of crocheted yarn to simple squares she was supposed to give to Carmen to use as potholders. She'd hidden them in a shoebox beneath her bed. There were only a dozen of them by the morning she woke to discover the trailer, porch and all, had disappeared.

"Mom!" she'd said, running into the kitchen from her bedroom where she'd noticed its absence from her window. "Mom, look! The hive's gone!"

Carmen looked out the tiny window above their sink, let the tip of her spent cigarette hiss delicately into a small drop of water, and said, "I'd heard that woman was having a hard go of it." She caught the eyes of whatever boyfriend it was sitting at the table with his coffee. "I guess it just got *too* hard."

"But it takes a truck to move a trailer and they didn't even have a car. And noise. It takes noise. I didn't hear anything."

"Me neither," the boyfriend said, crossing over to the sink to see for himself. He whistled like an imbecile when he saw the empty lot. "Now ain't that the damnedest."

Carmen shrugged, swatted his hand from her rear, and took on the pensive look she could get before she started drinking, and then again, when she'd been drinking so long, she was as good as early-morning groggy.

"People do all sorts of things, Helen. Lives are full of secrets we don't tell just *anybody*. They popped in from nowhere, and that's where they've gone back to, I guess. If it isn't a miserable life," she sighed, "it must be kind of nice. A gypsy's life."

"Gypsies!" Helen spat, imagining the skinny old lady in a turban, imagining there was a crystal ball hidden somewhere in that trailer and they'd never shown her. She wanted to tear her mother's tongue out but she just ran to her room, slamming her left fist against the washing machine on her way past because it made such a satisfying boom. Her squares were still under the bed, and she felt relieved.

"I guess you're going to miss that little friend," Carmen's boyfriend said when Helen re-emerged from her room in shorts and a tank top. She ignored him, found her flip flops beneath the TV table, and then ran out to the weed field where the trailer ought to have been. To find a clue. A note. All that was left, though, was a few paper cups, a giant mound of red ants that had been living beneath the trailer all along, and the places where the sewer and power lines came up through the ground. Now they were just attached to air and Helen felt sorry for them. It wouldn't have been difficult to acknowledge their existence, and her own, by tying a goodbye letter to one.

Deep cuts in the earth, where the trailer had been dragged away, headed toward the highway. She followed these empty gashes until they disappeared into gray asphalt.

* * *

The world: so full of the disappeared. It weighed on Helen through the days and nights. At a little past two on one of those nights she was wondering what it had been like for that girl to vanish over and over from life, and then Helen gave in. She did what she had been refusing to do during these first five days of self-imposed isolation and turned on Chakor's computer. Maybe she would look up hand-crocheted doll dresses and find a picture of the lost family, the back of her mind said, but when she opened up the Google search engine she typed in, *death woman "freedom reservoir."* The only tragedy marked by the Salt Lake paper at the lake happened a few years before, a toddler who had wandered into the lake while her parents argued about how to pack up their car. The rest of the stories were about fishing, were blogs about family camping trips.

Helen read a paragraph into the article about the drowned baby—it was the girl's birthday, her parents were teenagers, recently recovered crystal meth addicts—and decided not to read more. She stood up and walked to the north window, where she could make out the glinting of the stars and moon on the surface of Starvation Creek. What a dangerous life, even for people trying hard to save themselves from themselves.

Had those parents, she wondered, returned to the drugs after such a horrible thing happening? Had that little girl known her parents' arms weren't yet strong enough to lift her from the water and the rocks as soon as her head went under?

Better if that girl had struggled for air against the water's cold, and when none came she felt something incredible—felt her fragile legs switch into a fish's fins. And so then the most beautiful part of herself had swum away into the icy mountain waters, away from the terror of life, a deep mountain mermaid. It was ridiculous, but the best thing Helen could imagine.

And the woman she'd been searching for in the first place? Wherever she'd disappeared to wasn't public yet. If she escaped, perhaps she didn't want to be found. The worst possibility was that she'd somehow ended up back where she'd come from, and the second worst was that she was wounded somewhere along the shores of the reservoir, all alone, and that Helen had left her there to suffer for days. This guilt sent her finally to the Chipeta County Police Department's crude website in search of an e-mail address. It moved her to create a new, anonymous e-mail address. It took her a couple of minutes to do, a couple of minutes longer to write:

Date: Wed, 14 July 2004 2:33:15
From: incidentatfreedomres@yahoo.com
Subject: Please Check Up On Troubled Woman
To: police@chipetapd.gov

Dear Friends:

Monday night a beaten woman may have hurt herself out at Free-dom Reservoir—I heard gunshots and saw her with a gun. No other people were there but me. I did not stay to find out if she was okay because it was night and I was afraid she might shoot me. I apolo-gize for not writing sooner. If you don't find a body, and if you know somebody has been looking for her, please don't chase after her. She was trying to escape some kind of family violence.

Thank you,

Anonymous

---

* * *

The son Helen had given up for adoption before meeting Larry, she had always promised herself, lived with a family of Mormons whose earnestness and sense of God's strict limits on existence would serve to counter her own bad genes. Every time she went into Franklin she scanned the faces of thirteen-year-old boys with Billy's broad face or her mother's gotcha grin—two of the only signs of her relation to the boy she'd been able to recognize in the lone hour she'd held him in her arms.

That baby was so small it almost would have fit in a shoebox, but he was otherwise perfect. He was hot and naked. Just a day before the birth she had declared that although she understood she looked like the one in her swollen belly's state, she was not actually a cow, and would never become one. But in the hospital bed her boy's head searched around her chest like a blind puppy. His mouth latched on to her nipple and she didn't pull him away. He tickled and pulled as if her breasts were the one thing in the world he needed for happiness and contentment.

She hadn't read any books about childbirth. Helen hadn't even understood his latching on was a real *something*, a lucky milestone for a breastfeeding mom until years later when she tried so hard to have a child she could keep and she read countless articles on how harrowing the process could be. Sometimes the babies never latched on, some women hired breastfeeding experts in their despair, and yet her boy had wiggled across her chest and suckled with no prompting at all: a survivor.

He needs me, she thought, in the hospital. That much she understood. *This boy needs me more than he needs anything else.* She knew it for sure, and decided not to give him up. Sorry to the family the hospital had already notified of the birth, he was hers. It was her body filled with what the world itself had ordained this child needed. A blinding, crazy-powerful thought.

He suckled until he slept, and she hid her breasts beneath the sheet so the nurse wouldn't see—as if just hours before she hadn't looked directly into her most private parts and watched her boy's small head emerge out of it. She couldn't think of any names for the child, none that were good enough. When he woke forty minutes later, his eyes were wet blue-black clouds of another world that could focus on nothing. But his naked body rested against her naked belly, his hands pressed against her heart like he knew she would do the right thing and he had complete and utter faith in her motherly skills. She cried because contrary to all her expectations, she realized she had some. The fierce giant of a mother she had become in the space of a January blizzard understood she could, and she would live up to that small being's faith, so she rang the buzzer above her bed and asked the nurse to take him away forever.

Not because, as she'd imagined before that night, he was a wailing lump of her life's ruin, but because she would not be that for him. She was not, and would not be, another version of her own mother, who sobbed against the glass panes of the hospital delivery room for hours after her Helen announced that the baby's adoptive parents were already on their way.

"Keep her out of my room!" Helen demanded of the nurses. Since her mother's lack of sobriety was all too clear that night, they complied. Helen cried herself to sleep. But still: that was the part of her mother she missed in the years she stayed away. The mother who would sob and beat the ground like a Greek tragedy in and of herself, mourning for the woman her daughter seemed so incapable of becoming.

* * *

One memory leapt from the other as time passed in a blur, clutching at her growing hunger until she finally acquiesced and prepared herself a proper meal. There was a storm outside. She had spent hours watching the rain pounding into the creamy coffee-colored dirt, the gray clouds making the green of the pines appear bluish. It was an afternoon maybe a week into her exile. The endless cracking of thunder hugged her, smoothed the edges of her frayed thought process like a father's deep and faraway voice.

She found eggs in the refrigerator, and the stale leftovers of some of the homemade bread Ida gifted them for their wedding: she cut the loaf, tore out the middle of a slice, cracked the eggs into the center, and then listened to it all crackle inside the puddle of butter she'd let turn brown inside the cast-iron pan. A crackling and satisfied roll of thunder approved, and she shivered. And she was hungry. Finally hungry, and relieved to be so: her stomach had turned to acid with the bird-food diet she'd been on.

She'd made this same breakfast for both Larry and Chakor—the latter sprinkling the eggs with cumin and red pepper powder, the former with standard salt and ground black pepper. With both men she'd imagined making this breakfast, and more elaborate ones— waffles and yogurt and granola feasts—for the children she'd hoped they'd have together. She found it unbelievable, on this afternoon, that either man actually existed.

In her impatience at seeking out the spatulas she'd lost sometime between flipping the bread and finding a plate she used her fingers to lift her meal out of its cradle. She cried out an *ouch* into air that hadn't held a human syllable in days, that seemed overwhelmed with her simple exclamation. A bright red welt had blossomed on her wrist, across her veins, where it had met with the lip of the cast iron. Having tossed her food onto the plate beside her, she danced, shaking her hand, to the freezer and opened it: no ice.

Of course, no ice, she remembered: Chakor took his drinks at room temperature—even the beer he occasionally shared with Herman. "It's unhealthy to drink iced things," he'd explained to her early on, when he'd sent an iced glass of water back with the waitress at the grill. She'd laughed at him, imagining he was surely joking, but he just shrugged a little impishly and said, "You can think it's weird, but it's no use arguing against Ayurvedic wisdom."

"Ayer what?" Helen asked.

"I'll show you a book," he smiled. "I might be struck down even going into it among such a varied proliferation of hamburgers and pork chops."

But they never got around to books, much. She'd listened to him rant about the war as stoically as if a hunk of who she'd been so long wasn't caught up in it, or they'd brainstormed their plans for the art center as they explored the hidden canyons and byways of Chipeta Country that he'd never have discovered without her—and whenever they could, they'd made love. Outside, more often than not, which she'd never, ever have done with Larry. And what she discovered on their forays in outdoor intercourse was that a person could feel sucked up into the world itself under great open skies, like they were kissing the raindrops and licking the nipples of the earth.

The feel of his large hands moving slowly across her body she missed. She missed the sense that he could contain her within the grasp of his long fingers and lift her up above his head into the shining visions of the world she understood he would spend his life exploring. But she missed Larry, too. His sultry hugs, the musculature of his limbs. Where Chakor was almost timid, relying on her invitations and her own forwardness, Larry was sure of himself. Though they kept their lovemaking indoors, he liked to surprise her, and their sex, when it was good, left her breathless.

Helen walked her food to the small wooden table by the kitchen counter and sat down, but the burn on her wrist throbbed. She didn't want to let the pain spoil this first meal in so long, and thought about venturing outside to submerge her whole hand into Starvation Creek, which was fed by melting snow in the high mountains. But what if she were seen outside the cabin by Ida or Herman? They'd want to talk to her, to ask her how and where she'd been—and there was nothing for her to say. The kind old neighbors were just sensitive enough not to come banging on the door, she was grateful for that, but if she were outside and they saw her, they'd feel obliged to stop by. And she wasn't ready. She wasn't ready to see anybody, and she didn't have to. Not really.

Instead, she ran her wrist under the water faucet, also icy mountain cold. Through the small window above the sink she scoured the mountain for wildlife and didn't find any. It made her sad. She thought once again of the woman who had fled—her stowaway. By now the police had gotten her message, and perhaps the woman's fate was known. Or maybe not. That would be the best thing.

Helen dried her wrist with a clean white dishtowel and sat at the table. When her burn throbbed she ignored it and she fell into the meal she'd prepared. Like an animal—she had never been so hungry—she ate it plain, with no spices whatsoever, in a few gulps. Astonishing, she thought, there wasn't more—and then she actually cut herself another hunk of bread and started another round of the same dish. The heat from the pan bothered the burn on her wrist, so she cooked left-handed, and kept the spatula in her sights the whole time.

Midway through her second helping, she realized there was something off with the eggs. A strong smell, the eggiest she could remember ever having experienced, a smell like blood, and she stood abruptly without finishing her food. A wave of nausea swept over her, but not so bad she thought she'd lose her meal. She walked over to the computer, touched a button on the keyboard to awaken it, and saw the logout screen from Yahoo mail. It took her a few moments to remember the password for the anonymous account she'd set up, but she got it.

There was a message written back to her.

Date: Wed, 14 July 2004 11:38:44
From: "M. Abeglan" <mAbeglan@chipetapd.gov>
Subject: RE: Please Check Up On Troubled Woman
To: incidentatfreedomres@yahoo.com

Anonymous,

The Chipeta County Police Department welcomes anonymous tips, which are one of the only surefire ways to receive certain kinds of information on certain illegal or dangerous activities. We thank you for your efforts at being a good citizen and will look into the matter at hand.

In every possible crime scene scenario it is imperative that we receive the most accurate information possible so as to perform our duties in the way citizens deserve. We would welcome further dialogue with you in this troubling matter you have described.

No bodies have been found at the site, but since we don't know where on the reservoir you saw the victim we can't be sure we looked in the right places. We don't have sufficient information to launch a full-scale investigation at this point, and as you might expect, we receive many tips from people with deranged ideas of what is fun. We are curious as to why you waited several days before contacting us if this was truly a matter of life and death.

At your service,

Lieutenant Misty Abeglan

Helen blinked at the screen in front of her, and almost turned the monitor off, but then reconsidered.

Date: Tue, 20 July 2004 4:56:27
From: incidentatfreedomres@yahoo.com
Subject: RE: Please Check Up On Troubled Woman
To: mAbeglan@chipetapd.gov

Dear Lieutenant Abeglan,

It was near the second lookout point in from the road leading from Salt Lake toward Franklin. I am not lying. I am pleased you have not found anything tragic so far.

Thank you,

Anonymous

She pressed send, and this time, she smiled as she logged out and turned off the computer's monitor, but not its hard drive. This time she didn't even consider checking her actual e-mail account because the odor from the eggs had reached her, and was so strong she returned to the table, picked up her plate, and then emptied it into the toilet—an act that made her feel immediately less likely to hurl.

* * *

Helen, for the first time in days and days, opened the front door to the cabin and let the sunshine in. It was morning, and the birds were having a madcap time of it in their chirpings. As cool air entered the cabin's gloom, it eviscerated some of its heaviness. She stepped out onto the porch, and almost tripped over the duffel bag in front of it. Unzipped, it bore fruits, granola, and another loaf of Ida's homemade bread. She hung it over her shoulder and picked her way over to the wooden armchair that looked over the creek instead of actually going down to it, because all this fresh air was making her a little woozy. Happiness, this mountain, this chair, this creek, this man, and she was smiling so widely it was almost laughter. She fished a nearly ripe plum out of the bag Ida had left, and bit into it despite its hardness. The slightly sour taste, the meat of it, was so good it almost made her cry. And unlike her adventure with the eggs, she ate it slowly. Every bite she savored, she chewed until the fruit's fibers had all but disintegrated.

She let herself have the moment, more sure with the delivery of the provisions that her neighbors were content to let her come out when she was ready. The sun slanted down onto the porch, grazing just the tips of her feet.

* * *

July 24, 2004

The last leg of the drive up to the poet boy's cabin in Black Elk set Carmen and Terrible right up against the sun, which was dangling down just low enough in the day's blue to near blind her. And the Nova was a godawful place to be stuck driving against the bright—they should have taken Terrible's truck. Not only had the damned dog chewed every goddamned pair of sunglasses she owned, but years before the driver's-side visor had fared even worse in the hands of Clayton Clark: now there was an ace it would be worth getting a new visor to forget. He liked swinging his iron-worker's arms fast, breaking whatever was closest to his fist because, of course, his brain was small enough to fit in it.

So he was a nine of clubs, really, not the ace of anything. Except for his penchant to punch things more than people, which she respected, Carmen would've demoted him further down the deck: a six, maybe even a four.

Disgusting. He *was* a four, and Carmen didn't dance too high up her own skirt to admit a four is just the kind of man that used to be enough. A Four of Shit and Bruises. If it hadn't been for her run-ning into Terrible at the Wave, on a mostly unpremeditated acci-dent, she'd still be tied up with that kind of asshole today. Because how do you know what real fire is if you've only ever touched those thin flames coming up out of a 99-cent bottle of lighter fluid?

"We're driving right into the sky's asshole," Terrible complained, squinting out against the glare from his spot in the passenger's seat. "You'll get a headache. It's not worth it."

"Shut up," she growled, since she agreed with him already. "Don't even start."

Of course she knew he was as worried about Helen as the rest of the world: there was G.I. Joe yammering over the phone about bullshit, blaming Carmen for bullshit. And the boss lady with her nasal, near-British voice, and that rich lady's stutter. "I . . . I . . . *um* . . . it's just that I haven't *heard* from her in *days*, and . . . and . . . you know she's just generally, um, *so reliable*. I think of her like . . . like . . . you know, we're very close."

"If you went to the Ivy Leagues, lady," Carmen said back to her, "you were taken."

"Um," the woman replied.

Carmen was mad. She had had enough by then but saved the poor lady the trouble of expressing herself further by promising she'd go see Helen the next day. If she didn't, she figured, she could expect calls from India, the U.S. Army, Mission Control, the Quorum of the Twelve, and whatever little shop it was that wanted to offer her wayward child $49.99 for a gold-capped tooth. The girl had laid low long e-fucking-nough.

And best of all: the worriers had rotted out her own sense of well-being with their venom. It was all very lovely, but what Carmen wanted to know, was what godforsaken animal on earth didn't drop its tail and lick itself when it needed? "Does not a jack's ass in the whole damned world understand that when little Miss Helen fucks up, she hides?" she said aloud to make herself remember she was the one person who was right not to worry. After all, after giving up Carmen's baby grandchild as a teenager Helen had hidden from her mother for *five years.* Five.

Terrible knew better than to respond, and had, besides, spoken his mind already on the subject. He wasn't a sayer-of-things-twice kind of man. He was the fifty-one-years-old silent-and-ugly type: bent nose, crooked back, smashed-up figure all around. Skinny as a pipe cleaner, and that's what Carmen had always thought he looked like he'd been used for, like his body had been used up cleaning the residue in too-small spaces his whole life. The antithesis of flash.

Not a winning dating profile was the polite way to put it, but he was her Ace for goddamned sure. And here was the cabin, finally, and she hit the brakes and peered up at it.

"That's Jimmy Hensaw's old place, up there, isn't it?" she asked Terrible, and he shrugged.

"Beats me," he said. "You're the one knows these things."

That was true. Carmen had never been to Jimmy's but had been at the Meek's a few times in the seventies and had driven past it—a shoebox, more or less, made of logs. She followed the tiny little road up to where her daughter's ridiculous taxicab sat dusty in the drive. She left Terrible in the Nova, and banged on the door of the cabin as loudly as she could to scare her child back into her senses.

"It's the police!" she yelled out, rattling the doorknob that turned out to be locked, "it's the U.S. Army, the end of the world, the last days of Christ, and for God *sakes I'm getting married!* Did you hear me, Helen?" She heard her daughter's hand flipping the lock on the cabin's doorknob, a sound that relieved her but that didn't induce her to lower her voice when they were standing nose to nose.

"You're going to have a daddy!" she shouted right into her daughter's face.

She got a blanked, gray-faced little goldfish kind of stare.

"Looks like somebody swiped your freshwater for Smirnoff, little fish," she laughed, but she reached her hand out, took the girl's cheek in her hand, and searched her eyes for signs of life.

"You found me."

"I try. Heard about your whereabouts through the great wine." Helen almost smiled at the joke from her childhood. She turned her head back toward the Nova. "Terrible! We're staying!"

"You had him worried sick," she said to Helen.

The cabin's air smelled like bad sex or a long sickness, and about made Carmen lose the watered-down Bloody Mary and English muffin from breakfast. The window above the sink opened, she discovered, as did the two in the corner of the room where her daughter had evidently been nesting: half a dozen different emptied glasses, snotty Kleenex scattered around like bird shit, food crumbs, and a godawful hand-crocheted blanket. With both the windows opened wide, and the cross breeze settling in, Carmen felt she could now neatly wring her daughter's neck.

"Jesus, Helen," she said, instead, crossing the room again to see what was keeping Terrible. He was coming, but Helen's arm had become one with the doorknob, so Carmen covered it with her own.

"The whole world wants to know what's happened to you," she said, and then her daughter had already wrested her arms around Carmen's neck in a vicious sort of body clutch and was sobbing onto her shoulder like the child she'd never been. Her fool fiancé came inside empty-handed and so she made her thumb into the top of a bottle, over Helen's shoulder, tipped it to her mouth to guzzle, and then pointed him back outside to the Nova's glove compartment.

"There, there," she was patting at Helen's back, "you're gonna be all right."

*　*　*

Even as she watched her mother lighting up her Pall Malls inside the cabin, as her mother poured herself a JD and water, the older woman's presence was welcome. Terrible busied himself in the kitchen, pulling out drawers and pots and rifling through the refrigerator.

Instead of diving into the details that brought them, Carmen plunged into the plans for her own wedding—never stopping to explain what had changed her mind about the state of matrimony she railed against the whole time Helen grew up. Now all she wanted to talk about were details.

In any other state of being Helen would have resented this, but her mother weaved the story of her fantasy wedding into the air that had been filled with so much dread, and Helen was grateful. Even when Carmen flung purple rings of cigarette smoke around the room like circus props, Helen refrained from asking her to smoke outside.

"The Starvation Blues Band is going to reunite," she said. "The wedding will be in the old Presbyterian church."

Helen couldn't help bugging her eyes. "You're getting married in an abandoned building?"

"On Halloween," Terrible called in from the kitchen, and Carmen burst out laughing.

"Jesus, didn't you take just one drive around Smoot's Pass for curiosity's sake? Gary and Glennis Cowan bought it, what was it, five, six years ago, Terrible? They rent it out for weddings and special events. Done just a beautiful job on it. We're getting a lady minister in from Salt Lake, too. A Unitarian to come shake things up a bit down here."

Helen had a hard time imagining any remodel of the old church that wasn't a complete teardown—but then again, if it was remodeled, and even if it wasn't a real church, she had a whole second set of doubts about her mother choosing to be married in it by anybody who hadn't mailed away and gotten their marriage license from the back of *High Times*.

"Well, Terrible used to raise hell shooting at the Mormon church's bell when he was growing up," her mother explained, voice already soggy and warm from drink.

"Mormons don't *have* steeple bells," Helen said, and Carmen burst out laughing again.

"That's what they kept telling him, but it never stopped him, and now he's got a fondness for churches. And the truth is I *myself* don't get around to marriage often, and won't mind God being around to see, even if it is just leftovers."

Why did she emphasize *myself*? Was it because she knew Helen *did* get around to marriage often? Helen stopped breathing, suddenly certain there was an ulterior motive to her mother's arrival: Herman or Ida must have told Carmen about her wedding with Chakor. She braced herself for the accusation, but to her surprise—her disappointment—it never came. She just found out Carmen's dress was to be sewn by a friend of hers who made a living making intricate costumes for Renaissance festivals. They were going to cook a goat by burying it in a hole on top of coals, and Helen would get to be the matron of honor.

"For your dress, wear whatever you want," her mother generously proclaimed. "There's no way it's going to outflash mine."

"You're really getting married?" Helen said, and the full-tilt smile on her mother's face, which Helen had never seen before, answered the question.

"Vittles," Terrible said suddenly enough to make Helen jump.

When he set a pot of mashed potatoes in front of the two women, her mother lopped three-quarters of it onto Helen's plate and said, "Eat."

* * *

Carmen watched her daughter devouring the potatoes like a starving person. She was haggard, greasy-headed, smelled like she'd been dunked in body odor, but was still somehow just incredibly beautiful. The sunlight fell through the man-sized window in the middle of the room right into Helen's profile, sure, but it was something else about her, too. Fuzzy, despite all the gray in the lines beneath her eyes.

"Jesus Christ, it's aglow!"

She shouted it out, and then even louder, viciously out to Terrible who was smoking on the porch: "Goddammit, put that thing out! Put it out!"

"What?"

"Put. It. Out!" she growled, and he did, knowing that voice. He stomped it beneath his boot and came inside to stare her down, and she wasn't ashamed to be crying. Sobbing, really, while both Terrible and Helen—neither being among the sharpest quills on the porcupine's back—gaped.

"A grandma!" she said. "I'm going to be a real grandma!"

The confirmation she needed she watched dawning slowly, beautifully on her daughter's face, and then she saw that look mauled by the thoughts that followed. That girl would never know how to let the world make her happier, and this thought burst Carmen's bubble only the slightest bit. "It don't matter," she said.

Helen looked at her mother, the spaced out way she did, the exact spaced-out way she behaved when she was with child before and she had to make a decision.

"Blink," Carmen said. "Take a breath." Helen did.

"I mean it," Carmen said. "It don't matter and now's not the time to worry. This time, this grandbaby of mine is whosever's you say it is, nobody's but ours if that's the way you want it." Her daughter's expression remained fixed and faraway. "It's what you *wanted*, Helen. *This is what you want.* Be happy."

Part Three

Date: Wed, 27 Oct 2004 10:54:22
From: eharris@bluehope.org
Subject: Silo
To: cmotes@yahoo.com

Dear Helen,

The architects e-mailed me drawings this morning and I'm also showing them off at the board meeting this afternoon—I was so excited I wanted you to know. I just found out Diana Speckart is having her *entire* home LEED certified and retrofitted with everything from solar panels to on-demand hot water heaters while they're vacationing in China this summer. This means our timing is perfect: converting a grain silo into the Rural Utah Blue Hope Cultural Arts Center (we *do* need to come up with a better name) is exactly the kind of thing people are very interested in these days. I'll present it as our way of paying homage to the rural landscape *and* to Native American spiritual beliefs (by keeping the interior a circular shape) and she'll be gaga over it. And you know she's the domino that will knock the others over. I fully admit at first I was skeptical of the idea: but good work!

Emmaline

PS: I saw Charles Krenzler at a dinner party the other night, and he mentioned that you've gotten a few serious bites on your house already. Congratulations! From the sounds of it, I might see you far sooner than either of us expected. And you know I'm *expecting* you to stay with me when you get to town. Don't worry about movers: my brother-in-law is in business with a sweet man who owns one of the smaller companies in town, I forget the name. But you're covered. Don't worry your pretty little head about carrying anything heavier than your sweet child around . . . .

Date: Tue, 02 Nov 2004 08:34:43
From: cmotes@yahoo.com
Subject: Re: Silo
To: eharris@bluehope.org

Em,

Here's a second shot at the last part of the purpose statement—we used a paragraph from the e-mail you sent last month as a starting point at today's meeting. "Rather than teaching art randomly, the Arts Center will teach Native American and pioneer culture forms half the time, and explore the artistic expressions from regions throughout the world during the other half. Our children will embrace and explore their own and each others' traditions while also increasing their knowledge about art forms and philosophies from places as far-flung as Asia or Africa. Instead of demanding their own art be unchanging, we will encourage them to enrich it with the inspiration they take from this broader contact; to converse and look outward, rather than remain inwardly and parochially focused."

We can discuss this all in more detail soon enough, of course: I'm arriving November 6th on Continental at 12:35. I'll take a cab to my house (no need for you to come get me) because I still need to get an idea of what to tell the movers, even. Then I can drive my car to your house around dinnertime?

I can't tell you how much I'm looking forward to the appointment with your massage lady!

Yours,

Helen

Date: Mon, 15 Nov 2004 12:21:05
From: eharris@bluehope.org
Subject: Re: re Silo
To: cmotes@yahoo.com

Helen,

Randy Pitts finally got back in touch. He'll take Larry's case, but neither of us has been able to get in contact with you by phone. You CANNOT disappear again. AND DO NOT SIGN ANYTHING the company gives you. Copy everything and overnight FedEx them to me. I don't need to stress how IMPORTANT this is to make sure you get everything you deserve.

Emmaline

Chapter Twelve

January 7, 2005

Helen was waiting at the bottom of the elevators for arriving passengers in the Salt Lake City airport. Christmas and New Year's hadn't been taken down yet, and travelers were holiday weary. The scene Helen had constructed for the airport reunion was based on the one in Shirley Temple's version of *The Little Princess*, where Sara finds her shell-shocked father in a London veteran's hospital and sobs when he doesn't recognize her, pounding at his chest with her cute, plump fists until his amnesia lifts and he begins mumbling her name.

The call had come in Houston, while Helen was watching one of the movers hitch Larry's motorboat to a truck bound for a large storage unit in nearby Conroe. She hadn't even looked for a house in Salt Lake City yet. The phone's ring bounced off the empty walls like a trapped bird and she almost hadn't answered.

Larry had been riding off-base in a jeep that fell under heavy shell and mortar fire, a teenaged voice told her when she did pick the phone up. Her knees collapsed. More fell from the teenager's mouth, words she understood on a one-by-one basis, but words like the beads scattering from a broken necklace: all in the wrong order, none coming together into a cohesive form she could take meaning from.

"I don't understand," Helen said, over and over. The boy at the other end talked more, and then it was thirty minutes that had passed. Mr. Muhammad, the moving company's owner, walked into the kitchen to finish things up, and he yelped when he saw her pregnant body splayed about on the floor.

"Ms. Motes," he said, alarmed, and his strong hands were already wrapped around her shoulders. He was a wiry African-American man, stronger than he looked because of his line of business. He locked his eyes into her own, looking deep into her face, and she saw him.

"He's lucky," the boy was saying on the other end of the phone. "The surgeon he was riding with didn't survive. She was blown to smithereens. And then your husband was left for dead, and that's lucky, too."

Mr. Muhammad was saying, "Let's sit you down out on the steps, here, Sister," but the phone cord wouldn't stretch, and now it was already January seventh and Larry was coming home.

The people from ThunderVox told her to bring a sign with her name on it. She had forgotten, though she remembered to wear a shirt that resembled one Larry had chosen for her on a vacation to Portland a couple of years earlier. Red with large yellow flowers. The original shirt's neckline drooped; it was a form-fitting knit. The clone she was in, she'd picked up in the maternity section of the Wal-Mart in Chipeta. It was rayon, tight around her newly giant breasts, but slightly flowing around her stomach which had poofed out like a popover. In Oregon she and Larry walked along a gray and rocky beach, and he'd said she was the only bright spot for miles. They had held hands the way people who don't live by the sea do, and they were happy.

All the doors opening and shutting in the Salt Lake airport's baggage claim ushered in too much of miserable January for anybody to unload their layers, and so her shirt was actually barely showing beneath her navy wool pea coat. It was nearly noon and

Larry's plane landed at eleven-thirty. Snow was fluttering around the valley, making up for a long morning of sunshine and clear skies. Every third woman in the airport was more pregnant than Helen would ever be. Nobody paid the slightest bit of attention to Helen's lonely form.

Until she'd gotten the bad call she'd felt almost like she could take the rest of her life to make the decision about what man to keep. The mutual absence of her husbands seemed eternal. Chakor's mother's tumor was slow-acting and he nursed her. His idealism was increased by his struggles. That was the kind of man you married: Chakor was the right father to have in such a dangerous world, she'd think, but then Larry would offer up short, quiet updates about his work with the doctors. It was the strength, the acknowledgment of a bad choice and the move to repair it that made him the right father for this child.

Her baby was due March 22, and her stomach was growing, and it had pushed her will to make the decision away even further.

Now her eyes were focused on the elevator. Now the choice had been made for her. Larry would be delivered to her by another man. He was incapable of coming to her himself. Every time the elevator doors opened, she flinched.

* * *

It was Emiliano Sweeney's last week at the worst job on Earth. He was pushing around yet another mangled old guy, this time through the Salt Lake City airport. Blond and blue-eyed families were hugging each other, chattering away. Yodelers, they looked like. Fresh plucks direct from the Alps. In the two days he'd spent with poor Larry Janx, the guy hadn't said anything except *piss* when he had to piss, and *fuck* when he knew he was fucked. Sadly, that wasn't even very often. Most of the time Mr. Janx just stared off into the distance.

"It's the perfect job," he'd actually told his granddad. "Thirty hours a week and I get *benefits*. I'll be learning about the Defense Base Act, figuring out how it applies to these contractors coming home. I'll know something real about federal law before I go back to school."

This is the way the job had been sold to him, and it was how he was selling it to his family—but the old man was a veteran himself and didn't buy it.

"Jesus Christ thought he had the perfect job, too, *m'ijo*," he'd told Emiliano, "and he ended up a virgin with his hands and feet nailed up to a scarecrow's cross."

"I know who'd nail *you* to a cross if she heard you saying that," he'd snapped back. "And things didn't turn out so bad for Jesus in the end."

"God Almighty had His back," his grandpa had said. "Whose gonna have yours?"

"Whatever," he'd sighed, but he wasn't going to be brought down by little minds afraid of opportunities. That's what he'd told Rosa. With the first paycheck, he'd bought her a tiny pair of pearl studs and she got a special extra pair of piercings in her ears so she could wear them all the time.

"A lot of good that did me, didn't it, Larry?" he said to the drooped man in the chair in front of him as he pushed the down button for the elevator.

No good had come of the job, except the money, which he needed for law school. He was a cross between a nurse, an insurance adjuster's lackey, and a cemetery-plot salesman. A scam artist. For the first few months he figured if people were going to be so stupid to trust him, they deserved what they got. But the job was bad vibrations. He wrecked his car *twice* in the past nine months, and Miss Rosa Flores had left him for a man who *didn't* travel all the time. Whose job *wasn't* convincing families their damaged kids were not nearly as fucked up as they obviously were. Rosa had ordered lobster on their anniversary and Emiliano fell into a full-fledged panic attack watching her crunch and tear away at the dead food's limbs. He'd excused himself to go to the bathroom three times, and on the way home she told him she couldn't handle it anymore. Just like that. Now she was three months' pregnant. If it wasn't his, she was cheating when they were together. She was blocking his calls.

The elevator was filled with a young family with a stroller and at least five older kids under eight years old. He shoved backwards into the small space and it was overcrowded. All their rosy faces froze up, and it was obvious that either his brown skin or the sight of Larry or both had killed their buzz. He wished Larry would tell them they were fucked, and when he didn't, Emiliano made up for it by remaining there in the middle of the elevator after the doors were opened so the family had to slink out around them. Momma jammed her stroller into the side of the wheelchair on her way out, Daddy pulled the older kids out behind him and they were all holding hands like kindergartners. It reminded him of the day his abuelita had melted a candle into his brother's ear and pulled out a long, dirty string of earwax.

"Larry?" a woman right outside the elevator said. Emiliano took her in as he shoved his foot in front of the elevator door that wanted to close. She was heavyset in a way that looked all wrong on her, and obviously overwhelmed. Eyes opened so wide they looked drugged. Emiliano pushed Larry toward her.

"*Larry?*" she said again, and he could see the lady trying not to cry. He admired that. Larry, for his part, looked up at his wife, sighed, and closed his eyes.

Mrs. Janx turned to Emiliano, her brow wrinkled in a way that asked him to explain Larry's reaction. What his reaction meant, though, was nothing. Not a thing. "Mrs. Janx," he smiled, holding out his hand. "It's a real pleasure to meet you."

"Motes."

"Excuse me?"

"I'm Mrs. Motes. I didn't change my name." Something in her tone made him uneasy, and so Emiliano instinctively took a half-step back. Just last month a mother had blackened his eye with a three-ring binder. It had just healed.

"Oh, I'm sorry," Emiliano said, with the empathetic eye contact and sweet voice he'd been coached to use in the workshop on grieving family members. "My own mother kept her name, as well," he half-lied. "I should've read my notes more carefully."

The words were lost on her. She was staring her husband over like he was the wrong furniture, her eyes resting a long time on the empty pantleg beneath his right knee. He saw her dread.

"They told you he's got a prosthetic, but it's just a starter one," he nodded, pointing down at the black case dangling from the wheelchair's handlebars. "It's a great leg but it gets sore if he walks too far in it, or wears it too long. We just sat down and took it off, that's what held us up a little. But it's right in this bag, I'll show you."

The woman squinted at Emiliano as he bent to unbuckle the case, and he felt again like he was about to be clocked. He sighed and straightened. Off on the wrong track, and he shook his head at himself.

"You can touch him," Emiliano said softly, and it was the right thing on a couple of counts. You were supposed to encourage them to make physical contact quickly. The longer they went without touching, the more likely they'd demand housing in a long-term care facility. Some sick fuck had actually studied it, come up with that statistic. But at least in this case it's what Mrs. Motes wanted to hear.

She bent forward and rubbed her wet face against her husband's. Larry's eyes shot back open. He looked at her with relief: it was the most human reaction he'd seen from the man.

"It's your wife, Larry," Emiliano said, leaning down toward his head like they talked all the time. "Say hello." There was no reason not to give the woman hope and he never knew exactly what these cripples were capable of.

Larry looked from Emiliano to his wife and back again, his confusion obliterating the sweetness of the moment. The woman kissed him on the lips, God bless her, but he jumped back, startled. She kissed her fingers and ran them across his cheeks, and Emiliano couldn't help but be moved. This woman wasn't going to let her husband slip away, and that was the best thing for everyone involved. A rubbernecking group of yuppies passed by, their skis in tow, and Emiliano glared at them. Then, right as he was about to suggest Mrs. Motes follow him into the conference room the company had rented near the Southwest terminal, the lady took Larry's right hand, stood, and rested it on her belly.

"A baby, Larry," she said—and her strangely proportioned fat suddenly made sense. "It's *your* baby." The poor lady said it like she thought it would bring him back, and Emiliano felt a panic attack coming on. He breathed deeply. He wanted to run. This was the last week he'd have to endure this shit.

Larry was looking at his hand on her belly, moved it around its curve, and let it fall back into his lap.

There was a giant manila folder full of forms for the woman to sign in his briefcase. He told her to follow him to the conference room, and began pushing Larry forward. She followed alongside them, her hand resting on the back of the chair. The room was shabby as they always were. He parked Larry in a corner, and began setting out short stacks of paper on the wooden desk between him and Mrs. Motes.

"I'm only signing the release form today," she said.

"Who told you that?" he asked.

"My lawyers."

Now Emiliano looked at *her* like she was the wrong divan. He'd had no heads-up about this. "Just a minute," he sighed, and left the room to call Harrison, his boss. He dialed the number, and stood just outside the door thinking, good for her. Good for her, but what a shitload of work it made for him. He was put on hold just as soon as his call was answered.

"Larry," Mrs. Motes whispered like Emiliano couldn't hear, like he was the *police*. "Larry, can you hear me?"

He didn't want to listen anymore, and his heart was racing so he headed down the hallway. His father was a labor organizer who made shit for a living, and his mom taught second grade in the south-side ghetto. Rosa and all the support she got from her double-doctor family had a lot of nerve to judge *him*.

* * *

After Helen rejected both her and Terrible's offer to let them go to the airport, Carmen had set her annoyance toward the scrubbing of the floor in the loo with a bristle brush. It was the last step of the deep clean the house had undergone in the last few weeks—partly in preparation for the full house she was about to become hostess of, but mostly because she had been on a manic upswing. Quitting all her vices at once had transformed Carmen into the evil stepmother and Cinderella all wrapped into one, and she'd been working herself to the bone. But Carmen would handle it. Helen was not going to keep this grandbaby from her.

The phone's ring caught Carmen midway through her scour of the tub itself.

"We're coming back, now," Helen said, her voice wound up like a hot ball of wire.

"How is he?" she asked, ogling a three-inch-long string of greasy, rotting hair that she'd liberated from the drain.

"I want to beat the weather," her daughter said. "We should be there by four."

"Get a hotel, we'll pay," Carmen said, but Helen had already hung up.

If ever there was a month-long period she needed a drink, it was now, but she was keeping her promise: no cigarettes, no drinks before nine at night when her grandbaby would be in bed. It was a nun's life, and she was being forever tormented by a demon pregnant daughter.

What a fucking shame, too. The girl was not Miss Perk before the call about Larry, but she could be rallied. The week before she'd run off to Houston to sell their house, Helen had *finally* begun asking questions about her wedding and volunteering to help. Carmen had moved the wedding a week forward a couple of weeks, from the twenty-sixth of March to the twelfth, so the baby wouldn't be expected anytime during the ceremony. This had touched her daughter, and as a reward, Carmen had *finally* been allowed to accompany Helen to the doctor's visit in which the nurse told her daughter her baby was no bigger than a beer can.

"A *what?*" Helen had hissed, and Carmen had proved her worth by dragging the girl from the room and directly into the car. Having worked at the senior center six years, Carmen understood it was never in a patient's best interest to cuss out a staffer for a matter as insignificant as bad taste.

Helen was quiet in the car, as mad at her mother as the woman who'd misspoken. Some people, Carmen wanted to tell her, would appreciate the woman's levity. Instead, in a stroke of brilliance, she said as deadpan as she could, "Just think, the next time we come in the kid could be the size of a pipe bomb. Wriggly as a rabid squirrel."

Helen made a slight choking sound and Carmen cringed, but when she looked over: *finally* the girl was repressing a smile.

"Peaceful as roadkill, lips as provoking as two lines of cocaine," Carmen coaxed, and her daughter burst finally into the freest kind of beautiful wild laughter Carmen hadn't heard from her girl in decades.

"Coochie coochie Coors," her Helen whispered, and then they continued on with this the whole way home. A boy they'd call *Itsy Bitsy Budweiser,* a girl *Princess Olympia Light.* Their jokes were puns worse than Carmen was used to, but their laughter was deep, and it was the right damned medicine at last.

The mother-daughter team had burst in on Terrible, who'd just come in from carving a special set of cabinets for the new city hall building in Smoot's Pass. He'd grumbled out of the living room and into the kitchen, having all but ignored their story, and Carmen was about to follow him to the kitchen and box his sorry-assed ears for spoiling the mood when he showed back up in the living room with a bowl of Fritos, some onion dip, and laugh lines alit at the corner of his eyes.

"Jesus," he beamed. "Look at us."

Helen relaxed into the sofa, Carmen sunk into Terrible's arms, and they were a family. There was hope for the girl, her mother thought, and then after the house in Houston sold the call came in and ruined everything. Just like he'd been doing the whole decade they were married, Larry squelched her daughter's attempts at happiness.

Jesus H. Christ, Carmen wanted a cigarette. As she put all the weight of her arms into washing away the grime behind the toilet, now, she told her brain to take what it could get from the bleach fumes instead.

* * *

Ernie watched the woman in the parking lot surveying the distance between the wheelchaired man and the opened door of her minivan for two or three minutes before deciding he should approach her to offer help. Not six months before he'd offered a young lady advice on a lawnmower at the Home Depot and was berated like a child for having the nerve to suggest that she hadn't done her own research just because she was a woman. His new neighbor, an older woman who spent an awful lot of time at the gym, had taken offense when he'd blown the snow from her sidewalks and driveways. It was what one neighbor did for another in his day, especially if one had a blower and the other didn't. But today he made good and sure the lady in the parking lot was flummoxed before heading over to offer a hand.

"It sure is a cold day out," he said, in greeting, extending his hand out, "I'm Ernie. Ernie Forsberg." She reached out to clasp his hand, smiling gratefully, and he saw she was pregnant and not just a larger woman, like he'd thought. He blushed, ashamed for having not helped her out right away, like he had been raised to do.

"Helen Motes," she said.

"Well, it's a pleasure to meet you, Mrs. Motes," he said, looking down at the man to prompt her for the introduction. He could see she was new to this, and he felt bad for them both; he'd been there himself. "And this must be your husband?" he said for her, looking down for the first time into the face of the man in the wheelchair.

"Oh, yes!" she said. "That's my husband."

"Your husband."

"Larry."

"Larry," Ernie said, and extended his hand down, and the man just looked at it.

"He can't . . . " Mrs. Motes began.

"Of course."

"He's just back from Iraq," she said.

Ernie regarded the young man in the wheelchair anew. Not as young as soldiers came, but still in his prime. He found it strange the man hadn't been transferred to one of the bases in town, that she was picking him up from the airport. Then again, he wasn't even in uniform. Maybe he'd already been released from the service somewhere else, first.

"There's not enough room between the cars to get him in, is there?" he said. "Even in the handicapped spaces it's like that. They make parking lots like sardine cans these days, always out to make that extra buck, no thought for people's needs."

"I haven't done this before."

"You could pull the truck back a few feet and it might be easier to get him inside." Before she could move to do it, Mr. Motes was standing on his own.

"Larry!" she said, and the man hopped over to the open mini-van's door and sat on the vehicle's floor. Ernie laughed.

"You've got a fighter. A real, honest-to-goodness war hero, haven't you?" he said. "That's a good thing. Let's get this chair in the back and then help him up."

Mrs. Motes popped the back of her minivan open while Ernie attempted to fold the chair. He couldn't find the catch, which annoyed him: he'd spent twenty-five years caring for Annabelle and her MS. If there was one thing he had earned rights to do in his sleep, it was fold a wheelchair. He shook the newfangled thing, incensed that five years of new wheelchair technology could baffle him so, but he smiled up at Mrs. Motes when she came to help.

"I think you have to put your foot on that tab, and push here at the same time," she said. She was right.

"It required the old one-two," he smiled, as he began heaving it up into the back of the van. The chair was heavier than he'd remembered them. It was then that the teenager parked next to the Moteses came walking up and gave him a hand.

"Kind of an awkward weight," the girl said. He doubted she was old enough to walk to school by herself, let alone be set free on the streets with the wheel of a car in her hands. At least, though, she'd been raised right.

In a loud, overly enunciated voice she asked: "Do you need help getting up into the car, sir?" Ernie laughed. He looked that old.

"It's ours," Mrs. Motes said, appearing from the side of the mini-van where the girl hadn't seen her. "Mr. . . . "

"Forsberg," Ernie supplied again.

"Is lending us a hand."

"Oh, I'm sorry," the girl gasped, and then burst into a high-pitched squeal of sweet teenaged laughter, "I just assumed it was yours."

"Well you're a good girl," Ernie said, and the girl let out another peal of good-humored giggles.

"Don't let my mom know," she said. "It would ruin my image."

Mrs. Motes was staring at Ernie and his new teenaged friend a little wistfully and Ernie remembered himself and walked to the side of the van where Mr. Motes hadn't moved, and the girl followed him over.

"Are you a soldier?" the girl asked Mr. Motes.

"He was an interpreter in Iraq," Mrs. Motes said. "He actually didn't work for the military."

"A contractor," the girl said, solemnly, eyes widening. "And you're pregnant."

Ernie moved forward to survey the best way to get Larry up into the van's backseat but the wisp of teenager brushed past him and knelt down in front of Larry like she'd known him all her life. "Can you put your arm up here, sir?" the girl asked, thumping the armrest with her fist.

"He doesn't," Mrs. Motes said, but then Larry did as the girl asked. Grinning, she snaked her own head below his other arm and patted her hand on the truck's floor.

"Put your leg here," she said. "Good. Now I'm going to stand up and you have to use your leg and your arm to help get you over to the seat," she said to him. Ernie and Mrs. Motes watched, open-mouthed, as the two made the maneuver, which looked alien and beautiful.

"There you are," she said, "That was good. Can you buckle your-self in? Here's the belt. No? Well, watch me do it and maybe next time you'll get it on your own." The belt clicked, and near simulta-neously the girl had jumped out of the car like an imp, still smiling.

"My heck!" Ernie said, and then, to his horror, Mrs. Motes stomped to the van's sliding doorway and slammed it shut. A moment later she'd unlocked the driver's-seat door, and closed the two of them off into their own world with a softer, but definitive, thud. He had planned on offering to follow her home because her van was big, and the roads slick, but now he felt suddenly resentful of the whole scene, a feeling he hated.

"Poor lady," the girl said, as the van backed up. "But a contrac-tor! Wow! It's hard not to think he had it coming."

Ernie had no response.

"Nice to meet you!" she said, and left just like that, as well. He was halfway home before he got hold of how he was feeling, before he unburdened himself of the resentment he'd felt at being unthanked and upstaged both, in the airport parking lot. And then he laughed. He laughed at his own pride, and shook his head, and was happier than he'd been when he'd woken up at his son's house in Pittsburgh. At least he had a new story to tell.

* * *

It was a blizzard, falling harder all the time. Larry's head was leaned so far to the left she could only make out his shoulders and neck in the rearview mirror. It was hard not to believe he was pur-posefully angling out of her sightline and that he hadn't heard her tell him she was pregnant—because hadn't he heard the teenager? Hadn't he understood her requests and responded?

When the elevator door had opened on Larry in the airport she knew why they'd asked her to bring a sign: she might have walked past him, never suspecting the withered man dressed sloppily in gray sweats was the husband she'd seen months before. His brown hair was a grayish stubble. There was no gauze wrapped around his forehead, as she remembered from the Shirley Temple movie, as she had almost expected. His head did hang slightly over to the left, though, as if it lay on an invisible pillow. The rash on his neck that he'd come back from Iraq with in July had cleared up, but the skin itself seemed to sag more. Muscles seemed to have evacuated from his face entirely. It made him look like a fat man who had shed a couple of hundred pounds on a crash diet, whose body hadn't caught up to the change.

Helen inched along the highway leading toward Parley's Canyon at forty, thirty-five, and now finally, still well inside the city, at twenty miles per hour. There were a couple of inches of snow on the road. The red shine from the brake lights of other cars was flashing and the air between the snowflakes was a shining gray. Terrible had attached snow chains to the van two days before, at Carmen's insistence. Concerns about Helen's safety was one of the new leaves turned up in Carmen, one that made Helen bristle, though she was in no position to complain: her mother had actually cleaned out the bedroom she'd grown up in, had a ramp built into the house's side door, and made space in her life for Helen and the husband she had never even liked. It still stung to have Carmen suddenly coming through.

The heavily powdered highway was only offputting in the distant sense that somebody else, who hadn't grown up driving in this weather, might slam into the van after jamming down hard on their brakes. Otherwise, she had delivered Larry and herself up into the storm gratefully in her efforts at escaping the parking-lot Samaritans whose fault it was her husband had ended up in the back seat, behind her. What kind of person, she wondered, thinks a woman whose husband that has just come home from war wants to spend her first free hours alone with him where she can't see him?

Of course the girl probably thought Helen lived across town, in Sandy or Ogden at the furthest. If she hadn't spoken to Larry, known he'd understand, Helen wouldn't have hated her so much. As it was, things were infuriating all around. The ThunderVox rep had talked up her husband's ability to care for his own wound and to put on his plastic leg by himself like they were qualities he was selling, like she'd won the lottery. The guy had said it was *a pleasure to meet* her, this young man dressed in a lemon-colored dress shirt and an olive-drab suit. She had already learned in a series of phone calls with the company that Larry was *lucky* he only lost half of one leg—the other was rebuilt with steel poles. It was *fortuitous* their jeep was discovered within an hour of the accident. A very healthy sign that he'd already *regained* a partial ability to speak. It would be *easier* on her because Larry had shown initiative and learned to take care of his own limb. He could take it on or off, he knew how to clean his stump. She herself was *blessed* that the U.S.A. provided comprehensive insurance for contractors like Larry since World War II.

To avoid the tears remembering all this, Helen began closing her eyes tightly for a moment every ten seconds or so. She breathed and set one of her hands on her belly to comfort the baby inside when she heard a click.

The woman riding behind her with a gun had disappeared from the face of the planet. No articles in the *Chipeta Register* turned up about her, no illuminating information had been offered her from the officer she'd contacted, aside from a last e-mail in which she'd more vehemently suggested Helen find a better use of her time than sending the force out on wild-goose chases. She hadn't responded, and had stopped checking the e-mail from that account. Helen herself had begun to wonder if she'd hallucinated the whole episode in her panic, but with Larry in the backseat, hidden and unspeaking, she thought she hadn't. His presence felt eerily the same as the woman's had. She could have been speaking to either passenger when she finally hit I-80 and said, "It's good to have you back." He had replied with the exact same kind of hollow silence the stowaway would have.

By the time she entered Parley's Canyon the snowflakes flittered around the car like the ash from an angered and celestial volcano. They melted against the van's warm windshield, and its wipers tore at the streams of water left in their wake. The hot air from the heater gnawed at Helen's cracked sinuses and shredded cuticles. She puttered down the highway alongside only a few other cars, and turned the radio on. Guitars and a howling voice blasted into the van's silence at maximum volume so forcefully that both she and Larry screamed.

"Are you okay?" she said, having jerked the volume down to barely audible. "You screamed," she said, and noticed, too, his body had shifted. Hearing Larry scream lifted her mood to a manic happiness. He was now staring directly at her through the rearview mirror.

"I did, too," she grinned. "Scream." He just stared at her, though not statically. Larry's eyes scrambled around her face. It was death metal still playing very softly on the college radio station and she said, "Let's find something we can listen to."

She flipped through jazz, and classical, and pop, and alternative, finally settling on Cher: *Tonight you're gonna go down in flames, just like Jesse James.*

"We're going to make it through all this," Helen said, and he squinted. "We're married, Larry. We're going to have a baby. Do you know what I'm saying?" He moved his head in a way that Helen decided to read as a nod, and then he closed his eyes. Within minutes he was sleeping. Gray shadows and pale light illuminated the top half of his body. He looked like a *patient*. A sick man. A disabled veteran she'd never expected to meet except in passing on a street, on television. The observations deflated her spirits as quickly as his scream had inflated them. By the time they got near Park

City, they were out of the storm and the roads were no longer wet. She drove at least an hour.

"Piss," Larry said, from the back seat of the car, like he was reading Helen's mind. His hoarse voice rising from what Helen had assumed was a nowhere startled her. "*Piss,*" he said again, and this time the tone of his voice made it clear he was making a request. They had passed Orchard already, where Helen had wanted to stop but didn't because the thought of how to get Larry into the restaurant had baffled her. The sky was a scorched winter blue. They were fifteen minutes away from the rest stop at Freedom Reservoir, forty-five minutes away from Smoot's Pass where Terrible could help, and Helen gunned it.

"Can you wait?" she asked.

"*Piss,*" Larry said, slowly this time, like he was speaking to a rock. She told him five minutes as she screeched along toward the overlook. She slowed when she got to the rest stop, nervous because its quarter-mile-long drive hadn't been plowed since the day before. They inched into the parking area in front of the restrooms and by the time Helen jumped down into the thigh-deep snow and yanked the door open he had already unbuckled himself. Helen did as the girl in the airport had, and began commanding Larry: "Can you slide yourself down, to the floor?" she asked, "You have to use your arms to slide yourself down and we'll go to the bathroom."

He turned toward her and she lifted the armrest to make room. He put his arms on the seat behind him and his leg forward. As he shifted his weight, concentrating, he reminded her of Thumper, the blind three-legged cat she and Carmen used to have. He looked as oblivious to the world as the cat had, and his body was strangely graceful despite that.

Larry slid onto the van's bottom like a ballet dancer, and scooted up to the edge of the van with no prompting. Both legs hung over the side. Just his left leg disappeared into the white: his right pant-leg lay atop the crusted-over snow.

It was cold, the wind was whipping right into the cracks of Helen's coat, and Larry was only wearing a sweatshirt. The thought of his fake leg scared her too much to even attempt finding it, so she sat next to her husband and slipped her own head below his arm so her body might act as a crutch. Larry did not smell like cologne anymore; he smelled of sweat and sugar. And he didn't move to stand. When she stood, trying to carry his weight with her, he pulled back toward his seat on the van's floor.

"It's cold, Larry," she said, and he kicked his broken-off leg out in front of him and stared.

"You want your leg?"

"*Piss,*" he said; it was a moan this time. She guessed he had probably held his bladder a long time before even asking to go.

"Well you can go right here in the snow," she said, panicked, "I'll help you with your pants." When she reached toward his trousers, though, he shook his whole body, "No!"

She didn't know how to argue and so found the padded black case with his leg in it—she'd left it for him in the front seat, before her airport helpers had gotten involved. She opened it and set it next to her husband. Where his lower leg and foot had been there was a clean, smooth round stump that looked so healthy it surprised Helen. Then Larry set about peeling away what she'd imagined was skin, but what turned out to be a giant, one-piece, Ace bandage. His pale white-and-scarred tissue made Helen's knees buckle slightly enough that she pretended to stretch her own legs for nobody's benefit but her own.

His leg looked high-tech, nothing like what she'd imagined. A steel pole connected his foot to a giant tube into which she could see he was meant to put his residual limb. The foot was wearing the same boot that his right leg was and this upset Helen. Before he put it on, he slipped his hand back into his bag and came out with another sock. This one looked a lot like a man's tube sock. He pulled it on, and then fit his limb into the cup on the prosthetic, and then looked to Helen expectantly.

She sat next to him, again, and put his arm around her neck. This time when she stood he came up with her. She felt for the second time in minutes that he saw her as more an extension of his prosthetic than his wife, than any sort of person at all. It was eerie, but she let him bear down on her shoulder with the weight of Frankenstein, and they made it carefully through the snow, over to the men's room, which smelled of chemical toilet water.

At the door to the bathroom stall he went inside and shut the door behind him. Helen was beginning to understand there were some things he'd already learned—which meant that she was understanding, more and more, how much he'd forgotten. Then the sounds of a fight breaking out ensued as Larry gasped and struggled behind the door, he bumped against the walls a full minute before she heard the sound of his urine hitting the water. He sighed. She didn't know whether or not to wait for him or to come get him.

"Fuck, fuck, fuck," he said.

Today was the second time she'd ever heard the word *piss* coming from Larry's mouth, and she'd never heard him say *fuck* before, and the fucks were what made her cry. Not sobs, just patient streams of water stinging against the chill of her face. Inside the stall, she heard him shift to the toilet, and she herself leaned against the dirty sink.

She imagined the beaten woman walking in with her crying there, pregnant, waiting for her one-legged husband. It was dead quiet in the stall.

"Larry?" she said. It had to have been fifteen minutes since he disappeared into it. "Are you all right, Larry?"

She began imagining herself having to climb beneath the stall, belly and all, when she finally pushed onto its door, and discovered it unlocked. Larry was sitting on the toilet, pants down, shivering, though his head was cocked into the daze she understood was a kind of sleep.

"Let's get out of here, Larry," she said. "Grab onto my arms." Repeating his name, over and over again felt like it would speed up the process of his really being Larry. But he didn't budge.

"Larry!" she said, and she brushed his face with her hand, and he jerked to attention. "Larry, it's me, Helen. Larry, do you know who I am?"

"Helen," he said, absentmindedly clutching at the toilet paper roll.

"I'm your wife. You're in the bathroom at a rest stop," she said. "Let's get you back into the car, Larry."

He was like an anchorman whose earpiece had stopped delivering his lines, except that he didn't seem to care. He looked confused and nonplussed all at once—on both accounts, the opposite of the Larry she'd always known. Helen's tears started up again. In the Shirley Temple movie he would have noticed. He would have touched them and their wetness would awaken him, but in the movie playing out in the rest stop at Freedom Reservoir, even when he looked into her face he didn't seem to see it. She heaved him up and was relieved he hadn't defecated. She moved his hands up, to the sides of the stalls where he could support his own weight, and pulled up his boxers—strange since he wore tightie-whities before, since his penis looked like it always had. Maybe it was more solemn.

They hobbled, together, back to the car where she opened the passenger-side door and realized the reason the teenager had stuck him in the back, in the airport, was that it seemed impossible to get him into the seat. But then Larry surprised her, again, by grasping the top of the van's roof, and swinging himself inside. He almost fell backwards, but she shoved him in like they'd done this all their lives. She climbed into her own seat, moments later, and buckled Larry in from there, without asking, as the girl had, if he could do it himself. She kissed him on his icy lips, and his lips returned it a little. Maybe she imagined it.

As she crept back onto the highway, she smiled, though. She stole countless glances at him as she headed toward Carmen's. It was still Larry in profile. His strong chin, his Roman nose. Any moment, she thought, he could come to his senses and tell her how to drive.

Chapter Thirteen

June 4, 2004

It was the first day she saw Chakor. Or saw what she thought was a Mexican worker sitting in the middle of a row of a dozen white plastic chairs on Main Street, in Franklin, and holding up a *Bush Lies, People Die* sign. She thought: he's going to get killed.

"Nah," he'd said, when she'd got up the courage to walk over from the counter at Marion's Diner to warn him—and what made her do it? She'd never done something so forward in her life. "Nah, they just scream obscenities at me and flip me off," he'd said, and grinned.

A boy in a yellow Mustang vroomed past, screaming something as if on cue. And Chakor had thrown his head back and laughed. He wasn't screaming out anything himself, he wasn't even standing. This boy's idea of protest was lounging back in a cheap lawn chair, holding up his handmade sign, and drinking an iced tea from Marion's.

"Sit down," he told her, and she did. Just like that she had changed the course of her life, which she knew now, but not then. Then it was just curiosity that held her. She'd wanted the story about this thin, bright-eyed, happy protester with the shock of shining black hair that reached out toward the world, in every direction, all at once.

On TV activists were insane, wild-eyed, and so certain of their points of view they looked mean. They yelled, their voices screeching the will of the mobs they faced, even when they spoke of peace. It was the primary reason she'd never sought out a protest herself, though she felt sure nobody wanted the war to end as much as she did.

A teenage boy in a gray T-shirt and tight, worn jeans was walking by on the sidewalk between Chakor and Helen and the abandoned storefront of Erma's Office Necessities. His short hair and wide freckled face reminded Helen of a lot of the guys she had grown up with: a farmer's son (but not Billy's, and not hers—there was no resemblance). When this kid stopped in his tracks, Helen winced, ready for the ensuing fight.

"Mr. ChaCha! Mr. ChaCha!"

"Scotty!" Chakor said, smiling back at the boy. "Sit down, sit down! I've been thinking about you. How's your summer been?"

"Uh. No, thanks," the boy had said, eyeing the sign in his teacher's hand.

"Did you hear back from the U?"

"Still waiting," the boy said, looking at his boots for courage he now found. "You know, my brother's in Iraq and we're proud of him for it. It's an honor to serve."

"We published the poem you wrote about that," Chakor said, nodding seriously. "I still think about it."

"Yeah," the boy said. "Well, we're all proud."

Helen could see the boy liked Chakor, and she was impressed that Chakor had taken the kid seriously. Impressed more, perhaps, that the kid had taken a man like Chakor seriously: this was no small feat in a city like Chipeta.

Ida and Herman and a group of about ten other people crossed the street from the empty bowling alley's parking lot. They were carrying armloads of signs and a couple of coolers. Helen thought poor Scotty might run at the sight of the real hippies, but Chakor didn't even notice how he tensed up.

"Your brother's trying to take care of the country," Chakor was saying, "and I want the country to take care of your brother. Your brother deserves it."

"Mmmm-hmmm," the boy said, already walking away at a swift trot. "See ya, ChaCha."

Helen too stood to go.

"But the signs just got here!" Chakor cajoled, "You can hold up one of your own."

That was supposed to be her moment to say, "You know my husband's in Iraq and I'm proud of him for it."

But she didn't. She wanted to sit next to Chakor. She wanted him to smile over at her, and so she let Ida hand her a sign with a bleeding and maimed, maybe dead, Iraqi child on it and the words: *A War Is No Place To Raise A Child*. It offended her to the point of outrage, using the image of a child she didn't know even the fate of to make a political point. This kind of sullied, sordid sentiment embodied the reason she'd stayed away from rallies. She immediately rolled the sign up and held it below her arm like a weapon she'd defend if somebody tried to take it back.

But nobody was paying attention to her. They were listening to Ida, who she knew from childhood, though Ida didn't recognize Helen yet. Today Ida was sitting next to a woman Helen met that one day only. Her hair was bright red and Helen was startled to see there was a baby tucked into a sling on her chest, suckling on her breast right in the middle of Main Street. It seemed monstrous to her. With one hand she held the baby's head—it was that young— and with the other she managed to prop up a sign whose slogan Helen couldn't see.

Ida, in a dress she'd made out of an actual U.S. flag, was going on about her first husband, Rex Humphrey. He'd been the life of the party when he left for Nam, and he'd come back changed. He'd taken to sleeping with a gun beneath his pillow, no matter her protests. She stayed, anyway, because she was eighteen. She believed in duty. But then Rex got spooked by his dog in the middle of the night, and shot her before he was even conscious.

"I loved Rex," Ida said, "but Bingo was his *hunting* dog. He'd had her since childhood. The summer before he shipped, a man had kicked her in the ribs at a baseball game and Rex had beat that man to nothing in a blink. It took both teams to pry him off the asshole, though of course, their efforts were only half-hearted. Everybody loved Rex. If he could shoot Bingo, though, I was next. I left him. I'd have been a fool not to have. Poor old Rex," she said, eyes welling up with tears. "Shot himself in his mother's backyard a couple of years later."

Herman walked over to Ida and squeezed her on the shoulders. He kissed the top of her head.

"You did the right thing, Ida," the red-haired lady said. "I just read about a man who came back with a PTSD nobody could get him any help for. He stabbed his wife fifty times in her sleep. Fifty! Two kids sleeping in the room over, thank God he didn't remember them. Army tried to cover it up, of course. All-in-the-family kind of thing. Wasn't for the Internet we wouldn't know the hell these boys and girls come back carrying inside them."

Ida sighed, and Helen was disgusted. Not by Ida, but the redhead. She just rubbed her wrong, so Helen stood to go.

"It's just another crime of war," the woman said. "I swear to God our family's picking up and moving to Canada if Bush is elected again."

With that, a pickup truck loaded with teenagers came screeching by and Helen was hit hard in the chest by a water balloon, its liquid shooting up right into her face. Everybody scrambled around like chickens.

"Get the license plate! Get the license plate!" the mother was screaming into her knees. "They could have *killed* Bradley!" She was hunched down over her child, but it turned out Helen and Herman were the only people who suffered direct hits; everybody else's signs had deflected the attack.

Foul, skunkish water permeated the entire line of protesters now, and Helen herself felt it soaking into her skin, which terrified her. She jumped up to flee but Chakor grabbed her wrist. She turned to him and he was handing her a red flannel shirt. It confused her.

"For your face," he said, but then instead of giving it to her he cupped her whole head in one hand, and dabbed the water off her eyes and her cheeks with the other. She felt like a statue being rescued, like he was wiping away centuries of dirt. Inside his hands she brightened. She could feel it.

"You'll let me take you to the Grill for lunch, later?" he said. "For having taken one for the team?"

She nodded, yes. She blushed. She didn't say: "You aren't my team."

Chapter Fourteen

January 17, 2005

Helen developed a list of things Larry liked and hated. Staring at walls was on the list of things Larry liked because he did it all the time. Walking in circles around Carmen's house was on the list because he'd worn a path in the snow doing it. Help he didn't need was what he hated most, but it was unclear, from day to day, what that entailed since the people at the Chipeta County Rehabilitation Clinic taught him new things every day. What hate meant was that he was liable to swat at Helen or Carmen or Terrible if they tried helping him zip a coat or take his dish to the sink or groom himself. Long walks in the wheelchair he still enjoyed because he couldn't walk far on his prosthetic.

Temporary or not, the plastic and steel leg is what he loved most. He bathed himself each morning, then cared for the leg with a rag and alcohol. He lathered his stump with Vaseline, and then powdered both it and the cup of his prosthetic with baby powder. Mornings he washed the elastic bandage he wore at night to shape his stump; nights, last thing before bed, he washed the stump sock that had sat inside his prosthetic during the day so it would be dry by morning. He performed these duties in the bathroom sink, and he hung wet items on the shower curtain rail.

All this work Larry did tenderly, or so it seemed to Helen. All the love he should be feeling for his unborn child was focused on something temporary and plastic. It was a new body part, a ritual he needed—she could see that—but she still could not fight the resentment.

"He's taking control of his life," said Nurse Bettie Johnson from the clinic. "Be grateful." Bettie's hunch was that because Larry was so adept at learning physical tasks, his chances of returning to normal cognitive function were high. Loving his limb meant he would love again.

But he slept with the prosthetic propped up against the bed in Helen's childhood room, while Helen crashed on an air mattress in the den. She had lain next to him in bed the first night he returned from the Gulf, never having considered she should do otherwise. His penis hardened almost immediately and she moved to touch it—but he jumped back and slammed himself against the wall, wild-eyed, staring at her molten hand in horror. The thought of him strangling her in the night kept her from trying to sleep with Larry again: she did not fool herself into thinking she was on the list of things her husband loved.

She had proof of this. Due to Bettie's guidance, for instance, Helen eventually dragged her husband to a prenatal appointment to help him "feel part of the pregnancy." When waiting for the doctor, Helen undressed herself and stood purposely in front of Larry. She ran her hands across her taut, warm skin. Her back straightened as a deep pride welled up. He shifted his gaze. Not averted, because he wasn't rejecting her, she could see: shifted because her form interrupted the smooth surface of the walls he seemed to live inside.

That was also the appointment where Larry sat on the exam table, removed his prosthetic, and wouldn't budge from it until the doctor arrived and ordered him to. Because, of course Helen realized later, he recognized the white and metal sterility as his own. It was the appointment where the nurse's aide had assumed Larry was the baby's *grandfather*, and where Helen didn't correct her.

* * *

January 20, 2005

If the snow covering the lawns and fields between Carmen's and Peggy Smith's was a blanket, it looked chewed and torn in the places where brown grass and muddy brown spots poked out. Bringing sustenance to the maimed and disheartened ought to be easier, is what Carmen was thinking. Big-hearted soul that she was, she had driven over to Peggy's to pick up some jigsaw puzzles. When she went to start her car, afterwards, it wouldn't. The mile-long walk home, Carmen figured, would do her good but then she set the dogs in the Jameson's yard to yapping from their chains. As usual, they were tangled up all together, a humiliated land octopus with barking heads at the end of three of its tentacles. They were bound up so tight they constantly nipped at each others' heads and Carmen frankly found it a miracle the two smaller dogs, a Doberman pup and a terrier mix, hadn't become dinner for the giant Shepherd months ago. But of course, no matter how decrepit their owners are, she thought, it's hard to ruin a Shepherd.

"Trash," Carmen muttered, under her breath as she paused in front of the sad spectacle. Somewhere inside the trailer, whatever disharmonic torture that had replaced heavy metal as the young people's music of choice was playing so loud that it shook the ground. On a different day she might have thrown a rock through one of the windows because she'd screamed at these assholes about the dogs before. If she didn't mind being torn to bits she'd have set the beasts free months ago.

A curtain inside the back trailer window opened, and a dirty baby's face smashed up against the even filthier windowpane.

"Bah!" she yelled at it, stomping menacingly toward the kid with the ugliest arrangement of her face she could muster, rattling the plastic bag filled with puzzles at it. Her fondness toward helpless creatures didn't extend toward other people's children. Not if they were old enough to walk. When the one she was trying to scare didn't blink an eye, or change his expression despite her antics, Carmen felt a little sorrier than she was used to.

She was still thinking of the baby when she walked through her own front door to the delightful apparition that Larry was, sitting all by himself in the living room while Helen showered and Terrible was off at the grocery store. Her daughter took him into the Chipeta County Rehabilitation Center every day, but she hardly spoke to him, and it had driven Carmen to pitying him. She'd teach the girl how to pull him from this stupor by example, which was why she'd picked up the puzzles, why she smiled at him and rolled him to his place at the kitchen table just as soon as she collected herself.

"Now, Larry," she said to his dull face, "I'm walking into the kitchen to get myself a glass of tomato juice." His eyes followed her motion, "I'm unscrewing the lid, now, and pouring the tomato juice into the cup and I'm adding celery, a dollop of Tabasco, and splash of Worcestershire sauce, but no vodka even though I need some warming up. But it's not yet noon, you understand, and I've got principles to hold up. Look, I'll make one for you, too." And she did, and she set it next to Larry. He drank it up in a couple gulps, like he had been a Virgin Mary drinker his entire life. "Before we know it you'll learn to pour me my drinks!" Carmen nodded happily down at him. "Wouldn't that be a hoot?"

She knew better than to wait for an answer and instead spilled all the pieces from the first puzzle that crossed her hand out onto the table in front of Larry and her. The picture on the box was of a pile of snakes—no wonder Peggy had been so keen on getting rid of it.

"Now we've got to separate out the pieces with flat edges, Larry, okay?" she said. Rehab had sent papers home encouraging conversation and mental exercise for guys with brain trauma. Carmen picked up a piece. "This is the flat edge I'm talking about," she said, running her finger along it. "They go in this pile here."

Larry stared at her while she started sorting the pieces. She didn't expect more than this so early on. She told him about how a few years back they'd rented out an old stone shack on the other side of town to start a rattlesnake farm. Venom sold for hundreds of dollars an ounce. One night before they'd even figured out how to harvest the liquid gold, Terrible passed out on the couch inside the shack, and woke to realize he'd forgotten to put the lid on the glass cage the baby rattlers were in. It was three-quarters empty. Carmen found him hours later, crouched on a couch cushion, too frightened to move.

The whole thing soured Terrible on snakes and they'd gone out and released the ones that a couple of teenagers helped her catch in the salt desert outside town. After that some old man from Franklin rented it, and she'd warned him about the possibility of a few live rattlers inside, but he was an old ranch hand. Said he wasn't against a snakebite every now and again, for the old Arthur-Itis.

Larry listened, stone-faced as if he'd known his share of snakes, as if he'd in fact had a run-in with Medusa herself. But his eyes, Carmen noted, clutched at her words.

"Maybe you could use a snakebite, yourself," she said, raising her eyes at Larry. He must have taken it as a threat because he picked up a puzzle piece and put it in her pile, although it was the wrong kind of piece.

"That's what I'm talking about," she said with a smile, anyways. "That's just exactly it."

* * *

January 29, 2005

Larry's accident decided the trajectory of her life. No matter what else she'd done, she would not leave Larry, alone and helpless, to the world. All she had needed to do for weeks was write Chakor an honest, upsetting e-mail that he would survive. His poetry might improve for the trauma, she'd told herself. And Helen owed it to Larry to bring him back. She was determined to do it. Her mother pitied him, not Helen. Because Helen knew this was all temporary. She would use every possible avenue she could to get her husband back, most importantly fatherhood: Helen *knew* Larry Janx. He would not sit by deranged when there was a baby he needed to take care of. Even if the baby looked like Chakor, Helen's father was unknown. Larry knew that. The baby would pass muster.

The truth was that it could be either man's. Helen had not had unprotected sex with either Chakor or Larry in the months that mattered, except for that first afternoon Larry had returned from Iraq. But what were the chances that was it, after almost a decade of trying? No better, but no worse than the chances Chakor and she were the two percent of people who got pregnant despite the use of condoms.

What was clear was that although she loved Chakor, more and more so at the thought of never seeing him again, she *owed* it to Larry to give him a last chance, to let a child in his arms shock him back into himself. The problem was that she still could not let down Chakor. Not yet. Not for his sake, but for her own: his e-mails lightened the weight of Larry's current absent presence. Every new day she lived with her broken husband heightened her dependence on the fantasy world of what her life *might have been* had things turned out differently. Every new letter from Chakor made her remember that in his universe, her own life was a radically different thing than it was destined to be. She had not been able to break from his vision.

Today, she had brought Larry with her to city hall, where she checked e-mail on one of four publicly available, ancient computers. She hadn't brought him before, but the past few days he had been cooped up by snow. Today she'd allowed him to follow her into the cold. Of course, she'd intended to push him in the wheelchair, but he'd insisted on walking.

Now he sat hunched and exhausted in a chair next to the bookcase, and Helen felt guilty. Everybody had made it very clear to Helen that this first prosthetic of his was a "starter leg"—that when his stump had healed up completely he would receive a leg capable of walking two miles through the frozen mud on the streets between Carmen's and the library. She should have held her ground, and not taken him at all if he wouldn't sit.

The old city hall itself was about twelve hundred square feet, a building constructed from cement blocks and painted sage green. Across the street the newer structure strutted a more graceful composition: it was red brick and more governmental-looking, but still months away from completion. Inside the old building were two large rooms: one was for Mayor Lois Cooper and the city recorder to share as an office, the other was filled with a conference table and twelve chairs, and a ragtag library full of Louis L'Amour paperbacks and Alcoholics Anonymous literature. The computers were shoved into a corner of the conference room.

Chakor wrote to her on Friday nights, and Saturday mornings Helen came to the library to write back. The computer lab was manned today, as always, by Spike Wardle, the teenaged son of one of the six city councilmen. He always offered her coffee but otherwise ignored her, and for this she liked him.

Helen sat at her usual computer, and signed into her Yahoo account while Larry remained hunched behind her, staring at the spines of the books in the shelves like lost ideas. She hoped the creepiness of his presence comingling with Chakor's, even if it was only via cyberspace, would compel her to compose the letter she had not been able to write. What she told herself was that after she broke things off she'd still have the baby to look forward to. She still might have this bit of Chakor. At the same time, she couldn't imagine the baby even being born; not with her life in such a shamble.

The Yahoo account was full of unsent drafts of letters like the one she'd finally have to send. The only generous way to justify their presence was to insist it wasn't kind to break things off with Chakor until after his mother was dead. To make him feel alone in the one moment of their lives she could at least seem to be there for him would be unnecessarily cruel. For his sake then, not only her own, she should wait until the call or the e-mail when it was all over. He would travel across India for a few weeks to scatter his mother's ashes, to console the right relatives—why not let that be the time to tell him?

"I got an e-mail from Lloyd Bridges," she said to Larry, because though the letter from Chakor was there, opening it with Larry in the room felt more upsetting than she'd realized it would. "You remember going out on his boat, at Lake Powell, with the kids you used to take south? You always said he drove it like a blind man. Do you remember that, Larry?" she asked.

He nodded yes, but that didn't mean much. Larry had already learned that doing so was a generosity, an expectation of his caretakers, the way lifting himself into the car was. Helen would start out reminding him of any memory and get so nervous because of his vacant nods that she'd forget the details that mattered.

She stared at Larry in the room, as the bold letters of her new e-mail from Chakor stared her down. Her heart raced and she was actually sweating. She glanced over at Larry and realized he was still fully bundled in his winter gear. On the way over she'd been grateful the cold called blood into his cheeks, but now his face was flushed in the wrong way and she left the computer screen to help relieve him of some layers.

"Look at you, poor thing," she said. He knew how to take off and put on his coat and mittens, and usually wouldn't allow anybody help him; today, though, he let her. The walk had really worn him out.

"Why don't you rest your leg?" she asked, pulling another conference chair in front of him. Her husband actually complied with her suggestion—he lifted up the heavy weight of his leg, laid his head back, and closed his eyes. She felt guilty—she should have driven, or made him ride in his chair. Maybe he would nap, though, she thought, and kissed his head.

Back at the computer, she clicked onto Chakor's e-mail before sitting down. It was a long one and she glanced at Larry one more time before sitting and entering Chakor's world.

Date: Fri, 28 Jan 2005 18:04:22 -0600
From: "Cha Cha Kor" <desipoetics@hotmail.com>
Subject: Veraval
To: cmotes@yahoo.com

Dearest Helen,

When a man returns home to care for his dying mother, how is it that the fact of her dying can still surprise him? Her bones shrink inside her skin, her eyes are two dark and lonely planets, and her sister, my Maya Mami, sobs in the corner of her bedroom. I rub Amla oil into her hair every night, I caress her brain's shell like if I do it well enough it'll begin working properly. As if all it needs is coaxing. I've been doing this nightly, the last two months.

The good news is that the doctors have finally given permission for her to take a trip to Veraval. She wants to see her youngest sister and the Somnath Temple both, one more time in her life.

There are many stories to this temple, which is the most sacred of the twelve Jyotirlings of the Lord Shiva. The one here is like a giant, black, shining egg that they say used to hover in the air of its own accord. The temple itself has been destroyed by invaders seven times since it was first built, and the story is that the Moon God himself is the first person who built it, out of gold. It was to thank Lord Shiva for restoring his shine. The moon, you see, that naughty boy, had married twenty-six daughters in a household. That wasn't even the problem! The problem was that he had a favorite. His father-in-law cursed him for it, and he lost his shine. Chandra, the moon, prayed to Lord Shiva to restore his brilliance, and since a world without a moon would be darkness for everyone Lord Shiva relented. They say before the curse, the moon was always full; once a month, as he loses his shine now, he must return to the waters of the Arabian Sea, which the temple is built on, and pray and bathe to restore his light.

When I was a child, my parents and I went, and we stood ankle deep in the sea behind the temple—which I remember as a giant sand castle, and will be happy to see it again. What I remember better is the ocean lapping at our legs and an old woman who sold coconuts running and urging us out of the water. When I asked why, my father explained how so many children had been standing the way I was just moments before the sea sucked them out to their deaths. "What's wrong with you?" my mother scowled at him, for having scared me, but we all left the water. In the car we all laughed it off. Of that entire trip to India, that's what I remember most: standing at the lips of the Arabian Sea, the feeling I was at the brink of obliteration.

Veraval isn't just where the Somnath Temple is. Just a mile from the temple there is Triveni Ghat, which is the convergence of three great rivers: the Hiran, the Kapil, and the Saraswati (which does not even exist! It's mythological, but it still counts) at the moment before they enter the Arabian Sea. Lord Krishna was shot by an arrow nearby, and it is said he was cremated at Triveni Ghat. And so this holy convergence of rivers has been the resting place of my own family's ashes for generations.

I am glad we're taking her there. I think she won't let go of this world, of the pain that she wakes with day in and day out without the journey. Not that she won't die, but that she won't allow herself the peace of letting go—I am not the poet that would beg her not to go gently into the great night. And the idea of the moon bathing and regaining his glow in the water made up of my mother's ashes is one that will sustain me a long time. My whole life, I will have the pleasure of seeing my mother in the moon's shine.

Helen, the walls of this apartment feel drenched with sickness and sadness and hopelessness. I am homesick for you and I love you more every day. I love the pictures you send me, the words of wisdom and encouragement, and knowing you're there anchoring the other side of the planet so that if I come careening home from this half, I won't fall into an abyss, but into your waiting arms.

I love you, I love you,

I am kissing the screen,

Chakor

Helen read it several times. When she finished she worried Spike Wardle would come in and see her crying face and know the tears were for the absence of her lover, and not merely symbols of her grief. When she turned to check on Larry he was staring right at her, for how long he'd been doing it she didn't know. He was too far away to read the text, but he seemed perturbed.

"Hi, Larry," she said, wiping her face, defeated. Her first husband reached over for his jacket on the table, swung his bad leg down to the floor, and cried out in pain when it landed. Before she could make it over to him, he had taken the limb off, and was peeling back the sock covering his stump. She kneeled next to him and he didn't protest. His stump was red and looked like it had rug burn so bad he might bleed. The stump was also bony, bonier than she'd remembered, and she hoped something hadn't gone wrong. She looked up into his face, but his head had rolled back in the chair again.

It was Larry's world that felt unreal, the wisps of Chakor's were what she wanted to hold onto. She glanced over at the screen, still open to the e-mail, and felt like she was looking at Chakor himself. She turned back to Larry and whispered, "Just a couple more minutes," and he was so ghostlike she could almost see through him.

Helen returned to Chakor briefly, and wrote that she loved him, too. She told him about the plans for her mother's wedding, which was coming up in the first week of March. Carmen had at one point wanted to wait for the baby to be born so she could be the flower girl, but decided, instead, it would be best for everybody involved if her grandparents were good and married by the time the child arrived. Of course, none of this Helen could write to Chakor, who didn't know a baby was expected. She only described her mother's happiness, the crazy reception planned in the Legion Hall afterwards, and the difficulty Terrible had trying to convince her they would be roasting a goat in the frozen ground.

* * *

Moments. Larry knew. *The Empty Land.* Snakes. Sand. Helen, her wet cheeks. Fuck. *The First Fast Draw.* And then. Dr. Frank. *The Tall Stranger.* He had held her hand, her hand, *The Quick and the Dead.* Pink lipstick, pink lips, fire from nowhere. *Mustang Man.* Wet eyes. And that was. Fuck. *God Grant Me the Laughter. My Name is Bill W.* Larry Janx. Yellow pieces. Straight edges, his leg burned. *Showdown at Yellow Butte.* So much snow. *Runner get down from there! High Lonesome.* Horrible buckets. *The Strong Shall Live.* If it would, Dr. Linda Frank. Pink lipstick. *How the West Was Won.* No. Not won. *Not* Linda. Pink fuck, the melted tire. *With These Hands,* her surgeon's healing hands. Close them. *With These Hands.* Not burning. *The Lonesome Gods. Black Elk Speaks.* Shut them up. And it seemed, oh. Helen, the children, *It's yours, Larry.* Her wet eyes. *Don't let the motherfucker close them!* Close them. *The Big Book.* Close them, close them. Please. L'Amour. *A Trail of Memories*, this fiery leg, she's kissing the computer.

* * *

February 2, 2005

It is a cranky sonofabitch of an existence that folds a man up into the fat of his own brain the way it had for Larry. Terrible watched him, spent time trying to bore into the sadness and horror that had sewn him shut, and tried comparing what it was in front of him to the arrogant version of Larry he'd met before. He always came up empty.

They needed some kind of miracle and what they got was an infection in the man's stump, a new form of torture for an already wretched existence. Where he'd at least used to walk around like a zombie, he now sat coldly and glumly inside his chair, stumped as a stalagmite.

To counter this horror, Terrible had taken it upon himself to bring the man out on walks with him and Vera, park the wheelchair out on the ledge above the Highway 67 bridge, which had become for Terrible, something, and speak to him about why it was he couldn't stay knotted up inside himself.

He'd kneeled down next to Larry, never mind the wet and mud that soaked into his knees, held one of the man's cold hands in his own to force a connection, to help move the blood that wouldn't kiss the parts of his insides into something besides oblivion, and told him the story he didn't tell often.

"The dead tree up there on the ledge next to that group of boulders, you see it?" he'd whispered into the man's ear that was shining bright as ember in the cold. "No birds land on it. I swear upon the tar in my own heart I never seen one land there once since I started coming out here. There used to be days I'd come out, and I'd drink Hot Tops from the flask I used to keep. That's the most generic, the most sickly and deadly of all the cinnamon schnappses, Larry, which is already a godawful drink. But I didn't work much back then, and it cost about as much as a Q-tip. I'd lay down on that rock, plastering my back to its warmth, my face up to the stars, and I'd wait for a bird to land. And they never did. Not a single motherfucking parasite-ridden beauty ever touched one of them branches, and I told myself that meant something about what it was to live, and that's why it was I decided on that tree."

Larry seemed to be looking off toward the tree, you couldn't tell, and Terrible lit up one of the secret cigarettes Carmen would have wrung his sorry-assed neck over if she found out he had. Larry was good for secrets, though, and Terrible blew the smoke into Larry's red face, and the man jumped. Wrinkled his nose and stared into Terrible's eyes for the first time ever. He'd been waiting for the eyes to fall into his own and took it:

"Me and Carmen had fought one night, then, and I'd taken some of her Xanax, and I'd drinken a six-pack or two, and I came out here to hang myself from that tree.

"And before I could do it I saw that girl floating by in the river like an angel," he'd said.

"And it was not me, because I'm terrified of the murk, of the brown and the clinging of water I can't see to the bottom of. You never know what wants to grasp hold of your legs and take you down, you know? But it was something else, God or the Universe, for all I knew it was Porky Pig, but there was something sent me inside of the water that night, no choice I made, and I pushed in, and it was up to me to deliver this child up to the river's banks."

Larry's eyes had wandered, and Terrible needed them, he needed to be looking inside them, so he put his hands up to the sides of the man's face like he was going to kiss it, and cut the story short: "The point is that I saved her, man, I made it out across that shitty, smelly funk without drowning and we hit the shore and it was three seconds after that I realized what I'd done was save a *nothing*. A doll. And my fuck, I grabbed that baby girl by the heel of her fake leg and whacked her head right against the ground like an insane person, like she was possessed, or I was, and I screamed, and I was about to tear her head off and throw it into the waves when one of her little eyes flicked open, the other stayed shut, some water leaked out of the bottom of her somewhere. And I saw that I hadn't been tricked. That you never know what it is you're meant to save, and this girl, she wasn't a girl, this doll, this little Vera of mine was what I'd been given. And by God, I vowed to keep her."

He let go of Larry's face, and the man let it hang to the side the way he did, and right there and then is where Terrible wanted to let loose a tear or two, though he held back. He stood, and got back behind the wheelchair and started pushing again.

"The point I was trying to get at, son," he said to the man only a few years younger than himself, "is that you never know what it is that's going to save your life. But you got to let it, man. You got to let something save you."

They walked back into town, back to Carmen's, and up the ramp Terrible himself had fashioned for the poor man's chair. He wasn't in the habit of thinking things lost, anymore, but he didn't know about Larry. Something was happening inside that man's head, and Terrible wanted to crawl up inside it and let him out. But maybe he wouldn't be coaxed.

And then it wasn't a surprise, a few days later, when he watched Carmen insisting Larry help her with one of the puzzles she'd taken it into her head would lead the man back into the land of the living.

"What's that you've got in your hand, Larry?" she asked. "Is that a yellow? A yellow? You got to put it in that pile, Larry. That one, over there."

Sometimes the man did as she asked and sometimes he didn't. It was ten o'clock at night, this time, and Carmen was lit, and this was a moment Larry wasn't doing what he was told. And it was a moment Carmen wasn't having it.

"Goddammit, fucking Larry!" she hissed, "Give me that yellow puzzle piece right now or I'm jamming the table down your throat." The puzzle piece, Terrible could see, was clenched deep inside Larry's fist, but Carmen went for it anyways and Terrible stood to intercede, but not before she grabbed the broken man's usually limp arm and began trying to un-pry the fingers. And that's when Larry's other arm, his right fist, sailed up from its place in his lap and landed hard into the side of Carmen's face, as he shouted: "No!" It was one of about five words Terrible had ever heard coming out of the man's mouth. Carmen screamed, and Helen came running out of her room.

"He hit me! This motherfucker hit me!" Carmen was screeching, and crying, too, and Terrible had already moved the once-again-limp Larry into the living room, puzzle piece still in his fist.

Helen had run to her mother with a wet rag, was sopping up the blood that was leaking from a split lip, and saying, "Oh my god, oh my god."

"He tried to kill me, Helen! Did you see that, Terrible?" Carmen was screaming, "He'll try to kill you, too!" His own heart had pounded in fear a moment or two when it happened.

"Give me a look at that lip," he said to Carmen, and there wasn't a lot of damage: nailed by a weak left hook. "Nasty cut, that's all," he said.

"Nasty? Nasty!" Carmen was unhinged. "Goddamn you Helen! What is it about this man that makes you think he's going to raise a baby with you? What in the hell is going on in your mind to think you can take care of him at all? He's not safe here, we're fucking not safe here. You really want him better? You want him to get better? Send him to a fucking institution where they're trained to do it, but not here. He can't be here."

Helen held onto her belly like a life raft.

"You get me that goddamn puzzle piece, Terrible," Carmen was saying from beneath the rag covering her mouth, still sobbing, "Or I'm gonna shoot that motherfucker in self-defense."

Chapter Fifteen

February 2, 2005

His aunt Gulu lived in a three-story concrete house with walls painted beautifully in the bright colors Chakor associated with the homes of people living by the sea. She was a widow, but her two sons, their wives, and two grandchildren lived with her—though the family drama in that household was that the younger son wanted to move out on his own. It wasn't an estate they lived in. There were just three part-time servants, a family: a married couple as old as Guluben herself, and their young granddaughter who came twice a week to sweep and cook and garden. Chakor's mother lay on a bed on the second floor with windows that faced out toward the ocean that was a mile away. The servant girl had hung half a dozen pretty glass and seashell chimes in the room. They clinked like small, generous voices whenever the wind blew through the open windows. It was nothing like the stuffed-up room his mother had lain in, in Gandhinagar. It wasn't a day after they arrived that his mother set herself, finally, upon the task of dying—her thoughts turned toward the lives she'd leave behind.

"*Mane gabramanyu karanke chokri na sodhyu ane have mara hath ma ganga pani raku chu,*" she said to Chakor just two hours into her stay, and for the next several days, marriage was all she wanted to talk to him about. His aunt and cousins, even the children, took up the matter themselves as well: you're going to marry a Gujarati girl, aren't you?

The absence of truth that had become a lie began working its way into Chakor's conscience. The black stench of his unsaid followed him around from place to place, into the pale, sunlit air of his mother's room, up onto the rooftop where he wrote short poems among the solar water heater and laundry lines. It followed him into the Somnath temple itself during the only hour-long excursion to it his mother had the strength to make. And the day finally came in which it was clear to everybody in the house that his mother had turned. Her breathing took on a soft crackle, as if a well-worn paper bag had been traded in for her lungs. He understood that the brackish, runny weight of his secret was infusing the air all around her, obscuring her path to a new life, and he confessed to his mother only. He whispered his secret into her ear, worried she wouldn't hear, because her face had become a mask of strangely smoothed out skin. It seemed larger to him than it had ever been before. Her eyes were focused on images he couldn't see, and she hadn't responded to anybody's questions in hours.

It was ten minutes after he spoke, when her hand was in his hand, and his head was cradled against her arm, that she said, as if the words he'd spoken had just arrived: "A wife?"

He described the ceremony to her in a low voice no wandering or eavesdropping cousins or their children would be able to hear—how it had been Vedic, how Lord Shiva had been in attendance out on the mountaintop. His Ma's face had softened during the story. He watched as she pulled herself back into this world. It was a deliberate and obvious gesture, the strength of which he would remember the rest of his life. Her eyes fell on him, finally, fell away from wherever else they'd been focused on, and she smiled. "Go home," she said, each word she uttered sounding like boulders. "A fool. To leave her. To see. Your mother." And then her eyes rolled back off into that distance they'd been in, but the smile on her face remained at least a minute before it was swept over by deep currents.

Still, though, Chakor continued talking, telling his story, speaking in Gujarati with fluency he had never had. He whispered about Helen, her kindness, her spirit. Her connection to the land she'd grown up in. *"America che ena Matadesh, ena gam budha padosi chie, akash ma ek so karod sitaro, Himalaya jeva parvat, ane aju baju apna ghar che Vrindavan."*

He whispered for over an hour, cousins popping their heads in and moving on. He only stopped when his Amit Mama came into the room and Chakor could sense it was his turn to tell his secrets.

Chapter Sixteen

February 3, 2005

It had never felt right making the new Larry spend time in the home that the real Larry had found too uncomfortable to bear after forty-five minutes. Real Larry had no associations with Chakor's place and Helen could see, now that he was sitting in a wooden chair on the front porch, it had been selfish of her not to have brought him up here all along. She should be the one to suffer the brunt of the discomfort, not her husband, who would only know the cabin as the mountain-encrusted wonder that it was.

"What if you go into labor out there on the mountain in the cold of February, Helen?" her mother had asked, furious. "You think a mountain lion's going to know what to do?"

"Ida's a midwife," she'd said, which she wasn't sure of but it seemed very likely. "They're a stone's throw away if I need it."

"And what are you going to tell them? That your husband was falling all over himself to see the love nest you flit around in while he was being blown to bits?'

Larry was sprawled across the couch behind them, so Helen had said, "What the hell are you talking about? You don't know anything."

"You never have," her mother scowled.

Helen *didn't* know what she was going to do: it wasn't as if she had time to fully plan even her temporary arrangements in just the last twelve hours. A day ago she was resigned to living with her mother, by midnight Larry (and so she) had been kicked out, and today she was using Chakor's cabin as a temporary base. Until she found something better. What other option *was* there?

The way Helen figured things, Chakor's mother was dying but still alive. When she did pass, he'd have to stay another month or two to perform a series of familial visits and rituals—he couldn't just hurry home. That gave Helen a month to find appropriate housing somewhere in Franklin. Not Salt Lake City, because if all went well the Blue Hope's cultural center would open in the fall and she'd be its first director. All she had to do in the next month was set up the March interviews between Emmaline and the three visiting artists—and give up, finally, on Chakor's participation in the project. All she had to do was hope her baby waited long enough for these things to happen.

She'd left Smoot's Pass angry, in the unforgiving cold of early morning, and then shopped at the Safeway in Franklin before heading up to the Black Elks. Since it was Chakor's cabin she refrained from purchasing meat, out of respect. Nothing about the way Larry acted suggested he'd even notice.

Helen had been pleasantly surprised to realize the drive leading up to Chakor's door was cleared clean. She knew Herman had a pickup with a plow hitched to the front of it—there wasn't another way to really live out there in the winter—and figured it was he she had to thank. When she climbed out of the minivan it was just past noon, and the sun shone out like one magnificent, honest eyeball.

Larry had used the walker he'd gotten the hang of in the last week to make his way over to the porch all on his own, though he was painfully slow, careful about the ice. Except for when it was swiping at something, Larry had become excruciatingly careful with his physical body. This caution at least reminded Helen of the real Larry.

This morning he'd hopped up the stairs on the porch, using the banister for support. Another good sign, she thought, as she held him off from falling into one of the two wooden porch chairs until she'd brushed off the sparkling layer of snow that had blown onto it. With him settled, it had taken Helen several trips to unload the car, but the activity invigorated both Helen and the baby, who was running a marathon in her stomach.

Larry appeared immediately brightened. She'd taken him inside but after about twenty minutes, he'd stood up from his chair and used his walker to move over to the door, open it, and return to the wooden perch he'd sat in when they first arrived. Helen had followed him out and insisted he don one of his wool sweaters, and cover up with a thick cotton blanket Chakor had bought in Mexico. That's where Larry was, now: sitting alone outside, free of another person standing over him, she realized, for the first time since the ill-fated walk to city hall, the walk that had induced Nurse Johnson at rehab to scold Helen in a near-scream.

"You knew not to walk that far, and it had been sore already that whole week!"

"I didn't know that," Helen said, about the latter point. "He doesn't even let me look at the stump, I *told* you. . . . "

"I told *you* to give him autonomy, *not* to ignore his physical condition," she scoffed. "You had no place in ignoring it, or in letting him walk *two miles* in snow."

"It wasn't snow," Helen started, before holding back: she hadn't wanted to lose Bettie's friendship. She didn't want to fight her. Helen gave in, though she still blamed Bettie for giving her a false sense of Larry's abilities in the first place.

Now that she was here, up at the cabin, facing the real prospect of Nurse Bettie's face being the only friendly one she'd see on a day-to-day basis for the next few weeks, she was grateful about her own foresight. She took it as another sign she'd made the right choice in coming here, and this made her happy as she left Larry to take in the mountainscape, and she set about making the cabin's interior appropriate for the two of them.

First, she plugged the automatic blower in and filled the plastic mattress. She'd decided that since there was only one room, and since her giant belly made rising from the air mattress every morning nearly impossible, and, finally, since she felt wrong about allowing her husband to sleep in her lover's bed, that Larry could begin sleeping on it. Maybe in a week or two he'd feel well enough, he'd have changed enough, that they'd sleep together again, in a new house.

When the mattress was filled, and she turned the screeching machine filling it off, she heard voices out on the porch and knew who it had to be.

"Helen," Ida said, when she walked onto the porch. "You're back."

Herman was crouching on the ground next to Larry, as if deep in conversation.

"This is my best friend from Salt Lake," she said. "His name is Larry. He's just got home from the war."

"Mmmmmm," Herman said right into Larry's face. "Wrecked you up pretty good there, brother." She imagined they'd already tried and failed at conversation with him.

"He doesn't have family besides me," Helen said simply, pleased they had taken to Larry instead of reacting badly. "And he helped me so much when I was a runaway that I couldn't leave him in an institution."

* * *

The new car wasn't the first red flag; just for today it was. Before it had been stories about Helen driving the man people were calling her husband around town. At Herman's insistence, Ida had let the rumors be. She had waited. Now she let Helen invite her inside.

Herman tried to help the poor soldier stand, but the man clung to the chair he sat in: "*No.*"

"Quite a grip," Herman chuckled, patting his back. "I can keep the man company out here. Sun never did me any harm."

Ida nodded and pushed past Helen. Maybe it was better they were alone, she thought, as she filled up a teakettle, hoping some hot steam would calm her. Helen entered the cabin, the sun behind her so that her face and giant stomach were lost in shadows.

"World sorts itself out without your being in the middle of it," Herman had reminded her crossing the hill to the cabin. "You know it better than I do." It was true: she was always telling *him* to leave well enough alone.

"Not everybody buys a new car to cart their friends around in," was the first thing out of Ida's mouth, anyway.

"Yeah," was what Helen mustered.

"So how's Chakor?" Ida sat at the small wooden table she'd given to him when he first moved up to the mountain.

"He's on a pilgrimage with his mom," Helen said. "She won't live much longer."

"Not a lot of men would have even gone," Ida said, and Helen nodded. What Ida had hoped, what Herman had convinced her to believe, was that Helen wouldn't *need* to lie. That there would be a clear and maybe terrifying truth the girl would tell, and then Ida could do what came very naturally to her: work toward a harmonious understanding of events that would lead toward forgiveness.

But with lies, there was nothing to do but stir them up and swat at them: "I think a man that would travel across the ocean to care for his sick mother, just days after his own wedding, is also the kind of man that would want to be here for the birth of his baby. Don't you?"

"He's coming," Helen said, trying to force cheerful. "There's still time."

"It's one thing to hide a wedding from your family: I don't imagine he'd hide the birth of a *grandson* from his dying mother, Helen," Ida continued, shaking her head. "I also *know* Chakor wouldn't leave you all to yourself, pregnant, in the winter up here."

The conversation continued on along these lines, Ida throwing darts and Helen dodging them as gracefully as a hog on ice skates, though it was Ida's heart sinking lower and lower as Helen talked; she was no fool and Helen was sailing so far from the truth.

Her granddaughter Ashley thought she was crazy not to call or e-mail Chakor, and maybe Ida would have if she could have. But for the second not-so-insignificant-time in two months—the first time meant the loss of a job with benefits at the Forest Service for Herman—her technophobic nature thwarted her. She had no contact information for Chakor. That was it. He left his e-mail address, but she'd thrown it away in a fit of righteousness because she didn't have e-mail and didn't want it; she'd just decided to wait on communicating with him until she saw him.

"You're *kidding*," Ashley said, flabbergasted that a person might trust her friendship so much that she'd let months, or a year pass by between contacts. But that *was* the world Ida lived in; it was the world Ida loved and banked on, and now it was the world that made it difficult for her to help her dear friend get hold of his life. Perhaps Ashley would know how to find him, some way, she thought, as she cursed herself.

As she continued her tirade aloud: "You listen good, Helen Motes," is what she was saying now. "Chakor is the son we didn't have, got it? We love him and we said we'd look after you and you've been traipsing around with a veteran everybody says you're married to."

Helen gasped, which made Ida feel better: it meant the rumor was just rumor. "It's not my place to tell secrets," she relented, "and

I know damned well who you're *really* married to. But you're lying to my face and I can see it."

"Lying?" Helen said, tears bursting forth. Herman had warned Ida to be gentle with her pregnant hormones, but what of it? The whistle blew and Ida stood to tend to it. She brought out teabags from a giant pillbox in her purse, placed them into the unmatched mug collection Chakor had proudly amassed in his time in Utah, and poured the steaming water inside them.

"Larry's Mormon," Helen said. "He doesn't drink tea."

"I think that's the least of his problems," Ida hissed. "It's cold out there and unless you had the forethought to bring up some Postum or hot chocolate, this is better than nothing. Besides, it's chamomile."

"Drink this up, Buddy," Herman said with relish. "It's the good stuff. Chamomile from a friend of ours in California. She dries it out and puts it into these bags. It looks store-bought, but it ain't."

The soldier took the glass but didn't sip. He held it in his hands, and looked down into it.

"I *didn't* tell Chakor about it," Helen said in a near-whisper, patting at her stomach from the cabin's door, and Ida turned, stone-faced. "I thought he'd be back sooner and figured he should have his last days with his mother in peace."

Ida just stared up at her and stood to go, Herman following suit.

"And Larry is my ex," Helen continued softly, almost too softly to hear. "I lived with him five years, and when he went to Iraq I was the person on file. But Chakor knows he existed. He knows I broke up with him before I came out here. I didn't expect, I didn't realize I'm the person left to take care of Larry."

The ex was still staring into his tea, Herman was harrumphing.

"I couldn't just let him rot in an institution."

"Okay," Herman said. "We'll check in on you."

Ida wasn't sure what to think. Something about Helen was off, but maybe it was just the hormones. Maybe Herman was right, and she ought to give the girl room.

* * *

February 11, 2005

Bettie Johnson spent an uncomfortable part of the morning waiting on Dr. Yung to call in a larger dose of pain meds for poor LeRoy Humphrey, who was moaning almost incessantly because of his back. It took everything in her not to *accidentally* slip him an extra dose of Percocet, but Lynn Fry was on unpaid leave for making just that accidental mistake one too many times in the last quarter. Bettie was fond of her job. And the boys here needed her to smooth what she could of the bureaucracy's blindness to their plights, and so she let LeRoy suffer.

Annie Ball had agreed to let the man lay down on an empty bed in one of the physical therapy rooms so that his groans wouldn't upset the rest of the guys. Most people in the County Rehab were good people. It was just the callousness of the doctors that burned Bettie up. She put in another call to Dr. Yung's office because it was Friday and if he left without calling in, which happened more often than an ordinary person would like to think, LeRoy wouldn't get a wink of sleep the whole weekend.

Bettie stood and walked over to the table where her three traumatic brain injuries sat all in a row like Russian nesting dolls: Larry the war interpreter was the oldest, Russell the farm injury was ten years younger, and Hansel the Marine was ten years younger than that. All had the classic thin, worried faces of the TBI patient. The same dazed sadness. Larry was the only one who could hardly speak, and ever since his wife had let the nasty infection on his leg get out of hand, he was the only one who needed a walker. It would be a couple of weeks before the guys in PT would let him use the leg in-hospital, probably another month until they let him take it home. All this and his determination to defend his country despite his age made him Bettie's favorite.

"How's it going, boys?" she asked them. They'd had physical therapy in the morning and now they worked on crosswords—brain teasers to help reconnect misaligned wires.

Young Hansel looked like he belonged in high school. The guys' crosswords were culled from the pages of a children's workbook. As usual only Larry had finished, and now he was looking inside the top of his pen, thoughtfully. Bettie picked up his work: it was filled with random letters, but also a few words, this time: *lipstick, sand, hand*. No obscenities.

"When you got here," she said to him encouragingly. "You filled *all* the squares with unconnected letters. Now you're finding words. That's good! It's good you can write them out, even if you can't say them." He didn't even look up from inside the pen and she wondered what fantastic world he'd found inside it.

"Are you thinking about Helen? A trip you took to the beach?" she asked, and Larry gave her the invisible smile—the look in his eyes that said if he were who he had always been before, he'd appreciate her taking an interest. She pulled out another sheet from the workbook for him and set it down. *F, Q, P* he wrote like his hand had been burning to get them out, like it made all the sense in the world. His penmanship was gorgeous—he was the only one of the patients raised when handwriting was still considered a subject in school and it showed even square by square.

"Beautiful handwriting," she told him. Russell had filled in half a dozen right answers, and Hansel was almost done. She praised them both, as lavishly as she had Larry; all in all it was a good day for the lot of them. The phone rang and she dashed to the counter to answer it.

"Oh, thank heavens, it's you," she said to Dr. Yung, and she filled him in on LeRoy's predicament. "No, he's not faking it," she sighed, when he asked. Her TBIs did not fake moans! What a ridiculous question. As soon as she hung up, she buzzed Annie and asked her to administer the medication, even though the fax with Dr. Yung's orders had not yet arrived. Half of protocol was enough for Bettie. Maybe by the time for group therapy, LeRoy would feel good enough to participate. The doctor's returned call lifted Bettie's spirit.

"You guys have another fifteen minutes before we head off to group," she said to her man-dolls. "Roberta is leading it today. You like Roberta," she said, though she had no idea what any of them liked. Still, she was a strong proponent of inserting right-thinking into whatever parts of their brains would take it. She bent over LeRoy's folder and began scribbling notes, and when she stood, Larry's pregnant wife was waddling through the door, snowflakes dotting the navy wool on her coat. Her eyes were bright from the cold.

"You're early," Bettie said.

"It's already started snowing in the mountains," Mrs. Motes explained. "I wanted to make sure we got up before the roads get bad."

"That sounds right," Bettie smiled. Mrs. Motes was a bit of a space cadet, but a good girl who tried. "And there's nothing wrong with taking a Friday afternoon off, besides. You can celebrate Valentine's a day or two early." The sour look on the woman's face made it clear the subject needed changing, and so she added the first thing that came to her mind: "I still wish you didn't have to trek back and forth from the Black Elks in this weather, though. It's too much. You should make up with your mother." As soon as the words left her mouth she worried she'd blundered again, but luckily she got a smile from the poor woman.

"Well, if the storm breezes by as quickly as it's supposed to, I'll be meeting with a real estate agent tomorrow morning about a couple of houses in town."

"Oh, that's fabulous, honey," Bettie said. "That's just perfect."

"I hope so," Mrs. Motes sighed, "I'm ready for something perfect." The poor doll looked so lost that it near broke Bettie's heart.

"Did you take a look at the good work Larry's done?" she asked, handing the first filled crossword to his young wife. "He's written some words down this time."

Mrs. Motes scrunched her face and Bettie's heart broke even more.

"I told you, sweetheart, letters are a good start," Bettie said. "And those words! They mean a lot. He might not know what words to put in the squares but he's recalling vocabulary he doesn't say, and to me they sound like they're from the same memory. Just knowing letters belong in the squares, his being interested in finishing the project, in learning, that's all such a good, good sign."

Helen sighed, "I'm so sick of 'might,'" she said, resting one hand on Larry's shoulder, the other on her stomach and the child who might never know its father.

* * *

February 12, 2005

It snowed a foot overnight, a peaceful, silencing snow. Dragging Larry in and out of the minivan all to wander through houses he didn't know would just confuse him, would be exhausting and cruel, Helen had figured before leaving the cabin. At the last minute she'd opted to let him stay home. Why not give him a few hours on his own? It might be good for him, she'd told herself as she made him two sandwiches and a hot thermos of Postum, the roasted grain drink Ida had reminded her about—she'd always known it as

"Mormon coffee" growing up. She'd never known Larry to drink it before, but now he drank oceans of it.

Helen had dusted the snow off his favorite wooden porch chair, left his meal on its giant armrest, and helped him into it. She'd waved to him as she backed from the driveway using the method the real Larry had long ago taught her to do in the event there was no shovel and a lot of snow: she rolled back toward the driveway's exit six inches, then forward toward the cabin six inches, then back a foot, then forward six inches, and back a foot again. Painstaking, but the housing search was too important to risk getting stuck in the snow.

By ten she had cleared her driveway and was mightily relieved to see somebody had already made a one-way path down the mountain with a pickup plow. She'd crept through the narrow path at ten miles an hour to what she knew must be the chagrin of the Mack truck riding her ass and made her appointment.

Now, she was on her way back home. She was eager to get back to Larry, and she was thinking about how she needed to find a new real estate agent. This one knew something, had decided something cruel about who Helen was. She didn't make eye contact, didn't even ask about the pregnancy as any other person meeting an eight-months-pregnant lady would. Carmen wasn't a gossip, but maybe Ida and Herman had been talking. Or maybe nobody had: Chipeta County was small and had a long memory. Maybe the lady knew something about the first baby she gave up and disapproved.

The roads had been plowed over but were soft and slick again because the wind had blown new snow onto the path. Nobody else was out, not on the mountain roads, so the going was slow. It gave Helen time to move on to worrying again, now about the husband back up the canyon.

She shouldn't have left him alone, she was thinking now. Not for so long, at least. Because no matter what they said at rehab, Larry Janx's brain was no less damaged than it had been a month before.

Her husband said *food* or *piss* when he needed, and *no* or *fuck* when he was upset. He had no words to express contentment, though on occasion he picked up a random word from a conversation and repeated it back to whoever uttered it. The only difference between now and then for Helen was that she no longer cried because half his vocabulary was profanities, or because Larry treated her like a cross between the Invisible Man and a tool.

Jesus, it was stupid leaving him. But then, he adapted. He was an adaptor. He always seemed to become comfortable in whatever situation he was in. It took him a week of depression at losing his prosthetic, a week of fiddling with the walker, and now, he used it like it had always been part of him: not only had he learned to leave the cabin on his own, but he'd walked a few times around its periphery by himself. He was fine.

He was so fine, really, that the physical therapists had begun suggesting he be fitted for a new, more permanent prosthetic, rather than returning to the temporary one he had come home with. Give him a month to let the wound heal, they suggested, and then set him up with a leg meant for a man as robust as Larry wanted to be.

Of course this is where the gap between Larry's mind and his body terrified Helen, and she was still only halfway home when she began thinking about his rage, how it still erupted whenever he was frustrated or annoyed. It had resulted in a couple of broken glasses at the cabin, a bruised thigh from the day at city hall—which she lied to her doctor about—and of course, Carmen's broken lip. Helen feared living alongside a more mobile Larry in such a remote area, where her judgmental, hippie neighbors were the only people to turn to in case of an emergency. They *were* living up to their promise to Chakor: they were looking after her. She had come home one day, for instance, to discover a wheelchair ramp built off the side of the porch, with strong rails. But they weren't speaking to her. She hadn't seen them once in the nine days since she'd arrived.

In Franklin they would move in next to regular people, hope-fully sweet Mormon families all around. Even if they heard rumors about her, they would honor Larry's service, they might take him to church Sundays, and they would keep an eye out for his fledgling family. He was a member of the priesthood as all Mormon men were, and they would help Helen take care of him: that was the strength of the Latter-day Saints. And Helen would take it. She would take that though she was still betting—less now than she had at first, but still betting that Larry's mind would recover when he held his baby in his arms.

There were moments early on that Helen had thought of as hopeful. Larry's continued relishing of the outdoors, for example. Then she realized it wasn't real glee he felt. He did listen to snow crunching beneath his boot, he did look over his shoulder to watch the trail his walker and footprint made behind him, but these ges-tures were just the psychological equivalents of ghost limbs, behav-iors his body loved when it was somebody else.

It wasn't Larry. Just like when he stood, suddenly, at the kitchen table like any two-legged man might: he still only had one leg. If he was lucky he'd fall into the table and right himself. If he wasn't his momentum would send him careening face-first into the floor. It had happened a dozen times, at least.

This thought, the thought of him falling right off the porch because of his ghost limb, is what made Helen freak out about leav-ing him, yet again. The day had actually produced two very nice possibilities, one she may have taken on the spot had she chosen a real estate agent who deserved the commission. Still, as she made her way back up the canyon, she was imagining that he had decided to go off on a walk and had fallen. She was imagining him the way she'd seen a corpse on TV once: snow crystallized on his eyelashes and eyebrows, eyes frozen open.

She didn't speed, but she went the speed limit despite the roads. Larry, at least, was swaddled in long underwear, a sweater, and a parka. She had seen to all of that before leaving. If he hadn't moved, and he hadn't gone back inside, the worst that would have happened was not much. Maybe he'd taken his gloves off to eat his sandwich and then forgotten to put them back on. A little frostbite was probably the worst that could happen.

Unless he fell: and this was plaguing her until she turned, finally, up to the cabin. He was in his spot—cozy enough, and she almost cried for relief. Her plan had been to park at the base of the driveway and avoid getting stranded in the snow, but a path just the size of her van had been cleared, which meant her grumpy friends knew she'd left Larry to his own resources. She felt ashamed anew.

"Larry!" she said when she'd dismounted from the minivan's tall seat. "Hey, Larry! Let's get you inside, huh?" She said it loud enough to ensure Ida or Herman, if they were still around, would hear. Would leave. "I think I've found us somewhere you're going to like," she said, as she approached the cabin. As the door swung open. As Chakor came running out.

"Helen!" he said, the force of his voice made her scream, stumble back so fast she fell backwards, hard into the shoveled snow, onto her behind. The baby protested by jabbing her deep in the ribs.

"Helen, I'm back," he said again, and there was a sob of what sounded like rage in his voice. He bounded through the knee-high snow like a two-legged antelope, graceful and awkward and dangerous, a jumble of antlers. Helen scrambled up from the snow and tried running back toward the car but he grabbed her hand and tugged, and then she was staring into his face. When he cupped his palms around her own face and drew it close to his, her mind was filled with a scene from *The Silence of the Lambs*: the ripping of a woman's tongue from her mouth with a man's teeth. She jerked her head back.

"It's only me," he said. "What are you afraid of? It's *me*." He petted the sides of her face, he kissed her with soft, warm lips, and drew her body toward his own for long seconds only, because that was all the time he needed to gasp, "Oh my God!" To fall down to his knees, his hands now seeking out the perimeter of the globe on her stomach and to begin sobbing into it.

"Oh my God, oh my God," he was saying, and she had no idea what he was thinking, but she slid the diamond protruding from Larry's ring toward the palm of her hand with her thumb.

Though he hadn't bitten the tongue from her mouth, he may well have. She still couldn't make her words come, so she stood there like a statue. Like Larry. The grin on Chakor's face was as wide as the mountain range itself when he stood. He said, face still covered in tears, "You are such a brave, brave woman"—and the words dropped Helen's heart to her guts. He kissed her again, under the full sight of her first husband, and nothing inside her resisted kissing him back.

"You're white as a ghost," he said to her. "Your lips are icy sweet."

He took her right hand inside his own and she let him lead her up the porch and past Larry—whose mittens were indeed off—into the cabin, which smelled of cardamom and garlic. He began warming her ears and her face with his hands.

"I'm going to take care of you," he said, tears again ebbing into his voice. Her shoes he removed like she was a child, kneeling down in front of her. "I'm so, so sorry. I'm so happy and so sorry I was so selfish, my mother said it."

By this point, Helen was ready to think Larry himself must be invisible out there on the porch, that by some trick of light or desire Chakor hadn't seen him. When Chakor turned his back to close the cabin door she slipped her first wedding ring off entirely and zipped it into her coat pocket.

* * *

February 12, 2005

Chakor announced he would be returning to America as soon as the ashes were laid. Later in the year, he said, he would return to make the pilgrimage his mother was due. To his surprise, his family hadn't protested; they could see he was exhausted and he'd proven his devotion already.

It had been on purpose that he hadn't gotten hold of Ida or Herman, which he knew he could do through their daughter who lived in Franklin. Ida was the worst secret-keeper there was, and he spent long days relishing the look on Helen's face when he would surprise her with his unexpected return. To make the trip home, Chakor had asked a more distant friend, Edward Colorow. The man traveled weekly back and forth from Salt Lake to Chipeta County. Edward was kind, in his fifties, an elder in the Ute Tribe, and had insisted on driving Chakor all the way up to the cabin, despite the snow.

"I like to get out in the mountains, hey?" the old man had said, but when the path to his own house was mostly covered in snow Chakor had convinced old Edward to let him out at the head of the drive, where he thanked him profusely for his efforts.

"We'll have you over for dinner one day soon," he'd promised, for the hundredth time that day.

"Goodbye, Cupid," the man had laughed, backing back out into the drive. Chakor followed the wheel tracks he imagined Helen, his Helen, had made earlier in the day, when he saw the man out on the porch and wondered, suddenly, if his wife had actually subleased out his cabin and moved down with her mother, as she'd said she might.

"Hey, there!" he'd called out to him. "Hey!"

When the man did not reply Chakor got nervous. You never knew how a white guy on a porch in Chipeta County would react to a brown man hiking up the drive, and something about the man's posture seemed off.

"Hello?" he'd called out, "I'm a friend!"

The man just stared. Though he didn't move or make a threat-ening gesture, the stare itself was eerie. Briefly Chakor considered crossing the small hill between his home and Ida and Herman's but his curiosity was too much. Helen would know from his bags that he was home, if she did still live here, and he'd miss seeing her reac-tion at his return. He set his things in the space tire tracks had made in the drive, earlier in the day, and waved again.

He walked all the way up to the porch, smiling and trying to appear unassuming. At this distance he realized, from the blank depth of the eyes in the man's face, that there would be no response. The man was turned toward Chakor but didn't seem to register his presence in a way that warranted reaction.

Chakor climbed his stairs, and then knocked on his own door, just in case. When nobody answered, he let himself in. His key still fit, but it was unlocked, anyways. Immediately it was clear Helen was the primary occupant. Her suitcases were in the corner, her hairbrush on the table beside the bed. He noticed the air mattress, too, and the wheelchair in the corner of the room. It hit him, sud-denly, who this man had to be.

"*Larry?*" he said back outside, on the porch. The brief flash of light through the man's eyes was enough of an answer—was clearly all the kind of answer poor Larry had it in him to give. "Jesus, look at you," he whispered.

He bent down and stared into his face: stubble on the cheeks, a noble chin and nose, a physique that he could see had once been formidable. He stood when he was afraid the man would be able to read the part of his thoughts that weren't generous—the part that marveled, yet again, over how Helen had chosen him, had cho-sen his skinny, brown, flyaway frame over the man who must have been, when she was making that choice, almost Hollywood-rugged in his bearing and looks. The part of Chakor who was beaten up and shunned as a small Indian kid growing up in Port Arthur by the little-boy versions of Larry couldn't help relishing getting the girl.

"I'm Chakor," he said softly to him, "Helen's Chakor. It's my cabin, here."

Larry turned his head up toward him at his voice, but otherwise offered nothing. Chakor marked how in the few months since he'd seen the man sobbing violently in the backyard in Houston he had changed so completely that Chakor hadn't recognized him on sight. In Houston, it was true, Larry had looked obliterated; watching him had shamed Chakor. Now it was all worse.

"I just got back from India," he said to Larry. "I wish *you* could tell me what happened." The man seemed to nod. Helen would fill in the details of the story, much of which seemed obvious except exactly how Larry had landed on Chakor's own porch. Thinking about Helen, Chakor looked back down the driveway and sighed. He clomped through the snow to the side of the house and found his shovel frozen against it, and began clearing a path out to the street. It was easy work. Helen, or Herman, he imagined, had kept the driveway clear until that morning, so it was a dry snow. The scraping of his shovel against the ground produced a gritty, satisfying noise. Chakor relished, as well, the light sweat the labor produced. He'd spent the best of three days sitting in buses and airplanes and Edward's truck.

Shoveling took longer than he remembered. It was not so easy to skim the blade along his rocky, dirt path as it was on concrete sidewalks. The sound of his scrapings was the loudest one on the mountain since the birds were migrated and missing, and Starvation Creek was frozen. No cars were out, so he didn't even hear the occasional grumbling of a motor making its way up or down the canyon. He'd spent so many months looking forward to this, and now here it was, and he didn't know what to do with the absence of noise. Every so often Chakor glanced up at the silent man whose breath puffed out in front of him in small clouds. The weirdness of the man's presence was formidable. They were total strangers and most intimately connected all at once.

When he'd cleared the way to the road he turned to admire his work. His path was hourglass in shape: wider at the turn in, which could be tricky in the snow if there wasn't enough room, and again even wider at the area in front of the porch. He'd learned the importance of clearing that portion of the drive well enough to enable a U-turn after a neighbor almost smashed into him as he tried to back out, last winter.

Chakor's body burned with the heat of work, and he was sweating hard. He was thirsty and ran back up the drive to reinvigorate himself. He'd arrived at eleven and it was one already. After nodding to Larry, he let himself inside his cabin and put on a pot of hot water to make some old-fashioned American coffee. He drank four glasses of icy well water from his tap in the meantime. When the coffee was brewed, he poured Larry a cup, which he left black since it fit with the rugged image he imagined Larry had once endeavored to keep. His own cup Chakor loaded with cream and sugar.

"Coffee," he said to Larry, who accepted the cup eagerly. He held his hands against the hot sides, and Chakor realized they must have been freezing. The clean, burning cold of the day sunk into Chakor's lungs, as he relaxed in the chair he dusted off for himself, and he was so grateful to be back home he almost cried. After ten or fifteen minutes, he touched his visitor on the shoulder, and shook his own head toward the door to invite him in. Larry understood, and reached out for his walker. When he stood Chakor realized for the first time he was missing half a leg—how could Helen have possibly kept this from him?

Inside, they drank strong coffee together for the better part of an afternoon. Chakor had moved the kitchen chairs to the window overlooking his frozen creek, and he felt comfortable in their silence: Larry thinking who knew what, and Chakor teetering between being bowled over by the generous nature of his wife who had the capacity to care for a man even when she'd left him, and the uneasy feeling that there was more to the story than he could see.

But he was happy, still. The mystery itself reminded him of his wife, was part of his attraction to her. There was no way to deny that. And at the base of whatever Larry's presence signaled, Chakor understood his wife had cared for him, too. Had been so determined her husband should be unhindered during the time of his mother's death that she hadn't shared any of her own pain, or troubles with him. This, at least, was the best approach for him to take. A small part of him was proud, even if it also felt foolish, to think she expected enough of Chakor to think he'd allow this man, this broken man, a place in his house to recover in. He smiled generously over at Larry, and said, "It's good to be back. You're welcome here."

When the sun began making its way toward the upper mountains, Chakor finally stood—buzzed from the coffee, exhausted from his return. He poked through the kitchen cabinets that had been beautifully touched and rearranged and lived in by the woman who was his wife. They weren't the same as when he'd left them, a thought that seemed somehow marvelous. He found a bag of brown lentils, and decided they'd do well enough for a simple dahl. When he began chopping an onion, and garlic, Larry had stood, bowed his head toward Chakor it had seemed, and returned to his station at the porch.

* * *

Outside the fallen snow. Warmth in mittens. *Wait here, I'll be, I'll be, I'll be alone.* No. *I'll be.* No. Fuck. This wooden chair. This dull sun. Honest Abe born in a cabin. Crunching snow. Black boots crunching, crunching bones, fucking crunching. No.

Breathe. *From India!* Helen's cold nose on the forehead, a kiss, *I'll be, I'll be afraid, I'll be, I'll be, Helen!* The crosswords were not so wrong. *Now you're finding words, that's good.* Not only letters. *My TBI guys.* She had them, too, *poor kids.* Dr. Linda Frank. He had held her hand. *The Quick and the Dead.* Pink lipstick *so I still feel human, it's silly.* And that was fuck. *My sunflower, it's silly. I need to nurture.*

Stop. The cold cabin, right here. In the snow a ribbon? No. *My TBI guys, keep trying.* Keep trying. *It's your baby. Your BABY, do you understand me?* Yes. He snuck his daughter across the desert to save her.

In the snow a *rabbit!* Yes. Vanished. *Good job, Larry!* A rabbit. A *bunny* rabbit. Pine trees for Mr. Lincoln's Logs. For *Helen's Chakor.* No empty squares, fill the buckets. *Put the reds here, damn it!* So many missing shapes. If what it was on the plate, if a name lasted: pink lipstick, *just here, just to stay sane, our families,* burning beneath tires.

Sun. *Showdown at Yellow Butte.* And it still seemed. Black coffee, bitter black fuck the *Words of Wisdom.* They seem. *You're welcome here. But where could she be for so long?* One steady hand lost in sand. Lost. He'd held it. Helen said *I'll be back.* Yes. *I'll be back.* That doll, *our girl,* he said. Linda's sunflower, she said *I need to nurture something that was never broken.* Thank you, square buckets. *You've got to let something save you.* These round, shining legs.

Chapter Seventeen

October 11, 1997

Helen had been strong when she gave her boy away. She had the strength of teenagehood when she did it. She knew her boy was a survivor, like she was. Even when she was a twice-married woman she told herself she could still feel his heartbeat inside the rhythms of her own heart: she believed herself because she knew she had done the right thing. But for months after her miscarriage, the loss of her second child, she wouldn't leave her house. Her baby's death was an indication of her own unworthiness, she knew: the universe had finally caught up with her to punish her for the miracles of the birth of her first healthy son and the husband who loved her despite everything.

Larry's grief had been formidable, too, but it had soon transformed into the healing realm of the corrective: we should try again. Helen could not hear that. She was high-strung, and just a few months past twenty: not old enough to understand that some of life's setbacks were more cruel than others. She quit showing up at work. He brought home romantic comedies, ordered in dinners, he even hired a maid; but then it had been six months, already, and her depression began to seem unnatural and destructive, and Larry had had enough.

He gassed up the car, scooped his protesting young wife of the perpetual nightgown into his arms, and dropped her into the backseat—consciously channeling his caveman ancestors as he drove off into the sunrise. Into the mountains east of Salt Lake City, and then south toward Chipeta County: Helen thought he was taking her home to her mother, but then Larry turned off the state highway a few miles before they would have hit Smoot's Pass. The turn he took was so obscure that she knew exactly where he was heading, and it scared her.

Just a few months before, on the first and only trip Helen and Larry ever took to Smoot's Pass, Helen had introduced the route to him. It led to the Picnic Cliffs, a six-mile-long ridge of boulders piled atop each other, about a few hundred feet high. As a schoolchild Helen had searched through the boulders for Easter eggs, as a teenager she had kissed Billy Cooper in the crevices between rocks during a midnight kegger. But she brought Larry there to show him what was truly remarkable: the petroglyphs, seven or eight hundred years old, left by the Fremont Indians.

National Geographic and its smaller counterparts often featured information on the petroglyphs scattered throughout Chipeta County, but the ones at Picnic Cliffs weren't impressive enough to bear mentioning. They had thus become as intimately the property of the Smoot's Pass locals as the family portraits hanging in their living rooms or the tuna casseroles in their grandmothers' refrigerators.

Half a mile down the unmarked road that paralleled the rocks, on that first trip, Helen saw a glimmering white object in the desert. Instead of stopping where she usually did, she drove on to inspect what they discovered was an ancient oven left in the middle of the sage, shot to smithereens by what she imagined were the current lot of local teens. The whole stove hadn't rusted over from exposure yet, but it had been out long enough for the metal ripped by bullets to have taken on rusty red hues, the same color as the soil all around them. It was beautiful to her: an object of local, living art, a welcome addition to a wonderful and magical space.

But Larry didn't know that. He didn't know Helen was imagining what it would have been like to see the bullets sparking into the old stove, how it would have felt to shoot at it, and he wondered aloud about what kind of moronic idiots would aim gunfire at a metal object that could ricochet off the oven's frame and maim, or maybe kill somebody. Helen kicked the stove and the oven door fell open, releasing a slobber of Coors cans that startled Helen into a scream. She laughed and took her husband's hand to show him the nearest boulder with petroglyphs on it—the most accessible one, at the bottom of the nearby hill.

Larry whistled at the drawings—a dozen bulls etched into the sandstone, a few men with headdresses nearby—but seemed thoroughly unimpressed. Which was part of the reason she didn't want to show him the other rocks, even though she knew he'd enjoy the climb up the boulders. It was also why his reaction to Lovers' Note would enrage her.

"What's that," he asked, innocently enough, pointing over to the small, graffiti-covered boulder next to the one with the petroglyphs on it.

Helen smiled to look at it. None of the writing on it was so old that Helen recognized it, and she wondered whether some local grandfather came out and cleaned the rock every year or two, or if the paint was simply no match for a few seasons under the elements. She hadn't forgotten about Lovers' Note, but she hadn't thought of it earlier in the day when she suggested they see the petroglyphs. Most of the writing was of the John heart Katie variety, and the teens seemed to be keeping to the old rule that forbade insults and profanities. The initials and doodles were in baby blues, fluorescent greens, purples, reds. There was even an impressive orange that was almost exactly the same color as the rock itself: its MA heart RM took on the aspect of a secret message written in invisible ink.

"What the *heck*?" Larry said again. "What kind of rednecks did you grow up around?" he wondered, shaking his head. "Who would even *dream* of desecrating a historical site that should be protected by law?"

"Fuck you," Helen said, because she hadn't weaned profanities from her vocabulary when she was angry, yet. Larry was taken aback.

"Oh, come on," she'd said, softening a little. "The kids leave the petroglyphs alone—they're not even writing on the same rock. Lovers' Note has been here since I can remember."

"But that doesn't mean it's right to write on it," he said to her, the way he would speak to a child, eyebrow lifted.

"The Fremonts were writing notes about *hunting*," she said. "These kids are writing about what they *love*."

"Desecrating a historical artifact with meaningless garbage."

"Don't be an ass!" she said. "*You* barely glanced over the petroglyphs before getting bored. These kids're joining in."

The argument hadn't ended with that trip—it had entered into their relationship to stand for whatever moral disagreements the couple had. Helen took a handful of chocolate raisins from the bulk bins in the Wild Oats store in downtown Salt Lake, and she was showing her ancient artifact-defiling roots; Larry referred to a book offering a new accounting of the Mountain Meadows Massacre as liberal historical revisionism, and Helen proclaimed his historical understanding stuck at the petroglyphs.

On the day Larry drove straight from Salt Lake to Lovers' Note, he was as resolute in his silence the whole way. Helen couldn't figure out what he was doing, but she refused to ask. He got out of the car, which he'd parked in the same place they'd parked the first time, opened the trunk, and set off toward the rocks. Since Helen was unwilling to get out of the back seat, and he'd left the trunk open, her view of where he was going was blocked. She was part angry, part afraid, and part stubborn.

It was an hour, maybe, before he showed up, again. She was sitting on the hood, still warm from the drive, drawing the stove in a lined notebook in her efforts to show him she didn't care where he'd gone off to.

"Come on," he said, tugging at her sleeve. She didn't resist, and followed him to Lovers' Note. She had imagined, over on the hood, he had cleaned the writing off the rock, but that wasn't so. Since he hadn't written anything in paint she couldn't tell what he'd done for a minute or so—she stared a long time before seeing it: perhaps the only full sentence she'd ever seen on the rock, etched in stone like an actual petroglyph: *Larry and Helen raised a family.*

For some reason, Helen believed it, scraped so deeply in the rock people a thousand years unborn would read it. Helen knew she would love her husband forever.

"I'm just writing the truth ahead of time," Larry said, grinning, "to save myself a trip back."

Chapter Eighteen

February 21, 2005

Helen didn't care: Chakor was blissful, needed medicine. For two soul-replenishing weeks she dropped Larry at the rehab clinic and wept relief the whole way home. Wept. The only drawback was in knowing that Chakor would discover what he miraculously had not, so far, and that day would come, and the sorrow would return—that was all.

For now, she had him. He rubbed her body with oils. He sang folk songs, American and Gujarati, to the baby inside her stomach. Onto her tight belly he drew pictures of animals the baby would be surrounded with in its home on the mountain, and didn't the baby deserve that? Didn't her child deserve to hear a male's low, vibrating voice addressing it lovingly? He recited poems off the top of his head. Chakor said her body was luminous like a lamp stoked with ghee. Her shape forced them to be inventive in the bed, arms and legs locking in new ways, his thin long fingers cupping her breasts.

All while Larry sat outside on the porch. Not one iota of guilt rattled her. Her happiness was maniacal, as if she was an escapee from some sordid asylum and she would be damned if she didn't get her time singing and dancing in the streets before she was picked up again.

Helen *deserved* a respite. Larry deserved it, he deserved the way her happiness had transformed her relationship with him for the better. It was like she could love and care for him more deeply because his wasn't the only love she was bound to.

For the first time since he'd returned she chattered as much to Larry as Carmen had. She rained down stories nonstop on their trips to and from the clinic. At the dinner table, both she and Chakor made efforts to include Larry in conversations. She talked about the Blue Hope Arts Center and her hopes for it, or her anger at her mother since Larry had always appreciated that topic. She even told him about the way she'd imagined little cities beneath the lumps of snow when she was a child, eventually spooking herself so much she had spent an entire winter inside the school library, at recess. It didn't matter what she told him. It was all good for Larry.

These days would cease. They'd have to because she couldn't have two husbands. Chakor's presence had ignited that wonderful feeling that was all him inside her: a very particular sort of wonder and astonishment and generosity. Imagining him not a part of her life was easier when he was, actually, absent. Now the thought was like the loss of magic: the long years of disappointment she'd felt, as a child, upon understanding no unicorns or crystals would ever crop up in her life and transform it into something wonderful.

She had so much less experience with Chakor than she did with Larry. There weren't the kind of memories built up with him that she'd had a decade to create with her first husband. And so it was easy, in his absence, to blame this temporal thinness of their relationship on Chakor.

With him back, she felt sorely how much she wouldn't get to make those memories. She wanted to make the best of what time they had left because, despite all this—the last magic she had—she still thought she could maybe save Larry. The baby might. She would not give the idea up.

For now, Chakor could be distracted by tears whenever he began to push for information about Larry's stay, about the fight between Helen and Carmen. He still felt guilty for having left her, he still felt the thrill of discovering what he thought was his impending fatherhood. When it was all through he would hate her. He would move away and be more learned in the ways of love. Until that moment she would build a love reserve inside him, and he wouldn't know where it was from, but he would draw from it in the sad months that lay ahead. This was her plan for him.

And so: it was Helen's right and her duty to make crazy, explosive love, it was. Sex better than any she'd had before—whether it was due to the mysteries of her swollen body, or the thrill of being touched one more time before she was relegated to a life with a man who might never remember her name, she didn't know.

When Larry was at rehab, or on the porch, when he showered: they waited just long enough for him to shut the door behind him before falling into the sheets together, tearing at each other's limbs, fighting against the distance that had separated them so long. Another man, not Larry as he was, would have noticed. The new Larry didn't. He likely wouldn't have blinked twice if they'd just continued on when he wandered back into the cabin, though they didn't. The door would squeak open and Chakor would roll from bed and dart into the bathroom—partially out of respect and partially because it was thrilling to sneak.

Even during the nights they held off, Chakor hung a beautiful purple tapestry he'd brought back from India around the air mattress, which they moved to the same corner of the room Helen had hibernated in before she knew she was pregnant. The curtain cut off a lot of light, but it was too hard to put up and take down, and they didn't. Chakor never crossed into Helen's bed until Larry, they were sure, was sleeping. And then they silently—as silently as anybody has ever made love—caressed each others' bodies. The game was to try to make the other person stifle moans, to whisper into each other's ears at just the barrier of sound.

* * *

March 4, 2005

The woman pretended against it, but Terrible knew she was morose. She sat a long time every night after work, fiddling with Larry's puzzles. Sighing and carrying on about the girl choosing a deranged invalid over her mother. The phone calls between the women were strained, his fiancée was depressed, it was a week before their one and only wedding in the universe, and he considered his resources.

What he knew was that the Indian boy whose name he always slaughtered and had given up trying to pronounce had shown back up. He knew Helen was living with both men in a tiny cabin in the woods—a fact he understood to be a direct result of her kinship with Carmen, because only a Motes woman could manage sinking their fangs into a rotten melon like that. And he understood the girl was more likely to invite killer bees into her home than her mother. And there was a decent pile of unopened baby gifts left in Helen's room, relics from a baby shower cancelled when her husband turned up in pieces. It was five-thirty on the Sunday before his Saturday wedding, and Terrible had had enough.

"Goddamn it, woman!" he said to Carmen. "Get in the car."

"What's that?" she asked, motioning toward the half-dozen gifts he had in his hands.

"What does it look like?" he said, and the look on her face told him she had no idea, which he liked. He grinned.

"We've got a grandbaby coming that needs showering," he said. "Better late than never."

With that the woman perked up and cackled, which sounded good to his ears. She grabbed her purse and kissed him, which perked *him* up. By the time they reached the cabin the sun was down, but Carmen was so giddy she made him park on the road in case Helen saw the truck and refused to let them in. Not that she wouldn't climb through the window if she had to, Terrible knew.

He gave his fiancée the honors of pounding on the door. The delight on the Indian kid's face when he peeked out it tickled Carmen, Terrible could see. The kid threw the door open, "Carmen! Terrible!" he smiled, "Man, I've been wanting to see you, but Helen . . . ."

"Carmen?" Helen said, coming up behind him. "What are you doing up here?"

"I've come for my puzzle piece," she said. "I got a great big gaping hole where the cutest little partridge's head is supposed to be."

"We wanted to get this party out of the way before the wedding," Terrible said, jiggling the bags of presents up to distract the girl. "You up for helping Helen open some gifts, Churkker?"

"Chakor," Helen said.

Chakor opened the door wide, dodging Helen's efforts to stop him, and Terrible and Carmen piled in as the girl set forth that the baby was the only appropriate topic for conversation. Chakor broke the rule by asking about the wedding. Carmen said something, and Terrible looked around the cabin, which seemed a lot more cheerful than it had in winter. Chakor was a good little housekeeper, Terrible could see: he was clearing their dinner dishes while Helen sat on the bed sorting through presents. When Carmen dropped the hint that she'd skipped dinner to come up, he then began removing new plates from the cupboards.

Old Larry was relegated to a chair at a little table in the corner with a pile of crossword puzzles. Unfair is what Terrible thought, that he didn't get to help: it was his child too. In solidarity,

Terrible wandered over to pat the man on the back—and was surprised enough by his progress on the puzzles to say something.

"He just writes any word that comes to him," Helen said. "He's not answering."

Terrible nodded, but as far as he knew, that's all anybody ever did with words: make up the ones that came to them, when they came. Words were just words, after all.

"He's glaring at me," Carmen complained, as Helen tore the paper from the first gift to reveal a little yellow shirt.

"Oh, that's just his look," Chakor said. "He's not really glaring at anyone."

"I suppose he hasn't popped you in the eye, then?" Carmen asked.

"The lip," Helen said, and Chakor brought two heaping plates of food and set them on the small wooden table that he then dragged closer to where Helen was unwrapping gifts on the bed.

"Slow down," her mother said to Helen, as she was eyeing the food Chakor handed her with real fear. "The gifts won't disappear at midnight."

Helen ignored her, and Terrible, like Carmen, began regarding his plate full of strange-looking food: one mound of fluorescent yellow potatoes with black seeds on them, next to another mound of white rice covered in fluorescent yellow lentil beans.

"I wish I had some chapattis," Chakor said, "but we ate them all."

"Probably best," Terrible smiled, forking a potato and bringing it to his mouth. It was edible. He took another bite.

"We've been thinking about what to name the baby," Chakor said, then, glancing over at Helen who ripped open a large box. "Her middle name will be Madhuri, after my mother, but we wanted an American first name." Terrible glanced over at Larry in the corner. Helen didn't say anything. Nobody was even pretending to pay attention to the gifts since most of them were just little outfits or washcloths and such.

"I want the baby to have a big first name," Chakor said.

"We're not naming it *America*," Helen said, smiling. "Or Freedom, or Liberty, or Unity."

Carmen burst out laughing, "God I hope not," and Helen lightened up for the first time, smiling herself.

"You think I'm joking. These are the names he comes up with."

"No," Chakor said, maybe blushing beneath his brown skin. "I just want them to have strong *meanings*. I want the name to say something about my little baby, about who she is or where she's from."

"*Your* baby?" Carmen said, and Terrible braced himself. But it turned out his fiancée was more interested in keeping the peace than making a point: "I like Carmen for a girl," she said after a considerable pause. "It means 'singing orchard.'"

* * *

Ten minutes after they saw Helen's parents out of the house, Chakor was washing the old clay plates Ida had given him as a housewarming gift when she'd noticed he was eating on plastic dishware he'd bought at the Ben Franklin. Helen was gathering the wrapping paper and baby gifts.

The meeting started off as a pleasant surprise, but at some point Chakor had begun to feel uncomfortable. All night long there had been furtive looks between Carmen and Terrible, and Carmen and Helen, and Helen and Terrible—and when he'd try to catch somebody's eye to let them know he was noticing, their gazes darted out to anything that wasn't his own. Even when Helen had loosened up and starting talking more with her mother about the wedding, her parents kept glancing over at Larry. The whole night Carmen and Terrible kept opening their mouths to speak and then closing them.

As Chakor was rinsing out the sink, Larry stood and walked toward him. The older man was staring like he wanted to help and Chakor handed him a plate he'd just dried off.

"You want to put that in the cupboard?"

"He can't do that," Helen said, coming out of the bathroom, but Larry took the plate and walked to the cabinet where they kept them. He opened it, raised the plate up toward the cabinet, and then sent his hand flashing down to smash the plate onto the floor.

Chakor yelped and Helen screamed and dashed over to Larry as quickly as she could. The specific sound of the plate's collapse shocked Chakor—it wasn't a high-pitched and tingy noise, like a broken glass makes, but something more essential. It was thick and clattery and somehow understated in relation to the force Larry had used to shatter it—an observation corroborated by the four clean wedges the plate had split into, one next to the other. They even still retained the shape of a circle.

"See?" Helen said, running over. "He dropped it. His coordination is off."

"*Dropped?*" Chakor asked, unable to hide the anger and fear in his own voice. It wasn't the first dish the man had broken since he'd returned from India.

"Look at that!" Helen said, marveling down at the plate. "He made a four-leaf clover."

"Helen, Larry dropped the plate on purpose," Chakor said, "I don't know how he could have been more blatant."

Helen led Larry across the broken dish by his hand, and found his pajamas from the old hope chest they kept all Larry's clothes in. When she got him to the bathroom, Chakor began picking up the dull shards.

"It's not personal. Nurse Bettie says there's nothing personal about any of this," she said to Chakor, half an hour later, rubbing his shoulders with her hands. "Nurse Bettie says he still can't string moment to moment together, but that emotions catch up to him all at once. Even at the clinic he's swatted at the nurses who tried to get him off the treadmill fifteen or twenty minutes after he's off."

"This is getting dangerous, you know? Helping a person you cared for is one thing, but letting that person put you—put *you,*" Chakor said, his hand on Helen's belly, "in danger, is too much."

"He just gets frustrated. It's the only emotion he has hold of."

Chakor closed his eyes, face up to the black of the night, and let out a loud stream of air from his lips.

* * *

March 9, 2005

"You're talking about my wife! The woman who's carrying my *baby,*" Chakor was shouting right into Ida's face at the Wal-Mart in Chipeta, a few days later. Ida had held off criticism until then, certain the whole time the boy would come to his own senses, but he seemed bewitched. This morning when he'd told her he was going to run some errands for Carmen's wedding—what a farce!—she'd volunteered to come along.

"What do you know about her, Chakor?" she asked, as he piled plastic flatware into the grocery cart in front of them. She hated sounding like a close-minded, narrow thinker, but Helen had driven her to it. She was wishing upon wishing that she'd been wiser at the outset. To have had this conversation with him the year before, when he first started talking about marrying this girl. Then Ida had talked all about following his instincts and had given him a book of Sufi poetry despite her *own* instincts.

"She's my wife, that's who she is," Chakor said, lowering his voice. "I know she's going to be the mother of my child."

"Okay, fine. But tell me how's she gonna take care of a baby and an invalid? You have to make her make a choice, don't you see that?"

"He isn't living with us forever," Chakor said, thank God, as they moved down the aisle for the paper plates. Just the smell of the Wal-Mart was making Ida sick. "I need *purple*," he said, scanning the shelves.

"Helen can't live two lives at once. Don't you think she needs to make a choice *now*, Chakor? Before the baby comes?"

"It's her mother genes," he said, exasperated. "She's taking care of Larry because of her pregnant hormones, and when the baby's born we'll figure out what's next with that. He needs somebody, and we can be there for him. There's no purple."

"*We? We?* Chakor? He's not a charity case, he's not some cause—he's her goddamned ex-lover. And he's in the shape he's in because he volunteered, *he volunteered*—do you hear that—to go off to Iraq, not even for the military, but for one of those firms that's paid to torture people."

"You don't know what he did there!" Chakor said loud enough that a lady with a baby in her cart who was turning the corner toward him, veered away from the aisle at the last moment. "And I'm not in a position to judge him," he whisper-yelled, "even if he did. And it's good, it's a good sign Helen's looking after somebody. It's practice. She's nesting. And Larry's all right."

"Chakor," Ida tried, "Chakor, what about *you*? Why can't she practice caring for you? I can't figure out what's wrong with your brain. And him, his brain: that is *not* 'all right': he's lost his mind. He's *dangerous*. Carmen's not talking but I can tell you Helen showed up right around the time her mother turned out a fat lip. Herman saw her at the Safeway. And you and me both know for sure that if it was Terrible who did it he'd be the one needing a wheelchair."

"I don't want to talk about this here," he sighed. "We're only halfway through the list, and they don't have the right plates so we're going to have to try the Safeway."

"These have purple flowers on them," Ida said, piling almost the whole supply in the cart. "I assure you, they'll do for Carmen. And you need to answer me, you need to realize you can't have a man like that around your baby."

This time Chakor stopped the grocery cart and faced her. He was shaking with anger, but controlled his voice like a lawyer.

"I will say to you that of course I have wondered. Of course I know things aren't normal. But you need to understand my *mother* blessed my marriage. And now she's dead, and my father is dead, and my only nuclear family is Helen and my child. I need them both. I can make room, at this moment in our lives, for the unexpected. It's not easy having Larry there, but it's worse for him, I can tell you that. And do you know what? I *want* my baby growing up in a world where reaching out to the people who have been meaningful in our lives, even when we think our time with them has run its course, seems like the norm. I want the baby to see the strength of breaking with less forgiving norms in the name of common humanity. Our lives are complicated, Ida, and we make choices and accept each others' choices and we grow. I know you think that, too. And right now I want to focus on getting this shopping done so we can go home to my wife."

Ida didn't respond to him, but she followed him along, watched him put bulk spices and dried kidney beans and several fat jars of mayonnaise into his cart. She wasn't invited to the wedding and from what she could see, that was a relief.

* * *

March 11, 2005

Carmen was freezing her ass off in the cold waiting for her two-timing daughter to pick her up in front of the Legion Hall. She'd spent the morning making sure Terrible and the half dozen cohorts he'd lined up to help him set up for the reception didn't make any harebrained, last-minute changes to her plans. The boys were now busy digging two holes behind the building to roast the goats; she could hear the muffled sounds of their laughter from out back. Johnny Gomez was the one who'd done it before, and every so often she heard his voice rising up, barking orders, and it made her chuckle.

When Helen finally came driving down the street in her godaw- ful minivan, she was ten minutes late, but when she climbed in Carmen was relieved neither of her hangers-on were with her. It was the first time she'd seen Helen alone in too long—before it was Frankenstein, in the last few days it was always the poet following her around, trying to be helpful.

"Let's skip lunch," she began, though her empty stomach gouged at her ribs for saying it, "and get moving with the business of the dresses. I'm a busy woman."

"What dresses?" Helen asked.

Twenty minutes later the girl was standing in front of the bath- room mirror in the last of the four hideous gowns for pregnant bride's attendants that Jerri Ann Cooper had picked up for her, used, at the Deseret Industries in Salt Lake. Jerri Ann wasn't a close friend, but an old friend Carmen knew drove back and forth to the city a lot. She was a schoolteacher who spent her summers at *ren- dezvous*, trading beef jerky for beads and pretending her boyfriend Phil was a bonafide mountain man.

"You wouldn't believe it, Carm, but there was two five-foot-long racks of fancy dresses just for pregnant ladies there. This *is* the place for something, I guess, but don't ask me what. I think she's got some real pretty options, here," Jerri Ann had said, but Helen was now swathed in a long-sleeved, coffee-brown, faux velvet gown that made her look like a knocked-up, pale-faced Pocahontas—and it was by far the best of the dresses.

"You look beautiful, honey," Carmen sighed at Helen who was glaring at herself in the bathroom mirror. "That's the one for you."

"Why, of all people, did you send Jerri Ann?" Helen moaned, which is exactly what Carmen was thinking, but Helen had no room to point it out, and she told her so. "Wal-Mart is open twenty-four hours and you've had the better part of a year to pick something out."

"I know," her daughter mumbled. "This is fine." It was the tone of the word *fine* that made Carmen want to slap the girl.

"Yeah, it's *fine*," she snarled, "After all, it's just your mother's only wedding, and driving thirty-miles out of your way to pick up something half decent would really have been a drag."

"That's not—" Helen said, and sighed again before finishing her thought.

"Well, don't just stand there: take it off before you spill something on it."

"Sure," Helen said, and Carmen went to the kitchen and put two cold cups of the morning's coffee in the microwave, noting the time on the display's clock: two-thirty already. She was due to call the lady minister from Salt Lake at three to give her directions to the chapel and talk about the ceremony.

Helen came dragging her head into the kitchen and put her arms around Carmen, right as the microwave dinged. Carmen poured half-and-half into each of their mugs, and handed one off to Helen. "Thank you, Carmen. That was thoughtful of you to have arranged this for me. I've been out of it. I almost forgot Emmaline was coming Monday, when she gets back from Vail until she called me up yesterday asking directions from the airport. All the hormones are making me forget things."

"Hormones my ass," Carmen said, eyebrows raised, but with a smile. She had been young and stupid once herself, after all. "You're spending all your time juggling tweedle-dee-dum and tweedle-dee-dee. Speaking of which: I assume you understand only tweedle-dee-dee is invited to my nuptials."

"Of course," Helen said. "Larry wouldn't want to come. He's still twitchy in crowds."

"He's twitchy from sunup to sundown," she said, taking advantage of her daughter's attempt at sweetness. "Don't you imagine a second I won't call Family Services on the both of you if he does *anything* fishy after my grandbaby's born. I've got the number on my refrigerator already," she said, pointing at the number on the fridge. "I'm not bluffing." She wasn't.

Helen's face reddened and it looked like the sweetness was going to drain out of it, but she said, "I'm closing my eyes and counting to twelve," out of nowhere. "One-calm, two-calm, three-calm," she said.

"Don't tell me you're the one they've got learning to control your temper," Carmen sighed. "That's just sick."

"Nine-calm, ten-calm, eleven-calm," Helen went on, and then opened her eyes like she'd been invisible the whole time she was counting, "As I was about to tell you: Larry will stay home, and Chakor asked Herman Meek to sit with him while we're gone tomorrow."

"You forgot twelve!"

"Twelve-calm," she smiled, pouring a glass of water for herself, which made Carmen note that she hadn't touched her coffee. "I have to pick up Larry in a couple of hours and drop some papers off at the Blue Hope. Do you need a ride somewhere?"

"I'm waiting on a call here," Carmen said, pouring Helen's coffee into her own mostly finished mug. Helen was getting her things together, to go. She found a garbage sack from under the sink and fashioned it into a dress bag by puncturing the bottom with the dress hanger.

"So Herman's gonna have to miss the whole wedding because of Larry," Carmen sighed. "That's a shame."

"You didn't even invite the Meeks," Helen grinned.

"I didn't? I guess old Ida's going to curse me, then," she sighed. "Old witch."

Helen smiled. "Can't say I disagree. She is not a very open-minded hippie."

"Don't tell me she thinks there's something off in your asking your boyfriend's best friend to babysit your deranged husband!"

"Mom. . . ." The word coming from Helen's mouth was a lovely and foreign enough object that Carmen shut her own mouth. But then Helen didn't say anything.

"What?" she said, and Helen took a huge breath, and looked down at the table.

"They don't *know* he's my husband."

"They don't know?"

"Yeah."

"They *really* don't know?"

"I thought I'd divorce Larry first, and then I wouldn't have to tell him. I didn't want to scare Chakor away." She looked up then, and honest-to-God said into Carmen's face, "So don't tell him. You don't have to lie, just don't tell the truth."

"What the fuck is he thinking?" It was the first thing that slipped into her head.

"Larry?"

"Chakor."

"He thinks I'm doing a good thing," Helen said, and Carmen would be damned if the girl didn't actually blush at the mentioning of her lover's name.

"You meet a man you like, you were through with the man you didn't like, but you wanted to make sure the new thing took before giving the old one up?" Carmen said.

Helen vaguely moved her head.

"And now you're letting old Larry manipulate you into staying with his whole injured soldier act."

"You know it's not an act."

"Leave him, and we'll see what I know. But what is Chakor thinking? Who lets their girlfriend's ex-boyfriend live in their home? Especially since the boy thinks he's daddy?"

"The good guy," Helen said.

"No, the good guy is smarter than that," she shook her head. "Look at me however you like, but don't tell me you don't think it's about two shades closer to either moronic or creepiness than is right."

"Says the woman with a doll for a stepchild," Helen said.

Chapter Nineteen

March 12, 2005

Square buckets. Sleeping Helen. Hollow mattress cold against the floor. Larry knew. Helen's Chakor.

"Ready? Let's try to make it a mile today, okay?" His dead mother. Oil in her hair. *She rises with the full moon. We'll go out and see her, together, one night.*

Snow drift. "I'll sweep it off. No use slipping before we begin."

Warmth in mittens. Larry knew. His white down parka. *All dressed up like an Eskimo, Larry. Good work today. It's paying off, don't you forget it.*

One step and another. One foot, *same* foot, again and again. Mud spotting through the snow. *Lean into it. Use those arms! You sure ain't a spring chicken but you work like it. Good job!* Slippery. Careful. This man's red jacket, Helen's Chakor. *Not America or Liberty or Unity.* His long, skinny legs. Hands in his pocket, a wisp. Dry spring snow. Like sand.

"Look at that, Larry!" Whispering. "It's a doe and her fawn!" A doe and her fawn. Yes. Their black eyes, wet ash. *Ashes in the water, and now she rises with the full moon. I miss her.* Larry misses her. Clumping ice on the creek. The thaw. *It's your baby. Your baby, do you understand?* Yes. *Keep Frankenstein away from my black eye.* His own tracks like a monster's. Look.

"Did you drop something? No? You need a rest? I can find a log. . . . " Large bird's hands on his white parka. *Like an Eskimo.* A lucky clover. He drove his girl across the desert to save her. *We'll tell everybody we eloped at city hall. My uncle's from California. My baby.*

"Here you go, here's a spot. I know your arms get more tired when it's slick."

"No!" his own black voice, a melted tire.

"You sure?" One foot, same foot, two. *Your arms are getting so strong, Larry. Good job.* "I guess that's best. We need to make good time to get you set before the wedding."

One foot. *Her hands are full, but she should really have taken him in for a leg before now.* The chirping sky. The sun rising. Warming. Dry spring snow like sand, like her missing hand. Her lipstick, Dr. Linda Frank, *It's silly.*

I miss her. He missed her. *She never got to visit me here.* The hollow mattress cold against the wooden fuck. Wet, naked smells. *We need somebody while we're here.* And then his melted scream.

"Larry!"

The bush springing up from nowhere. Helen's Chakor running, "Oh my God, are you all right?"

Dry snow in the parka's neck. Scrapes and burns. Sand clumping the blood, *Can you hear me?*

Fluttering hands. Lifting the walker, aluminum legs. "You fell right into it like a chair!" His smile, wet ash. His black eyes. *Let's go for a ride.* A question.

"Stay still, Larry. You know, I think the bush is the only thing that kept you from falling into the creek. *My God!*" *The Lonesome Gods. The Quick and the Dead.* Larry was breathing. *You're a lucky man.* He breathed.

Helen's Chakor. His brown, thin boots braced into snow, into sand. Her pink lipstick, his skinny body.

"I want to throw my weight back so we don't both go toppling in. Put your hands around my neck and hold tight." His one leg,

Frankenstein. His strong arms around the brown neck, her hand in his hand. Wet fuck. This man's arms beneath Larry's armpits.

"One! Two! *Three!*"

Cheek against cheek. The boy's hot breath.

"I'm going to roll you off me. There. You're okay?"

Larry knew. He could sit. Grabbed his walker by the leg.

"Jesus!" his ashen eyes. His laughter, wings across the sunrise. *Good job, Larry. She rises with the moon.*

Chapter Twenty

March 12, 2005

The Saturday of her mother's wedding was a mess. After waking late to an empty cabin—Chakor and Larry were off on their morning walk—Helen had scurried to cook breakfast so they'd arrive home to something. That left her with just a few minutes to dress, and then right as she finally made it to the door her new cell phone, which she'd just plugged into the wall to recharge, rang. She answered without thinking.

"You didn't tell me what *gorgeous* mountains you grew up around," her boss said.

"Emmaline?"

"I can't believe I've never been to Salt Lake before. Such a pretty little valley. I spent the night in a hotel right by the Mormon Temple—when it's all lit up at night, it's a vision straight out of Disney, isn't it?"

As it turned out, Emmaline had decided to skip her yearly trip to Vail so she could support Helen at her mother's wedding. Next Monday, when Emmaline was scheduled to arrive for work at the center and when there wasn't a giant family event going on, it had seemed barely plausible that Helen could hide Chakor's presence from her boss. She simply wouldn't ask her boss to the cabin, would not tell Chakor her boss was in town, and if Emmaline wanted to see Larry, they'd visit at the rehab center. The plan wasn't perfect, but maybe doable. Doable *on Monday*.

"It's something I *wanted* to do," Emmaline was purring. "Don't you worry about me missing out on real fun, either. All that Vail trip has become is too many Tom Collinses and a lot of riding up and down the tram."

"The wedding will be over by the time you get here," Helen said, which was true. "*Tomorrow* we can drive out and see the new building. It's beautiful."

"Nonsense!" Emmaline said, "I'm in an exquisite little canyon now, just outside Chipeta. I just need directions."

"But you can't come," Helen said, cringing. "It's a *really small* event. Just Carmen's best friends. . . . Not that I don't appreciate your wanting to be here. . . . "

"Oh, I see. It's just that I've planned this, you know, this *surprise* for you for over a week, but I understand. I see."

"Do you have the directions to your hotel?"

"Gosh," Emmaline said quietly. "You sound *upset*. I don't want to make the day harder for you—I just wanted to help. Be the coat check girl, or something."

Helen laughed at the thought of it, despite herself, and looked down at the clock on the stove.

"*Oh shit!*" she shrieked, "Oh my god, Emmaline, I have to go!"

"Oh, God, you're in labor . . . *I knew it!*"

"No," Helen sighed, running toward the van with her cell, although the batteries still needed charging. "Call me when you get here, we can talk," she said, and hung up because she knew Emmaline would keep rattling on—she was a car phone driver. She saw Larry and Chakor walking on the flat trail by the river and waved as she tore out of the driveway, and down the mountain, already more than half an hour late for her appointment at Bobbie Lee's Bobbie Lee.

* * *

Ms. Kathleen Talbot was in her favorite place in the world: Bobbie Lee's cushioned chair, leaned back, listening to the girl complaining about her high school sweetheart *cum* husband of fifteen years, Brandon Hancock.

"He *knows* I'm the one picks the kids up from school and stays with them all afternoon," Bobbie Lee said, combing Kathleen's old gray hair up, folding it back into the turquoise rollers. "They *don't* miss me around the house because I'm *there* the whole time they are."

"That's true," Kathleen nodded, happily.

"*He* misses me. He misses the nookie he used to get anytime he thought he could add an extra twenty minutes to his lunch break."

"I'm not surprised," Kathleen agreed. Bobbie Lee was a real hair-tugger when she was upset, which she usually was. It was why Kathleen had switched over to the girl after going to feather-fingered LaRoo Calvert's place for two decades. These days her weekly hair appointments not only made her look presentable enough, but they were therapeutic. Bobbie Lee's yanking was a reverse sort of acupuncture. The blood really tingled and her old bones felt invigorated for two solid days after a session with Bobbie Lee.

"Without the extra money I bring in we couldn't have built that new patio he's so proud of. So what if the house isn't spic-and-span as it used to be?"

Before Kathleen could answer, Carmen Motes's girl, who Bobbie Lee had been worried was a no-show, came bounding through the door a clean forty-five minutes late.

"Just missed your mother, Helen," Bobbie Lee said, with a pull of Kathleen's hair. "I know who you are because she said you look like a knocked-up moose—that's her words, not mine."

"I'm so sorry," Helen panted.

"Oh, don't be," Bobbie Lee smiled. "Ms. Talbot is a half hour early for everything, so she took your place. At three I got a group of girls coming in for Spring Fling. If you'd come late at three o'clock, you'd be in trouble."

"Thank you," Helen said again, hovering in the doorway like a fat, frizzy-haired ghost.

"Sit down and read a magazine and breathe, for goodness sake," Ms. Talbot said to the poor girl.

"You've got time," Bobbie Lee said, and it was true the girl looked like she wasn't sure. "You'll be in and out of here in forty-five minutes flat. That's with a makeover, too—it's half-off for brides-maids. Then all you've got to do is throw on a dress and shoes, and you're there."

As if to make good on her promise, Bobbie Lee began yanking and curling Kathleen's own hair like lightning. The old woman faced the pain by focusing in on the younger Motes. The girl had left town before entering Kathleen's American History class at Union High, and she hadn't seen her since then.

"You *do* look ready to pop," Kathleen said to the girl. "If I was Carmen I would've waited a few weeks for the wedding so my grandchild could be in it."

The girl said nothing, her gaze affixed to the four elk heads hanging above Bobbie Lee's mirrors. Their presence was the second reason Kathleen herself liked coming in—it was just *different.* She'd been trying to convince Bobbie Lee to put a wig on one of them, but the girl said Brandon would "lose his shit" at the sight of it.

"Those heads are Brandon's. Bobbie Lee's husband's," Kathleen offered.

"He didn't see the use of me cutting hair anywhere but our kitchen until I pointed out we'd have the extra wall space to hang them," Bobbie Lee explained. "They creeped me out the first ten years of the marriage, but then they became my ticket to freedom. Isn't that funny how things go?"

"Yeah," Helen said, nodding blankly, having caught her breath and her bearings.

"It's like that poem about the road not travelled," Bobbie Lee kept on.

"Uh-huh," Helen nodded politely.

"I don't see it," Kathleen admitted.

"Well, the deer heads were this ugly, spooky road that I was stuck on, and now I can see how if we didn't have them, I'd be in a real mess."

Kathleen considered leaving it at that, but the schoolmarm in her wouldn't have it. "That poem," she said, "is about *choosing* an unusual path for your life from the outset, and how that's supposed to make your days more interesting. You married the boy you always knew you were going to marry, at the age all girls marry. The deer heads are just a lucky break. I, however, chose *not* to marry—and you know I could've—and that is supposed to have made *the difference.*"

"Maybe we're talking about different poems," Bobbie Lee said.

"No, it's the same poem. And the road that was supposed to have made *the difference* did not. The poem is wrong," Kathleen said.

Both girls were staring at her now, and it made Kathleen happy to see it. "What you want to do whenever you see two roads before you is take off down through the brush between them. Because God knows it's miserable being defined by a road, no matter how little travelled it is."

Both the younger women in the shop were looking at Kathleen like she had transformed, in the last sixty seconds, into an old coot. She got the same look from her students eight hours a day, five days a week, and had learned not to take offense.

"Let's get your hair under the dryers, Ms. Talbot, so I can start on Helen," Bobbie Lee said, but Kathleen stood proudly.

"Two roads are two lines," she said, looking from one girl to the other so her words would sink deeply into both of their minds. "The brush is everywhere else in the world. You think about *that.*"

* * *

GGs Special Events and Funeral Parlor delighted Davendra Dave, all around. The name of the church had made him feel slightly apprehensive, but it turned out to be a cozy little chapel right out of a John Wayne cowboy movie. Maybe one hundred people would fit inside, it was made of wood, painted white, and there was a little bell tower that Mrs. Cowan had agreed to let him sound when the newlyweds departed.

"Nothing is more American than ringing a steeple bell," he said to her, nodding happily.

Davendra had not left Hinduism. He had only done what people throughout the world do when they find themselves in another culture: added a new layer of meaning to the infinite others that were already inside him. One belief system would feed and nourish the other. He had performed two Unitarian baptisms, which he had not enjoyed, and one funeral, which he had: but this was to be his first wedding as a Minister in Training. Originally he was only scheduled to accompany Reverend Bethany Paul, but her appendix had nearly erupted the night before. There was no time to find a replacement. He was on his own.

"Shouldn't your name be Davendro," the bride—a wrinkled, fat, old woman—asked when he met with her briefly earlier in the day. "I was expecting a woman. That's what I asked for."

"I was expecting teenagers," he had shrugged, rather than explaining Reverend Paul's unfortunate circumstances. "Would you like me to put on a dress?" He was relieved when the lady burst out laughing, because sometimes his jokes flew over people's heads. The tone of his voice could sound more severe than he meant it to, but this lady had liked him immediately. He learned from her that she and her husband-to-be had not written their own vows, which was unusual these days, and that they wanted the ceremony short. Of course.

"Heavier on hope and goodwill than on God himself," she had said with a wink.

"A-OK," he nodded back. "I prefer them that way myself." It was no lie. He had only memorized the most basic of the Unitarian ceremonies, and had, in fact, worried the couple would request a more complicated sermon whose words he would have to read. Though he never looked down on the other priests reading the holy words from a book, doing so himself was a concession to this new kind of priesthood that he would not make.

Now, as he stood preparing for the simple ceremony, he gawked at the arriving crowd. They were mostly regular people. More threadbare than the members of his Salt Lake congregation, but still dressed up. Added in were a dozen or so men who had arrived on motorcycles roaring loud enough he had covered his ears. The riders walked in the picture of order itself. These men wore black leather vests over white dress shirts and dark jeans. The few in short-sleeved T-shirts had fat arms and impressive tattoos. No matter their attire, however, he was impressed to see all the men wait politely at the church's front doors for the arrival of their ladies, who had followed in cars. These women wore a bizarre assortment of dresses the likes of which Davendra had not seen since 1978, when he had arrived in America and loved watching Sonny and Cher singing on the television.

Most striking of all the guests to the priest and pundit, however, were the seven or eight couples who actually matched the church itself: they had dressed like frontier explorers, as if hours earlier they had been hunting bears. Men wore leather, like the motorcyclists, but their jackets were long sleeved and still the obvious brown of cowhide. And the women wore long, pioneer dresses. Eventually

Mrs. Cowan began arguing with one of these explorer types who had begun passing an old-fashioned pistol around to the people around him. Eventually she and the gentleman disappeared into Mr. Cowan's office, where they locked the gun until the ceremony was over.

"Reverend Dave," Mrs. Cowan said when she had come back, mispronouncing his name to sound like the common American man's name.

"Dah-vey," he corrected for the fourth time that morning.

"Reverend Duvet," she whispered, "the bride and groom are in their rooms, and I'm going to start up with the organ."

"Good, good, good," he said, smiling, waving her off. He was very excited already, then just as the music started a face he recognized slipped in quickly, to a pew in the back: the newlywed Chakor, back from India. He was pleasantly not-very-surprised, and winked at the boy's startled face as he listened to the old-fashioned American Wedding March ascend into the air from the church's electronic organ. The song, he realized, must have fallen out of favor with Salt Lake Unitarians. He had not heard it in real life, before—only on television.

He wondered where Helen was as he smiled toward the door through which the wedding party would enter, and then she stepped through them, first in the procession. It startled him since Carmen had told him her daughter would be the maid, and Helen's mother was supposed to be dead—but perhaps this was another Auntie-Mother, he thought.

Helen was a vision, strange and lovely: she was very pregnant and wearing another of the Sonny and Cher dresses. She carried a bouquet of daisies in one hand and a large doll dressed in a pretty white dress in the other. Behind her came the groom, in a black suit and top hat like Abraham Lincoln's, and the bride herself wearing a Victorian dress of scarlet and gold—as red, in fact, as any lengha or sari he had married anybody else in before. It all made him so happy he nearly laughed out loud. He cursed the American tradition of not taking photographs during a wedding. Nobody among his friends, Hindu or Unitarian, would ever believe what he had seen.

Helen's face paled as she approached him. He smiled to calm her down but she had a hazy look in her eyes he recognized from the first wedding he had performed in India, where the bride had fainted midway through the ceremony. "Why don't you sit in the pew, dear?" he said to her, and she did.

He turned, then, to welcome his motley crowd. The bride and groom standing before him were the ugliest he had ever married, and yet the rapture on the woman's face as he turned toward them was beautiful and sincere. He held back tears because of that look, because he was standing there in front of such a foreign and patient crowd, and because he knew he had made the right choice in expanding his priestly capabilities. Why everybody in the world neglected to spend the majority of their days performing wedding rites he would never understand.

* * *

Helen watched her mother's wedding with a growing pit in the little room there was left in her stomach. She could have sworn her mother had said the priest was a woman, but here Davendra Dave was, speaking in English and wearing a turned collar. If he were performing the ceremony in Sanskrit and a dhoti it would not have been more discombobulating. Any moment he might turn toward her and say something about having presided over her own wedding, and so she clutched Vera tightly enough to indent her poor little arm.

The room was filled with people she'd known growing up. They'd all aged like Carmen—as if she'd been gone decades rather than years, and she focused on that. On stealing sidelong glances at the fat and misshapen, jovial crowd who she noticed, unlike her, were rapt with attention—intrigued, she could tell, by this brown priest with a mysterious accent. She wondered where Chakor was. He had helped her through the mortification at having been tapped to carry Vera, but had then slipped into the chapel alone and she hadn't seen him on the way in.

It was good the priest asked her to sit, because she was hot. Sweat tickled at the edges of her puffy up-do, and she was on the verge of tears. Every particle of her being was involved in the effort of just sitting, not listening, but trying to look engaged and happy. If she ruined this day for her mother, no matter what she'd held against Carmen before, she wouldn't be able to forgive herself. The thought surprised her, but it was true.

As she began forcing herself to listen to the priest's words, she realized he was also nervous. There was an anxious tenor in his voice as he began stumbling through what was a very traditional, non-denominational ceremony. At some point to compensate, perhaps, he gained a lilt in his words and there was a beautiful quality to them, like she'd heard on the mountain during her own wedding. With each new sentence, though, perhaps as he was feeling more comfortable, the lilt became so pronounced that it began sounding more like a chant. Like he was chanting a Vedic ceremony in English. She couldn't see Carmen or Terrible's faces, so Helen stole a glance at the woman sitting on the other side of the pew from her to make sure it wasn't just her imagination—and saw the lady smiling, swaying to the tune.

"Does aaaaaaa-NNY MAN proTEST THIS peace?" Davendraji sang out, and she took the opportunity to look behind her. Her mother's usually unflappable friends had become wide-eyed and open mouthed and their expressions seemed to reach the priest himself, who cocked his head curiously, and then said in perfectly natural, accented English: "Then I now pronounce you husband and wife. You may kiss each other."

And with that, the church erupted with the hoots and hollers that had always defined her mother's set. The piano started up again and Carmen and Terrible—who she realized for the first time was now her *father*, the first father she'd ever had—walked toward the open church doors with their friends tailing them. When she turned to the priest, he was gone, and so she made her way through the crowd, which opened up for her since it was her parents leaving the building.

As the church bells started ringing, she watched Terrible lift Carmen in her crazy, beautiful red dress, and walk toward the matching black Harleys with fire-red sidecars, which belonged to Lou and Elisabeth Arnold. He dropped her into a car, they both waved goodbye, and everybody surrounding Helen cheered as the engines of the motorcycles revved so loudly that Helen jumped and they gave the church bells a run for their money. Then, her parents drove away: Carmen in the "Just" car driven by Elisabeth, Terrible in the "Married" car, and tin cans trailing behind the both of them.

"Helen!" Chakor called, laughing. "Helen! Let's go see Davendraji!"

* * *

Chakor could see his poor wife's eyes wide with fear at the prospect of her mother finding out she'd married without inviting her. For the last few weeks he had been pressing Helen to confess, but today was the wrong day. He clasped his wife around the shoulders and kissed her on the neck.

"Don't worry," he said. "I bet he'll leave before the reception."

A few minutes later, though, the couple found the priest and marveled with him about the coincidences of the world.

"No reason for me to drive all the way back to the city tonight," he'd said. "And I have been urged not to leave without trying the roasted goat, which as you know I cannot do. But I must admit I am curious about this custom."

"It's not a custom," Helen said. "I mean it is somewhere, but not here."

Davendraji nodded, smiling.

"Well I'd love to tell you about my trip, but we forgot to bring Helen more comfortable clothes for the reception. I have to drive up to the cabin."

"I suspect borrowing something from one of your girlfriends is not so easy these days, is it?" the priest chuckled, and Helen nodded.

"Will you join me for a beautiful drive, on a beautiful day?" Chakor asked.

"That's a great idea," Helen piped up, and an hour later they'd already dropped Helen off at Carmen's, and were pulling into the long drive at the cabin.

Watching Davendraji performing the wedding that seemed not particularly Christian, but certainly not Sanskrit, had dazzled and delighted and slightly upset Chakor. He'd known the man enjoyed sitting in on the Unitarian ceremonies—that's where they'd met, in the days Chakor was training in Salt Lake City to be a Poet in the Heartland. Still, the pundit had never suggested he had aspirations to join a new priesthood. On the contrary, they'd discussed how much the pundit missed performing Hindu rituals—and how he'd been rejected by the local Hare Krishna temple.

"I like weddings," is all the priest said now, when Chakor asked him about the switch.

They drove silently most of the way up to the cabin, and Chakor assumed the man was tired. He didn't want to talk about India since he was still processing the trip itself in the scraps and bits of time he had between freelance-editing journal articles and looking after Helen and Larry.

Not until the roads began winding toward the Black Elks did the pundit finally speak. He said, "I was surprised to see Helen had family. For some reason I was under the impression nobody was living."

"Oh," Chakor said, relieved the man had brought up the topic he hadn't been sure how to. "Yes. Well, we thought that since my parents couldn't come, and we were going to have a second wedding anyway, it was best to keep it a secret and just pretend the second wedding was the real wedding."

"And so this mother just thinks you have impregnated her unmarried daughter?"

"I guess so," Chakor said. "But it's a pretty nontraditional family."

"That is true," the priest laughed, shaking his head. But then he rested a hand on Chakor's shoulder and said, "Secrets are never best. They are an awful way to start off a lifelong endeavor. I am sure you know that."

"I do," Chakor sighed.

"Well, it is not my place to mention it to anybody. I know you were going to ask."

"Thanks," Chakor said, choking up a little because he had no parents of his own, anymore, and Davendraji was right.

"No," the pundit said. "This is not the day to spring that sort of news on a mother, is it? But it is right that you tell her."

This time Chakor started the silence by not answering, a silence that lasted until they drove into the cabin's parking lot to see Larry all alone on the porch. Chakor introduced him as an old friend of Helen's, a houseguest, and while he went into the cabin to find Herman—who wasn't there—the priest sat down next to Larry on the porch and began talking to him.

"He can't talk, not much," Chakor said. "He was wounded in Iraq and he's just living with us awhile. Herman!" he called back into the house, like maybe the man was deaf and hadn't heard him calling. Then he cupped his hands around his mouth and called out around the back, "Herman!"

"No," Larry said, shaking his head. "No."

"Man, he's upset," Chakor said, "don't get too close to him."

Davendra ignored him and began rubbing Larry's hands between his own.

"We had a friend watching him," he told Davendraji. "He's just left him here." It didn't surprise him that Herman had lapsed on his duty—he didn't even want to imagine how long Larry had been left alone—but it surprised him at how angry he felt about it. His eyes actually teared up.

"You have taken him in?" Davendraji asked.

"For a while." The priest's smile, then, the amount of pride in it as he looked Chakor over, nodding his approval, was finally the reaction none of his friends had given him in regards to Larry. It was wide open and generous.

"That's a wonderful thing," the man said, moving his own hand onto Larry's folded ones. "What a wonderful thing for you to do. I can see he appreciates it. Don't you? Yes, I can see you do."

It wasn't hard, then, for the two men to come to the same conclusion about what to do. Chakor had thought it was the right thing in the morning, even, and felt pained leaving him behind. When they asked Larry if he wanted to go to the reception, he stood with his walker and began down the ramp. Davendraji laughed in delight, and Chakor remembered to run inside to grab the wheelchair and a change of clothes for his wife. Both the priest and the soldier were already in Helen's van when he got back to it, and as he struggled to fold the chair, he realized it was the first time he'd driven Larry anywhere. Helen had always been insistent about shouldering the responsibility of taking him to his rehab classes, and he'd let her. But Larry was his responsibility, too; was his family in as much a sense as anybody else on the earth was.

"I am sure that this caretaking you do," Davendraji said, "balances out the bad luck the untruth of your wedding may have started."

And Chakor smiled. He looked back happily at Larry's sad, stubbled face in the rearview mirror, and believed what the priest said.

* * *

The reception would begin at seven and Emmaline took her time primping in the hotel room. The drive out had been *haunting*. The mountains were less domineering than in Colorado, where they seemed determined to shoulder everything—clouds, sky, each other—out of the way. Not that Utah wasn't grandiose. It was that, but also *relaxed*.

Her only quibble was that she had only brought her digital Olympia. Helen had given Emmaline the impression that Eastern Utah was uniformly and dismally desolate. Her descriptions of Chipeta County's population, too—along with a few *New York Times* articles about the rural ghettos of North America—had spooked Emmaline. She imagined the county a cross between the Dust Bowl, Wounded Knee, and a medium-security prison. That her hotel room would be robbed seemed inevitable and so she'd left her valuables behind.

Driving into Franklin, however, finalized her realization that she had overreacted. The Nikon would've been fine. Both the city and its inhabitants looked as though they'd been gleaned from a Norman Rockwell painting and Emmaline was entertained by this quaintness. Her hotel was newly constructed, if tacky and cheap-looking, and her suite was large. The young girl at the front desk had been courteous in her own way.

It was quarter past seven, and Emmaline was dressed and ready. She was wearing a very plain, moss-colored wool Jil Sander dress and simple black Chanel heels. Ordinarily she would have at least passed through a salon before a wedding, but the puffed hair and heavy makeup women throughout Franklin wore uniformly dissuaded her.

As Helen told her, the drive to Smoot's Pass took less than twenty minutes, and as she turned onto the small town's Main Street it was clear from the outset what a different community it was from Franklin. It still had the edge of seeming like sweet Americana, but here there were real trailers with weeds in their lots, and half the homes looked crumbling. There were no businesses except the gas station she had turned at—and of course, the Cultural Arts Center, which she was eager to see. It was halfway between Smoot's Pass and Franklin, on a side road—Helen had given her directions, but she didn't want to get lost.

At the second stop sign she turned right, as she had been directed, and realized the town didn't *have* streetlights. For a flash she was proud to be starting a project out here, and then she got very nervous when she saw what she knew must be the Legion Hall. It was a small, inelegant rectangle constructed from cinderblocks, and painted white. It was surrounded by motorbikes and jalopies. Her duty to Helen was the only thing that compelled her to stop and step out into the wet gravel.

A large group of workers were smoking in front of the building and she wanted to ask to make sure she had the right Legion Hall, but felt intimidated by the stares her arrival procured. Two of the women were also in dresses, but they looked thirty years out of date. They were too tight and hugged at the women's fat rolls, and Emmaline wondered if these were the same dresses they had worn to prom, as teenagers. She smiled fleetingly at them and upon stepping through the steel door and into the event parlor that looked like . . . what? She had no comparison; there was not a movie scene she could bring up to describe the guests or the impoverished room that held them. Swabs of fabric draped the ceiling and the walls, and though the lights were dimmed, Emmaline could see they were frayed and rotting from perhaps decades of use. Red-faced, happy people were dancing or conversing in small groups in colorful clothing that served as their own sort of animated and whirling decorations.

"I'm looking for Helen?" she said to a woman dressed for a day in the frontier west, whom she had caught looking *her* outfit over with an astounded gape.

"Who's looking?" the woman said, instead of helping.

"She's my employee," Emmaline sighed. "My friend."

Instead of responding to her, the woman scurried across the room, to the side of the dance floor where Emmaline caught her first glimpse of Helen, sitting on a stool draped in cheap crepe. An ancient woman sat next to her. Emmaline didn't wait, but followed the woman over, saw Helen patting her on the shoulder.

"Jeanie thought you were a health inspector who had heard about the goat," she whispered into Emmaline's ear as they hugged. Emmaline let the comment slide, unsure about how to interpret it.

"You didn't tell me it was a themed reception," she smiled tightly, and Helen laughed, sliding off the stool. Her stomach protruded gigantically from her bizarre ballgown.

"Sit down," Helen said, offering her stool, and as Emmaline gathered her thoughts Helen's body tensed up, and she said, "I'll be right back. Don't move."

Not like there were many places in this room Emmaline felt more comfortable in. She leaned back into the wall, and listened to the band whose music was almost laughably inharmonious, though the singer had a nice voice. She sought out where Helen had run off to around the time the song ended, and a soft, plump hand clutched at her own.

"I'm Fern Monks," the old woman croaked.

"Emmaline Harris," she said, "Pleased to meet you."

"I been coming to the dances at the Legion Hall for sixty years now," the woman yelled, though the band was taking a short break while the singer was going to "the crapper," he said.

"You must have been a girl when you started," Emmaline smiled.

"Not me," she laughed, "I was never young. But I did like the Friday Night Stomps. Every weekend this building was this filled up and more for decades. My parents came to dances at the old Legion Hall, and I married Lewis after meeting him at one."

"That's a lot of history," Emmaline said, relieved to be talking to somebody—it made her stand out less, she thought.

"They were marvelous, just marvelous. Just like this, until the television came along and people started staying home," Fern said, sliding off her stool.

"Fascinating," Emmaline said. "That's such a shame."

"At midnight the men shot their guns out into the sky like fireworks, and chills would run down your spine," she said. "*Chills.*"

"Don't tell me you're the one gave Jack Grimshaw the idea to shoot off his pistol," said a woman Emmaline recognized as Carmen from the gravel in her voice. She appeared from nowhere in a crimson Victorian gown that was actually very beautiful.

"I didn't have to give him the idea to shoot, sweetheart," Fern smiled, patting the bride on the arm as she headed off toward the ladies' room. "It was already there."

"She did!" Carmen gasped at the woman's stooped and receding back, seemingly oblivious to Emmaline's presence. "That old woman is gonna get the cops called out to break up my wedding!" she said. Just as Emmaline called out to her, the band started up a new song, and Carmen melted across the room and disappeared.

The room was filled with women who looked like Cinderella's stepsisters and men culled from the bit parts in Shakespeare's plays, which was to say, for the first time in her life Emmaline Harris felt like one of the girls sitting on the sidelines of a dance. People were drunk and dancing sloppily and shouting loudly—and a small part of the socialite longed to join in. Or more specifically, longed to *know how* to join in. This was a world that of course must exist, but that she had never conceived of, and the thought made her drowsily nostalgic. She had been waiting fifteen minutes for Helen when she finally stood to get her blood moving, and to find out where Helen had disappeared off to.

* * *

Helen intercepted Chakor as he made his way toward the stools by the dance floor. Her jaw was clenched, and she ducked his efforts to kiss her by grabbing his hand and yanking him into the small office at the front corner of the building.

"Are you all right?" he asked, and she didn't say anything. She took the brown paper bag with her change of clothes in it from his arms and began undressing in the dim light.

"What's wrong? What happened?" he asked, following her into the room.

"Hold the door closed," she said. "There's not a lock. I'm just overwhelmed."

He could see she wanted a moment to herself, but rather than standing guard outside the door, he stayed in the room, unwilling to give up this unexpected chance to see her lovely, exaggerated shape, the warm glint of her bare skin beneath the floor lamp's flickering light. A pregnant woman, he thought, was so beautiful because in her shape you remembered she was animal. You could see how she was kin to does, and cows, and stray cats—that heaviness of form, her dull movements were a direct link to the harmony of the universe, to the thing, to the life force connecting all things.

"You are a goddess," he smiled. She was in her new, giant black bra and had slipped on her funny-waisted jeans, and he couldn't help himself as he left his station near the door to kiss her.

"Mmmmm," she said, and he was thankful she hadn't pushed him away again. "You're drunk."

He laughed, and kissed her again, and then helped her slip her sweater over her head before lifting it and kissing her bare belly.

"It's daddy," he said. "Be a good little baby, and come see us soon."

"You *are* drunk," Helen laughed, pulling him up.

"I'm just happy. I'm having a good day."

"I'm glad you got to spend some time with Davendraji before he left," she said. "And he didn't seem too angry. Did you have a good talk?"

"Oh, no," Chakor said, his stomach twisting because in the glory of freeing Larry from the mountaintop, he'd neglected to think about this moment. "I don't want you to be upset, because I've got everything under control, so don't worry. But Davendraji's *here*. He's not going to mention anything about the wedding to your mother. He understands."

"Understands," Helen said, her shoulders tensing slightly. "Where is he?"

"Everything is under control," Chakor said again. "He's outside looking after Larry."

"*Larry?*" she hissed. "Larry is *not* here."

"We *had* to bring him," he said, but he knew from the way the blood drained from her face that Helen wouldn't agree.

He listened to her teeth grind as she thought, until she turned to him and demanded to know *why*, in a fit of controlled hysteria. Helen had already opened the office door and was peeking into the main room, looking frantically for Larry and Davendraji, and Chakor rested his hands on her head.

"Slow down," he whispered, his mouth right up against her ear. He told her about how they'd found Larry, all alone, how there had been no choice but to bring Larry.

"You should've stayed there with him," she hissed, and he had never seen her so angry. Her whole body was shaking. It didn't matter that he promised he and Davendraji would look after him. She would not relax.

"*Goddammit you need to get him out NOW,*" she shouted in a whisper. "You should leave now and drive them back up to the cabin."

"Come on, Helen," Chakor said, anger entering his own voice. "If his presence doesn't bother me, why should you let it bother you?"

"You don't understand," she said. "I want you to go. *All of you.*"

"Well, we won't!" Chakor said. "I have a *right* to be here, and Davendraji does, and Larry has a right not to be left in danger. We can play your game, Helen, but you can't make up all the rules."

"Chakor!" she said, and burst into tears. He was mad, but he went to her and held her.

"Come see for yourself," he said, wiping her tears with his coat. "They're not causing any problems."

He held her limp hand and led her out of the office, into the blare of Starvation Blues Band, which seemed to be getting progressively louder. He pulled her toward the front door, but stopped momentarily when he saw Carmen.

"Helen!" Carmen drawled, hugging her daughter from behind. "I love you, I love you, I love you!"

"I love you, too!" Chakor shouted at Carmen, but she had already crossed the room to where Terrible was talking with friends. Her dress had looked a little ridiculous in the full of day, Chakor thought, but in the night, with the dimmed lights, she looked like a queen.

* * *

They stepped outside into the chilly air, which was initially a respite from the stuffy, musky odor inside. Helen felt like the insides of her body had been scraped clean, but had given up.

"Where'd they go?" Chakor wondered. "Wait here, just a second," he said as he jogged around the side of the building to find them.

The drifting smoke from the goat roast and the cigarettes were nauseating, and she leaned against the front of the building. She waited a few minutes, avoiding the curious and friendly glances from her mother's friends, before wondering what had happened. Maybe, she was thinking, she should just come clean to everybody. She was tired of worrying, she was tired of hiding things. She took a few steps toward the corner around which Chakor had disappeared when she heard Emmaline's voice.

"Helen? Is that you?"

She turned to see her boss, who looked scared and wilted, and must be furious at having been abandoned.

"I don't know if it's me," she smiled, fighting back another round of tears.

"Oh, you poor baby," Emmaline said, because she was a difficult person, but generous too. Her boss picked her way through the gravel, that was not made for high heels, more delicately than Helen would have thought possible, to come to her. To hug Helen. "What are you doing outside? You changed?"

"Larry's out here," she sighed, "Come on." She held her boss's hand and walked around the corner of the Legion Hall where Chakor, Larry, and Davendraji were lit up by the deep glow of embers. Emmaline stayed uncharacteristically silent as they came up behind the men, and glimpsed what the men were so transfixed by: glowing red coals surrounding a shrunken goat's body. The beast evidently hadn't been butchered, only skinned. Its legs were folded to the sides, like it was sleeping in hell.

"Oh my *God*!" Emmaline whispered loudly, and all three men turned their heads over their right shoulders, like the move had been choreographed. "What *is* that?"

"*Cabrito*!" Johnny Gomez answered from the darkness. Helen hadn't even seen him. He stepped out into the light, grinning ear to ear, a giant carving knife at his side. "Wait ten minutes and I'll let the pregnant lady have the first taste."

The goat looked like a fire-breathing demon rising up out of the earth and she stumbled backwards in protest of the thought.

"I don't think you better even *look* at this, honey," Chakor said.

"A little late for the warning," Johnny snickered.

"I think I've seen enough, too," the priest said, turning abruptly, and smiling sweetly at Emmaline all at once.

"Me, too," Chakor said, and they turned toward Emmaline and Helen, waiting expectantly for an introduction. Instead of doing that, as she thought she was going to do, Helen grabbed her boss's hand and dragged her back toward the hall without a word. They entered, and walked back to the stools by the dance floor, which Carmen had dubbed the "grandbaby stoop." They were set out expressly for her pregnant daughter to rest on without feeling left out.

"My *god* that poor animal!" Emmaline said. "They didn't burn him *alive*?"

"Of course not," Helen sighed.

"This is really an extraordinary reception," Emmaline said, sounding sad. "I feel like everybody's grandmother."

Helen put one of her swollen, pregnant hands on Emmaline's thin and delicate one. They both watched the men come in. Chakor parked Larry in front of the gift table and sat down in the chair to its side, and Davendraji headed toward the bathroom. Left alone, one by the other at Carmen's wedding, Helen realized how much the two had in common: two outdoorsy, nondrinkers from conservative backgrounds who loved her, and were as out of place as Emmaline. She liked seeing them together, and wondered how they would have gotten along if Larry weren't mute.

"He's really bad off, isn't he," Emmaline said, resting her hand on Helen's shoulder after following her gaze.

"I don't want to think about it," Helen said, firmly, though what she didn't want to do was think about it with Emmaline. "Not tonight." Her boss nodded.

"Helen," she said softly, "I know I shouldn't have come. You warned me, you tried to tell me I would just make you more uncomfortable here, and I had no idea how out of place I could be in the world. I'm sorry I barged in."

Helen smiled over at her, squeezed her hand, but didn't answer. She was watching the three men—Davendraji was back from the bathroom, and sitting with Chakor.

"You know, I forgot to tell my mother something," she said to Emmaline.

"I'm here, I'll just be sitting here if you need me. Don't worry about me."

Helen didn't. Emmaline would be fine. Her mother, on the other hand, would not be fine if she bumped unexpectedly into Larry—and so she followed Carmen's loud laugh and tapped her on the shoulder. She turned from the friends she was talking to, and put her arm around Helen's neck.

"Two suitors and a sugar mama in the house, and none of them can get it together enough to bring a pregnant lady a drink," she sighed, dropping an already half-emptied glass of wine in her daughter's hand. "Now that's a raw deal."

"I was just coming to tell you about Larry," she said, handing her cup back to Carmen. "I'm not supposed to drink."

"One glass of wine is good for the kid," Carmen said, refusing the glass. "Good for my kid, good for yours. The band's taking a break in a couple of minutes and I was hoping you'd dance just a little bit with Terrible, first thing, when they get started up again. It would mean a lot to him."

"It would?" she said, but then she saw him coming over, skinny in his black suit, an all-out bashful smile on his face. Of course it would.

"There's the two loveliest ladies in the house," Terrible was saying then, drunk enough to have lost his usual bearing, and to squeeze mother and daughter together between him. Helen was happier for just a second than she'd ever remembered being. How simple she was, she realized. What a small request of the world to grant her a family. The thought sent her gaze back over to her husbands, to Chakor who she had never made up with since fighting.

"I'd be honored to grant you the only dance of the night," she said to Terrible. "Just let me go have a short word with Chakor before the music starts."

"Sure thing," he said, blushing, and she snaked over toward her second husband. Luckily he was sitting further down the same wall Emmaline was, and there were several couples leaning up against it between them. Chakor wasn't in her boss's line of sight, and so she kissed him and smiled.

"I'm sorry I'm on edge," she said. "I just wanted a simple evening, and I exploded."

"I know," he said, as the song ended, "but you shouldn't worry."

Then, from just a few feet away, a deep voice boomed into the small lull that came with the silence of the band:

"Hey, there, buddy, better not be messing with that."

They looked over: Lou Arnold was talking to Larry who was still sitting in front of the table. He had the mountain man's pistol in his hand.

"No," Larry said when Lou came forward to remove it, and the biker backed away, unsure of what to do.

"Don't tell me you left that fucking gun on the gift table, Jack Grimshaw!" It was Carmen, who had made her way across the room when Larry's actions had sucked all the noise from her party.

"I was *dancing*," Helen heard Jack say from somewhere near the door.

"Hey, Larry, just set it back on the table," Chakor said, stepping toward him. "Take a minute if you need to." And then out to the rest of the room he said, "He's okay. He doesn't even realize what he has."

Emmaline's face peeked out from behind Carmen as Helen took a step toward her first husband.

"Larry," she said, and reached forward to take the gun.

"No!" he shouted so loudly it scared her. She didn't know what to do, she couldn't move. Larry was still looking at the gun's barrel. Nobody was breathing, it seemed. After an excruciating period of this silence, his head snapped up, and he looked around the room. Bashfully, she thought.

He raised the gun up, and turned to his right to set it back down on the table in front of Chakor and her, but as it hovered in the air, in the seconds before he put it on the table, a Harley's engine revved up right outside the open front door, and the gun was sounding, and everybody was screaming, and Chakor fell back into the priest.

* * *

Lieutenant Misty Abeglan walked into exactly the kind of room a detective never wants to see: a man down with a head wound wrapped by a bunch of Rendezvous Ricks. His pregnant wife collapsed beside him on the floor, drenched in blood. Her drunken newlywed parents hovering above her. And to blame: a disabled war veteran being shielded by a man in a priest's collar. And as if all that weren't enough, there were five or six dozen intoxicated wedding guests all insisting their version of the transpirations were correct.

"Joey," she sighed to the husband she didn't have time to call, "don't wait up for me tonight."

The paramedics arrived at the same time she did—and so the victim had lucked out. Mr. Finnegan Thomas called in just half an hour before claiming a heart attack. The one time they didn't show for a Finnegan prank would be the time he was actually in peril, and then the lawsuit the man was determined to get hold of would be his. She'd come in to cite him, because he was a time suck. Today, though, his civic detractions might have saved a life since both she and the ambulance were just a couple miles out of town when the call for the shooting came in. They'd gotten here fast.

While the paramedics worked on the victim, Misty directed Simmons and Zubiate to round up the guests on the other side of the room and assess whether or not any of them knew anything the family didn't about what happened. Herkimer was left to begin cordoning off the area.

She left herself the hardest job: that of finding out which version of events the entire group huddled around the victim agreed on. As the paramedics lifted the victim's body onto a gurney she got her first sketch—the mentally disabled former solider had picked up an antique pistol left on the table as a wedding gift by Jack Grimshaw (surprise, surprise) and shot Chakor Desai in the shoulder as the victim had been trying to convince him to put it down:

Carmen Terren, drunk. "We were just everybody having a good time and then that goddamned deranged bastard shot Chakor. He doesn't belong on the streets."

(Terrible) Terrel Terren, drunk. "Man's got PTSD and the sound of the motorcycles made him jump, though I don't think he meant to shoot anybody."

Emmaline Harris, sober. "I don't know if he *meant* to shoot because he is a very responsible man, I mean he *was*. But Helen and Mr. Desai were standing *next* to each other, and I think that might be important. I mean, I don't *know*, but if it wasn't an accident, and, you know, it might have been, but if it wasn't, they were standing *together* and so who *knows* what he meant."

Reverend Davendra Dave ("dah-vey"), difficulties with the language. "I saw the panic in Larry's face at the sound of the motorcycles. I think he was not aiming at any of us and I was standing right with them."

Lou Arnold, drunk. "The devil was in his eyes when he aimed right at that poor kid's head and smiled."

* * *

As the police worked their way around her, the ambulance drivers made her stand back as they lifted Chakor up into a gurney. Helen prayed, concentrating on the baby in her womb and begging for it to stay put. In a movie, she knew, the pregnant lady always went into labor at a moment like this and it helped her not to panic, to dissolve entirely, to think about calming the child inside. *Everything is going to be fine,* she told it, *it's an accident. Your daddies,* she said, deciding not to concentrate on semantics, *are going to be fine.*

Except nothing looked fine from her vantage point on the outside of the room, *It's fine,* she said, but blood was caked into her jeans and forest green sweater. She refused to look at it, but she could feel it, the blood, sticking to her skin beneath her clothes. Everybody else was talking to the police officers that kept arriving. She felt like a ghost, wondered when it was she'd have to tell her secret.

"He's just in shock," said the ambulance man, startling her. He was a Ute with a short ponytail, and a fat, tired face that looked familiar, though she couldn't place him. They raised the gurney up onto its wheels.

"What do I . . . " she trailed back off into her daze. *It's going to be fine.*

"You could ride over with us," the man said, "or go home and get cleaned up, which is what I'd do. There's no help you have for him, right now."

She must have looked awful because he gripped her shoulder with his large hand and said, more forcefully: "Go home. Clean up. Get a ride to the hospital." Then he leaned toward her and whispered, "The police can't make you talk to them right now—calm down, take care of yourself." He pointed at her belly. "That baby's what's important, here. You know that. His daddy's shoulder is torn, and he'll have scarring on his face from black powder's tattooing, but he's gonna *be* just fine."

Larry was still sitting in the corner of the room, forgotten, and she wondered now, for the first time all evening, what would become of him. Everybody all around her was arguing about whether or not he'd shot Chakor on purpose. All the stories seemed equally plausible, and fragments of different voices with different theories buzzed in and out of her hearing like bees.

Don't worry, she said to her baby, and when the officer interviewing Davendraji left him alone, she made her way over to the pundit before somebody noticed she was available. She looked down at Larry's face, which was withdrawn.

"You aren't going to the hospital?" the priest asked.

"They said I should get cleaned up first," she said. "But he's going to be fine." She was so distanced from the event, her own words immediately felt like a line overheard on television. The room was emptying and she wanted to leave, too. She was marveling that not a single police officer had approached her.

"They're going to take him to the hospital psych ward," the priest said, nodding down at Larry. "But he didn't do it on purpose. I was sitting right there." Tears were in his eyes. "It's my fault he came."

"Punditji," she said, relieved to have somebody to comfort, but then she didn't have anything to say, and a policewoman tapped her on the shoulder.

"I'm Detective Abeglan," she said, and Helen almost swallowed her heart. "Could I have just a moment to take a statement?"

"I'm tired," Helen said, and tears welled up in her eyes. The policewoman's face softened, her eyes resting on her belly, and so Helen knew they still hadn't figured out what she'd done.

"All you need to do is corroborate what happened."

"No," Helen said, but then sighed. "Can I sit over there?" she said, pointing at the chairs. She didn't want the priest standing there next to her.

"Of course."

"I'm sorry to put you through this," the woman said, staring deeply into Helen's eyes and nodding. "I *will* be brief." Helen nodded.

"The suspect, Larry Janx, is an Iraq veteran with PTSD, and your husband, correct?" Helen nodded. "He's made a number of violent outbursts in the past?"

"No," Helen said, "he's just confused. I don't, I didn't think it was violence."

"And you and your husband live with the victim, Chakor Desai?"

"I'm tired," Helen said. "I'd rather do this tomorrow."

"But you live together?"

"Yes," Helen said. "Up at Black Elk."

"And you think there were jealousies?"

"Oh, no. No. Nothing like that."

"But Mr. Janx is your husband?"

"Yes."

"And the priest married your mother, Carmen, today, and not you, is that correct?"

"Of course." Detective Abeglan nodded, smiling, and Helen knew she could put off discovery another day. Her heart started swatting at the sides of her chest enough that she grimaced.

"Ma'am? Are you okay?"

"They're both my husbands," she whispered to the cop.

"What?"

"I'm married to both of them."

Detective Abeglan cocked her head to the side, squinted slightly, and nodded at Helen almost imperceptibly for a long time. "So you're saying that Larry Janx, who suffers from a brain trauma and has the emotional capacity of a child, picked up a firearm and it accidentally discharged and hit Chakor Desai?"

"Excuse me?"

"It was an accident," Detective Abeglan nodded. "So far as you could see."

"I *married* both men," Helen said more loudly this time, her eyes popping, her hands gripping onto each other like two drowning people in an ocean.

The woman leaned in and said, "This is a don't-ask, don't-tell state, Ms. Motes. My cousins still live out in Colorado City, and it's not the life my family chose, but like I said: don't ask, don't tell. *Zubiate!*" She called over to a thin-looking man. "We'll need to take Mr. Janx in for holding, overnight, and have him assessed." Back to Helen she said, "We'll take good care of him, Ms. Motes."

Helen felt scraped out as the policewoman stood, and headed over to talk with the others. Terrible walked up behind her and said, "Your boss is going to drive you to the hospital, and we'll join you shortly, with the priest."

Part Four

From the Chipeta County Register
Week of Monday, March 14, 2005

Sidenotes, Page 1:

Poet Wounded
"East" Indian Chakor Desai, Chipeta County's *beloved*, first Poet in the Heartland, is recovering from a gunshot wound at the Eastern Utah Regional Medical Center in Franklin. In the immortal words of Lord Alfred Tennyson, we hope for his speedy recovery and urge him: "To strive, to seek, to find, and not to yield" to this setback.

—See Page 8

News From the Police Blotter, Page 8:

Local "East" Indian poet Chakor Desai was wounded in the shoulder and face Sunday night by an antique Colt Dragoon shooting #4 birdshot at the wedding of Carmen and "Terrible" Terrel Terren. The gun was discharged by decorated Iraq war veteran, Larry Janx, who was rendered simple minded earlier this year in service to us all. Mr. Desai's wounds were not life threatening and he is expected to fully recover. No charges have been filed.

Chapter Twenty-One

March 14, 2005

Helen Motes slumped shivering on a mustard-colored chair in Chakor Desai's hospital room as he slept. The entire floor was overwhelmed by the noxious smell of a spilled bottle of Clorox. The walls inside Chakor's room were vaguely more pink than white because this part of the hospital had once been the maternity ward, and though the television worked, nobody had turned it on.

Chakor was the only patient in the room. His neck and the bottom half of his face were wrapped in gauze—Jack Grimshaw's horse pistol had been filled with birdshot that had sprayed out before it hit. Initially doctors were relieved to discover such light-caliber ammunition, but the bulk had hit into the nerve center of his shoulder. The rest had fanned out and tattooed his neck, chin, and cheek. It was all a mess bigger but less damaging than a straight bullet would have made. Chakor was all tubes and bed sheets.

Davendra Dave was speaking softly into his cell phone, rearranging his life in Salt Lake for at least the upcoming week. He felt responsible for having encouraged Larry's presence at the wedding. Ida and Herman Meek suggested he stay in their spare room, and he had accepted. Across the city Larry Janx was enrolled full-time at the Uintah County Rehabilitation Center. Social workers had told Helen that no matter the outcome of the police investigation, he would be best served by recuperating full-time in an institution.

Every so often a nurse walked into the room to check on Chakor's condition. They had kept him sedated so his body could heal, but he came to every so often. Helen held his hand during these moments, and he had made weak jokes about how if she'd hurry the baby up a little, they could share a hospital room and save everybody a wad of money. A month before, Carmen had told a different baby joke, drunk. It was the night before she'd kicked Helen and Larry out of the house. It was when she was still trying to convince Helen to quit worrying about who the father was—"Wait till he's born," she'd giggled, "and see whether he's brown or one-legged."

"Jesus Christ, Carmen," Terrible had said.

* * *

Not once did Helen imagine that the three reporters covering the seventy-five square miles of inhabited Chipeta County would neglect her. The same night Chakor was shot, however, the third-largest methamphetamine ring bust in the state's history played out in Franklin during a sting the DEA had spent months orchestrating with a few members of the local police department. A seven-year-old girl was nearly mauled to death by a prominent county commissioner's bulldog, earlier in the week, and three local teenagers had broken a longheld honor rule and defaced some cave art in Nine Mile Canyon. That was all the disaster the *Register* figured country residents could take, it seemed. The rest of the paper was filled with legal notices, special interest stories, and recipes. Nobody had even called Helen about the shooting.

Life had neglected to untangle itself for Helen Motes. She'd waited for her secret to unravel, as secrets must, but it would not. Detective Abeglan had refused to reveal her status as a bigamist, and had not spilled out her secret to the room full of wedding guests speculating about Larry's intentions. Helen's last hopes had rested on the week's edition of the paper. The reporters surely, she had assumed, would name Larry as her husband. With that domino toppled, Davendraji, Ida, Herman, or their children would discover the depth of her lies.

What it came down to was this: everything in the world disappeared. Babies and fathers. Little girls and broken women disappeared into reservoirs. Families into nowhere. Possums, wasps, insects disappeared. But Helen's secret remained, it always remained intact: the first inviolable thing she'd ever faced. And she hated it.

* * *

The birdshot entered like a rusty hammer thundering down hard from the heavens into his bones. It had dropped him down to his knees, and then the sting set in to his arms and neck. It was a poisoned boiling of a sting, like a tree-sized wasp was trying to store venom inside wounds he remembered as bright red. *Scoot!* he'd thought, his head commanding him to crawl from his body and shake the wounds from it like dust from a carpet, quick before they set in. He remembered waking in the black of his hospital room in the late night, his body a ruined sun nourishing a complicated constellation of bright green lights and transparent tubes. Then the faces of his loved ones floated into his field of vision, bobbing around it like grotesque and bloated balloons. When he slept, he was cradled by the presence of his mother. The wet, heavy scent of the sweet amla oil in her hair. The songs she'd sung him as a child. His father's disappointed eyes.

Larry had shot him. Probably accidentally—the last thing he remembered about looking at him was his embarrassed confusion. The question of whether he had done it on purpose or not, the question that Ida, Herman, Davendra, Carmen, and Terrible would not give up, Chakor rejected. His right arm might never function again. The spray from the birdshot would leave his chin and neck scarred—he would never be carded for liquor, never be sweet-faced, as his mother had called him, again.

Of his visitors, only Helen had been silent. His wife kept a mostly silent vigil beside his bed, refusing to interpret what he'd seen with his own eyes for him. They were never alone long enough for him to tell her *this is not your fault.* It wasn't. His wife had tried to shield a man from danger and from life in an institution by bringing him up to live in the cabin; she had tried to shield the world from the danger of Larry by doing the same. Carmen called him Frankenstein and the sad truth was that she was right to do so. Helen was the heroine who had taken pity on the monster, who saw his humanity before the disaster of Larry's mind. Chakor had been taken with her vision of the man—he had felt a strong, human bond, as if their hearts were stitched up with the same fibers. But from the outset he had known the impossible and dangerous nature of his wife's quest. He wanted her to know that. He hadn't found a way to voice his concerns, before, without seeming jealous, without her thinking he didn't understand the grand generosity of her vision.

If Larry hadn't shot *him*, his own fears insisted to Chakor, their baby might very well have been the thing the man had damaged. Chakor had been weak: he had been too afraid to voice his fears, and the universe had punished him for it. He would not, as the funny newspaper clipping had urged, yield to the setback.

He tried to explain all this to Helen early Monday morning, when Davendra left to take a nap and they found themselves both alone and conscious for the first time since the accident. He had been teasing her about how she ought to give birth while she was already at the hospital, but today she looked like it might happen. Her body looked ready for release.

"Have you seen Larry?" he asked her.

"No," she shook her pale, pale face. "Not yet."

Chakor nodded. If she had been to see her ex-boyfriend he would have understood—despite everything, even he wanted to know how he was doing—but he was glad she hadn't.

"But he's my husband," Helen whispered into her hands, like she was in conversation with them and he couldn't hear. "I have to go see him."

"Are you okay?"

"Larry's my husband," she said, still pale, but sitting up straight now. Looking him in the eye. He squinted and tried to figure out what she was saying.

"You feel guilty," he said. "You lived together a long time, and . . . ."

"He wasn't my boyfriend, he was my husband," Helen said, louder, nodding. "Larry was my *husband*, Chakor. We were married in a temple." She took a diamond ring from her Levi's pocket and put it onto her finger over the ring Chakor gave her.

"This was my ring first," she said.

The stinging that he hadn't felt since he'd been in the hospital—here it was a more throbbing pain—came back. Chakor closed his eyes, but when he opened them again Helen was sitting exactly where he thought: it was no dream.

"Larry was really your husband, not your boyfriend," he said, stung by his anger.

"Yes," Helen said, "but I didn't divorce him before I married you. There wasn't time."

"You didn't divorce him until I went to India?"

"I am still married to Larry."

The words settled slowly into him, the way water takes a long time to settle into the roots of a dried-up plant. But then the slow tears trickled from his eyes.

"And the baby?" he whispered.

"He came to Houston after you left for India . . . ."

Her hideous, hideous face stared down into his like an ocean monster's, but Chakor didn't look away. He engaged her empty eyes with his own as he grabbed the tubes protruding from his wrist and the gauze covering his face and neck and ripped at them, screaming with the pain of it, he ripped them. He tore at himself with all the sedated strength that he had and his screams, and Helen's screams, and the beeping of machines, and shouting of nurses didn't drown the thunder trapped inside his head until he lost consciousness.

* * *

When Helen entered her room, late Monday afternoon, Emmaline Harris was on a call with the front desk about the Internet connection she was supposed to have but didn't. The girl had let herself in with the key left at the front desk in her name. She walked into the kitchenette and started sobbing. Crying people were one thing, but sobbing people had always made Emmaline uncomfortable.

"Listen," Emmaline said to the man on the phone, "you take care of my problem, and I won't cancel the room charge on my credit card."

"I don't care if the sight of me *does* send you into tears," she said when she found her protégé and kissed her on her salty cheeks. "It's good to see you."

It took a few minutes to direct Helen into the leather chair by the window. Now her legs curled beneath the baby she was carrying, and her head was collapsed back into the headrest. In the dim light of four o'clock Emmaline noticed for the first time small specks of blood dotting Helen's shirt—not hundreds of them, but enough that Emmaline's heart jumped.

"What happened?" she asked. "What happened?" But Helen's crying had gotten worse, not better, she was sobbing up to the mint green ceiling uncontrollably, and Emmaline didn't know what to do. The blood on Helen entered viscerally into Emmaline, and her own bones, her own hands started shaking.

"There, there," she said, but she may well have been invisible. At the brink of panic, she ran into the kitchen and soaked a hand towel in steaming water. She twisted enough excess water out of it that it wouldn't drip all over the tile, and ran it over to Helen. The girl didn't reach up to take it, so Emmaline placed it on her forehead—and there was some magic in it. The flow of tears, the hysterical breathing subsided. Emmaline grabbed a cotton throw from the bottom of the bed and wrapped Helen in it, and then she waited. She could see Helen trying to control her breathing, and just watching her calmed Emmaline, as well. She pulled the ottoman toward Helen's chair, and sat down.

"What's happened?" she whispered, when Helen had been under the towel a long time. She could imagine, and probably not be far off, she knew—she *had* been at Carmen's reception. Her own friends hadn't believed her when she'd told them what happened during it—she'd finally faxed the police blotter from the local paper to Sydney Amis, who had convinced everyone she was playing an early April Fool's.

And still, the lurid and amazing story Helen began to tell was something Emmaline could hardly believe. What Emmaline wished at first, hearing Helen's story, was that she'd realized in Houston the degree of dire straits the girl had been in—not because her husband was off at war, but because her spirit was so dampened that she jumped at the first bright thing she saw, the first chance she got. As Helen continued unraveling her bizarre array of wrong turns and bad decisions, all made in the course of a few months, Emmaline felt something similar to what she felt when some grant came in from a disadvantaged person living on the edge of the world but determined to make the most of it. She thought: these shouldn't be this girl's best options.

Helen had been saddled with a drunken mother and no father, and she'd run away from that and built a life out of whatever brambles and twigs had presented themselves—that's what this bright spirit had been forced to do. All along, ever since meeting Helen, Emmaline knew that her husband, the soldier, wasn't what a girl like Helen would have chosen if she'd had options. He was what had presented itself, and the girl had been grateful.

But when she dared tell Emmaline it wasn't enough what had she counseled? *Stay with him.* She'd ignored this girl's assertion that grateful did not sustain her and so as Helen's tears subsided, as Helen described the man Emmaline thought was Larry's caretaker being rushed back into surgery, Emmaline understood she had, in a small and significant way, failed her protégé: Emmaline's vision of what was good enough for Helen was nowhere as ambitious as Helen's dreams for own life. For all her liberalisms and the money she shed off into the lives of the less fortunate, here Emmaline had waltzed right into the oldest, most tired failure of the liberal aristocrat. Now the girl was forty weeks pregnant and unsure whether the father was the man who almost bled to death when she told him the baby wasn't his, or the man locked in a nuthouse across town. *Learn this lesson,* Emmaline nodded to herself, *and something will come out of it.*

Emmaline believed that. She knew Helen had made her own bad choices—but Emmaline had failed to take the girl's life seriously. That mistake, she vowed, she wouldn't make again.

"I have an idea," she said softly into the gloaming. Helen sat still. "My idea is that you raise the baby with me. Your mother can come visit all she wants, but we need to get you out of here. You can move back to Houston, into my house—you can have your own *wing* and we will give your child all the options you never had."

Helen blinked, confused. "Houston?"

"Not the suburbs, dear. You'll live with me in River Oaks, in the middle of the city."

"I don't think so," Helen said, but Emmaline knew she was considering it when she asked, after a minute or two of silence, "but what would we do about the center?"

"We'll get somebody. Maybe even your poet will take it up—you told me, in the summer, a lot of it was his idea. But if he won't take it, somebody out here can get it going, maybe a graduate from one of the colleges in Salt Lake City. It doesn't have to be you."

Helen shook her head again. "I wish I could," she said. "But I can't just leave. You can't just destroy people's lives and then disappear. You can't. What about Larry?"

"Let's not pretend the medical care in Chipeta County is comparable to the care he'll get in a city with a *few* major medical centers," she laughed, because she could see it. She could see how she was right. "Helen, there's no place in Utah to step back and evaluate what you want or need out of life. You're buried here, you're already disappeared. But then you were given a gift, and you deserve to take it. Whether or not you choose to return to Larry, you'll know you're doing what's best for him for now. You won't have to see the poet—and you can let him get on with his healing without seeing you. The only center of your life will be the baby, and as you watch it grow, watch what she can do in the world, you'll have the time to figure those things out for yourself."

* * *

March 20, 2005

Carmen and Terrible were helping Helen move her things from Chakor's cabin. The old witch, Ida, had sent Herman over to make sure they didn't *steal* anything. Helen told Carmen that, and she'd had to bite her tongue: the man had lost his pretty face, maybe the use of his arm, his wife, and his child in the space of a few days—was he going to notice a missing teacup? Did Ida really think Helen

wanted to swipe his guitar and his inherited macramé wall hang-
ings now that she'd stolen his uncomplicated marital status and his
idealism?

These weren't thoughts she shared with anybody but Terrible,
who couldn't talk about it yet, himself. Chakor, the son-in-law she'd
always wanted and never knew she had, had barred not only Helen
but Terrible and Carmen from his hospital room. He'd written the
newlyweds a small note, in a shaky, scrawling hand: *This isn't your
fault, but forgive me if I can't see you, yet.*

The "yet" she found hopeful. When she saw him she planned
on telling him, straight out, the kid had to be his. After almost a
decade of trying with Larry how believable was it that one week of
sex had done the trick and not a summer of love with Chakor? At
the least, the due date made either man a possibility: why had her
daughter not given Chakor that small bone? It baffled Carmen. The
girl said she didn't want to give him false hope and Carmen had
nearly slugged her.

Terrible was running in and out with boxes, while Carmen and
Helen packed them and moved them to the front porch. Herman
sat on his high horse, out on the front porch, smoking a pipe.

"Nice to know you can sit idly by and watch a pregnant lady
heaving boxes," she smirked after fifteen minutes of giving him the
silent treatment. "You should've tried keeping your fat ass planted
there the other day when it would've made a difference."

"You . . . you . . . " he said, but then he clenched his teeth
together, and shook his head with a smile, like he'd just figured out
how to avoid a trap. "I'm not biting," he said, a look of distaste on
his mouth. He planted his eyes on the trees and shrubs that were
still brown from winter, but no longer buried in snow, and refused
to look back up at her. "Coward," she growled, and moved back
into the cabin for more. But he must have been taking blindside
glances at the unhappy family in flux, because he was the one who
witnessed the puddle of water forming around Helen's ankles as she

walked to the edge of the porch to ask Terrible to bring in some more hangers.

"What's that?" he said—the addition of his gruff voice to the quiet labor was audible even inside the cabin, but Carmen ignored him and hoped Helen would as well.

"Mom!" Helen screamed, "Mom! Mom, my water broke!" And by the time Carmen got out there, Herman had abandoned his seat and was holding onto Helen like the water might wash her away.

All four of them entered the cabin together, and as soon as they had Helen sitting, Herman was using Helen's cell to call Ida, who was down at the hospital. Carmen was on hers calling the emergency room.

"She needs to be walking around," Herman barked out thirty seconds into his call. "And wait until the contractions become regular."

"We're not supposed to go right away to the hospital," Carmen said in a loud voice meant to override Herman's. "We have to wait a few hours, until the contractions are a minute long, five minutes apart."

"Ida's on her way," Herman said.

"Oh no she's not," Helen and Carmen said in unison, and Herman whispered something into the phone, but put up no argument.

The first contraction ripped into her daughter so suddenly she screamed, doubled over where she was walking, and almost fell down.

"Just relax, just relax," Herman barked.

"You try relaxing with a sixty-pound ball tearing out of your anus," Carmen screamed back at him, while Terrible actually helped Helen to the chair by the window overlooking the river. He started massaging her shoulders and humming.

"Where'd you learn that?" Carmen asked, and he shrugged with a grin.

Just as soon as the first contraction was over, and everybody looked relieved, another one started right up. Terrible continued the massage and Helen moaned, it seemed, to the tune he was humming. It took them fifteen minutes of contraction pounding in after contraction, for Terrible and Herman to begin helping Helen into the van, and not twenty minutes after the labor started they left Herman to close up the cabin and raced down the mountain.

* * *

March 21, 2005

The baby was perfect, a little girl delivered in the backseat of Helen's van and wrapped in Terrible's flannel shirt before they reached the hospital. Dark-haired and dark-eyed but fair skinned. And two-legged. It was still anybody's guess at who the father was, but Helen figured she would try to sort it out, and this was new.

All she wanted now was to be with the baby and to be babied herself. She told Carmen she was returning to Houston just as soon as she was discharged, and that was going to happen at the end of the day. Her mother had been to the hospital to hold her grandbaby several times but she had stopped speaking to Helen. Jealous of Emmaline.

"You can fly out and visit," Helen had offered.

"You can fly out your ass," her mother had half-heartedly responded.

Just like before, Carmen couldn't see the difference between what she wanted and what the baby needed. The baby, for instance, did not need a plastic doll for an aunt. Helen had promised Terrible that the doll could accompany her to Houston and had even nodded approvingly when he announced Vera was already buckled into the van's passenger seat, awaiting the small family's return. But in Houston, she'd be a doll, again: a beloved, secondhand gift from her baby's grandfather—that was all.

The baby didn't need to grow up in a city where Helen knew she'd be ostracized just as soon as the news about her double marriage spread. There would always be the Detective Abeglan, but decent, normal people would think she'd done both the poet and the soldier wrong. And her mother: her mother meant well, she always meant well, but Helen couldn't count the ways on her hands a moonlight drunk might revert to a full-time one. And so Emmaline would be arriving at four o'clock.

Which was why it was a mystery to Helen when after she'd signed all the papers she needed—after she'd written down the baby's name for the first time—she didn't wait for her friend. Instead she cradled her tiny girl wrapped in the organic blankets Emmaline had gifted her, found her purse, and fled. There was a stairwell entrance just a few feet from her room and she slipped into it without any of the nurses who were supposed to be ensuring she didn't leave without a ride noticing. She pressed her shoulder against the wall to bear her body's weight, and inched her way down the stairs—an excruciating venture because of the hernia and the episiotomy that were results of her record-setting labor.

Minutes later she had found her car in the parking lot—space 101 A, right where Terrible had told her it would be. In the days before the wedding Chakor had not only already strapped in the car seat, but he'd taped black and white pictures of animals to the van's roof for the baby to see. She eased her girl into her place beneath the menagerie for the first time, and against her expectations, the child didn't fuss.

Helen had to lean back into the van's seat, because sitting down normally was too painful, and she must have looked like an old woman driving, though she didn't drive far. Within fifteen minutes she and the baby were unstrapped and she was hobbling through the doors of the Chipeta County Rehabilitation Clinic, newborn in arms. Larry was awaiting transfer to specialists in PTSD at the VA and Baylor Medical School in Houston. When Bettie Johnson saw Helen and the baby she burst into tears.

"I'm so sorry," she said.

It wasn't difficult to convince Bettie to let Larry out into one of the small waiting rooms. Helen wanted to think he had changed— that he wasted away, that that would give her proof she'd been a better caretaker—but he was just the same.

"Larry," she said. "Larry." He recognized if not her, the her she'd been to him all winter, and stood like he was ready to go: he was wearing a prosthetic again, and Helen hadn't even known.

"This is your baby, Larry," she said to him, and she walked toward him and lifted his hand and put it on the baby's nose, on her lips.

"She needs you," Helen said. "You need to get better. I want you to get better so I can tell you her name." It was true. Helen still hadn't uttered the baby's name, didn't know what it would sound like out loud.

A flicker, a pained expression in Larry's face looked like it was going to become a tear and fall and so Helen braced herself for the Shirley Temple moment, but it didn't come. The flicker did, the near-tear was really there, but then his face closed over like a lizard's eyelid. He walked toward the door and looked at her, waiting for her to follow him: he wanted to return to the mountain. Bettie heard Helen's sobs from outside the room and rushed in. Larry had slowly begun backing away from her, toward the door, and he didn't fight it when Bettie led him back into the hallways you couldn't leave.

In her arms the little creature from another world didn't seem to register her mother's distress. She nuzzled her face into Helen's chest, hungry.

Now it was twenty past four, and Helen didn't answer the call coming in from Emmaline: it made her feel steady not to. Her translucent-skinned girl, the most delicate thing she'd ever been entrusted with, rested in her arms. In another world Helen would return to her van and drive away—not to Emmaline, her savior, just off into the sunset that would care for her and her child for the rest of their lives.

In this world she called Bettie in and told her to cancel plans for Larry's move. Where would he find a woman who cared for him like Nurse Bettie, in Houston, she asked the woman, and the nurse smiled tears back at Helen.

"He won't get better care there," Bettie said, nodding. "I really don't think he will."

"He won't," Helen echoed, walking from the room, toward the parking lot. "None of us will." She had known that almost as soon as she announced she was leaving. What business did they have in somebody else's perfect world? Where was the life in that?

By the time she made it back to the van the little one was crying. It was soft and feathery, her voice. Helen climbed into the back seat with her and the girl suckled fiercely, another survivor. This girl deserved a father. There were two men and only one choice, she thought, two fathers and one choice. But it rang falsely, the thought. That was the problem. The old schoolteacher in the beauty shop had said as much. She'd said: head for the brush.

Helen's eyes focused on the animals Chakor had taped to the ceiling. They were simple black and white, and they reminded her of the petroglyphs at Picnic Rocks, and that reminded her of the Larry she would not send away to rot alone.

She was beginning to understand that she hadn't been able to choose between Larry and Chakor because, all along, she had wanted Larry *and* Chakor. She had been in the brush from the start, and she hadn't left it because it was where she wanted to be. Because Helen had learned something about brush, the high grass of it, the tinkling of grasshoppers, the pounding of jackrabbits crossing the roads intersecting it, the slow march of its caterpillars painted like clowns and built like war machines, the rabbits, the possums, the hornets, the wildflowers, the thorn and thistles: every demented thing that gets underfoot and trips you on the way to somewhere and leaves you entangled in bloody welts and bites amidst the diseases and troubles of humankind, all that stuff that charms you and kills you is also what makes life worth living. Helen didn't want the brush for the pain it caused, she didn't want to disappear into it, or to use it to set herself apart: she needed the rich scent of it to survive, its fullness. She could guide her child through it.

And Helen did have two husbands. She had married two men because she loved each of them, and one was now in worse shape than the other, but she wanted them both. Her baby was the product of both men and if the world could not see it, Helen could.

What if, Helen was wondering as she buckled their baby back into her car seat, what if she could still convince Chakor? The magnitude of the words and days it would take was not lost on Helen as she pulled onto the highway and headed to her mother's.

It was a lot of hope she was depending on, and it was so late. But it was only so late, it was not too late, and that was enough to get Helen home.

About the Author

Miah Arnold grew up in a house attached to the Three Legged Dog Saloon in Myton, Utah. She attended Carleton College and earned a PhD in Literature and Creative Writing from the University of Houston. Her stories and nonfiction have been published in the *Michigan Quarterly Review*, *Nanofiction*, *Confrontation*, *Painted Bride Quarterly*, and the *South Dakota Review*. She has received a Barthelme Award, an Inprint/Diana P. Hobby Award, and a Houston Arts Alliance Established Artists Grant. She teaches writing in Houston, Texas, where she lives with her husband, Raj Mankad, and their two children.